Without

or

The Search for the Gene Culprits

Studies in Austrian Literature Culture and Thought

Translation Series

General Editors:

Jorun B. Johns
Richard H. Lawson

Rüdiger Opelt

Without Pain

or

The Search for the Gene Culprits

Translated and with an Afterword
by
Lowell A. Bangerter

ARIADNE PRESS
Riverside, California

Ariadne Press would like to express its appreciation to the Bundesministerium für Unterricht, Kunst und Kultur for assistance in publishing this book.

.KUNST

Translated from the German *Ohne Schmerzen*
© 2005, Czernin Verlag, Vienna

Library of Congress Cataloging-in-Publication Data

Opelt, Rüdiger.
[Ohne Schmerzen, oder die Suche nach den Gen-Tätern. English]
Without pain, or, the search for the gene culprits / Rüdiger Opelt ;
translated and with an afterword by Lowell A. Bangerter.
    p.   cm. -- (Studies in Austrian literature, culture, and
thought. Translation series)
ISBN 978-1-57241-158-6 (alk. Paper)
1. World War, 1939-1945—Atrocities—Fiction. 2. Theresienstadt
(Concentration camp)—Fiction. I. Bangerter, Lowell A. 1941-
    II. Title.

PT2715.P45O4613 2007
833'.92--dc22

                                                        2007034693

Cover Design
Art Director: George McGinnis

Copyright ©2007
by Ariadne Press
270 Goins Court
Riverside, CA 92507

All rights reserved.
No part of this publication may be reproduced or transmitted
in any form or by any means without formal permission.
Printed in the United States of America.
ISBN 978-1-57241-158-6
(trade paperback original)

For my wife Traudl

A long path
In order to experience
The heights and depths
And the mystery of love
Together

INTRODUCTION

On the 60th anniversary of the end of the War, we remember the millions of victims of the National Socialists and hope that the horror of the war that they unleashed may never repeat itself. Sixty years probably also had to pass, before we were really ready to look at things and no longer brush aside what happened. In the beginning the perplexity was too great, as was the wish to forget. Belittlement of the suffering, however, does no service to the victims; recognition of the experienced torment is the first prerequisite for healing the wounds at some point in time.

So this is not a nice book that winks at murder and presents it as harmless entertainment. Rather, it describes with drastic devices what was done to human beings in the Second World War, and also afterward. Its intention is to show what violence causes within the soul and how the crime stories of the present are tied to the crimes of the past.

In order to achieve that, it is necessary to examine the causes of the contemporary historical events. In the process it becomes clear that we cannot push aside the fact that there were also millions of perpetrators who followed the path of war and violence with enthusiasm and conviction.

What transpired in the souls of the perpetrators? How could it come to pass that they felt themselves to be superior and in the right when they killed and tortured? How does this poisoning through violence affect the families, the children of the perpetrators? Only when we understand that, can we demilitarize the souls of human beings by tracking down and exposing the hidden rationalizations of the murderers.

Thus one intention of this book is to construct a psychological profile of some fictional perpetrators of the Second World War. As a psychologist, in that process I employ the technique of describing the course of events on the basis of the murderer's stream of consciousness, in a manner similar to that used by the criminal psychologist Dr. Müller in his book *Bestie Mensch* [The Human Beast]. The chapters from the time of the World War are therefore narrated from the point of view of the perpetrators, which does not coincide with my views in any way. Thus if you find in those chapters fascist and racist ideas, they are there in order to call things what they are and to make them visible, and not in any way to sanction them. The thought processes of the perpetrators are juxtaposed with the experience of the victims, because that is the only way that we can reconstruct the things that happened.

After the war, perpetrators and victims lived in the same country, in the same cities, bore and endured the shared history. What would happen if the children of the victims and the perpetrators met without knowing about their common secret? Would they be indifferent with respect to the past or would the experienced horrors be staged anew amid the fears of the present? In my psychology practice I experience again and again that people are broken by the fact that they have perpetrators and victims in their own families, and the unresolved conflict rages in their own souls. I expounded on that as a theory of family involvement in my book *Die Kinder des Tantalus* [The Children of Tantalus].

I now describe what such spiritual conflicts can look like in a concrete case, on the basis of the experiences of a fictional family from Linz, one that stands for many of my patients who sought an answer to their spiritual sufferings. Let yourself be captivated by a gripping crime story that begins with a murder and ends with the exposure of old family secrets and terrible truths. Quite incidentally you will become acquainted with the motifs through which the traumatic events of the past mold our contemporary behavior. This exciting reading material is a quick course in psychology that will automatically give you perspective about yourself and the personalities of your fellowmen.

Rüdiger Opelt, April 2005

1

Linz, November 1, 1991

"But I don't know the dead woman!"

The young man was beside himself with fear. He had no idea what had happened to him, and he could not explain to himself why he should have to answer for something that was completely beyond his knowledge. He began to fear and to hate the police inspector. Why was that man accusing him, when he really had not done anything at all? It was an insane world around him – or had he himself gone crazy?

"The dead woman was lying on your bed covered with blood. You yourself were lying next to her holding the murder weapon in your hand. That doesn't look good for you, my young friend, not good at all," said the police inspector. "We have everything we need: scene of the crime, murder weapon, murder victim, and perpetrator. The only thing missing is a confession on your part."

The young man wiped the perspiration from his temples and said, "But I don't know the woman. I've never seen her before. I don't know how she got into my apartment and into my bed. I have nothing to do with the matter."

"Yes, yes, that's what all our perpetrators say. Go over to the prison and you'll find nothing but condemned murderers who are just as innocent as you are. And who wants to admit that he succumbed to the frenzy of violence out of jealousy, greed, or the joy of killing? You wouldn't be the first one like that. As a police inspector, during the last thirty years I've seen so many things that actually don't exist at all, that your case won't shock me either. In contrast to the others, however, your case is as plain as day. The woman came into your house and you fought. You rested and then stabbed the woman with the knife. And we'll find out the motive yet as well, once you give your confession. Until then both of us must probably remain in this interrogation room. I have time, a lot of time, no matter how long it takes."

The young man felt the perspiration collecting in the small of his back. He did not know what answer to give the police inspector. The latter would not believe him anyway. He did not know himself what was going on. Could he still trust his own thoughts at all? Was what he thought he perceived reality – or had he transformed himself into one of those figures about whom he gave expert opinion with a professional eye? Had the insanity that he had to deal with day after day spread to him? Had the hallucinations that tormented his patients hopped into his mind like ghosts so that he could feel the torments of the schizophrenics?

In his distress he asked for an attorney.

Inspector Wimmer became cynical: "Yeah, I could let you go to the telephone. We would wait for your attorney and he would explain to us very calmly that you will not make any statement because you could incriminate yourself with any statement. But I consider that to be a waste of time. It will really be much more to the point if you soon remember what happened during the course of last night. You'll see that with a full confession you'll look the facts in the eye much more easily. Once it has occurred to you what took place, we can then also explain that to your attorney."

The young man perspired as if in a sauna. The policeman was the bath attendant who whipped the towel through the air to drive the heat of the infusion over his naked body. Without an attorney he would entangle himself completely in this muddled situation. And that was exactly what the man across from him wanted. After all, he was dealing with the Linz police and there was no joking with them.

He remembered the newspaper article about the case of Igor Fuego. Years ago the latter had been found guilty of murdering a barmaid. All of his protestations of innocence did not help him at all. Even when the only witness for the prosecution recanted her testimony, the case was not reopened. Why not? Didn't they want to admit that mistakes had been made or let a man go free once he had been condemned? Who knew? In any case he had to deal with an opponent who was hard to take.

Should he plead for a psychiatrist and have himself declared mentally incompetent? The longer the interrogation lasted, the more sensible that alternative seemed to him. You see, he was gradually beginning to doubt his own sanity. What he had experienced in the last twenty-four hours was so confusing that every thought that he could take hold of pressed him even deeper into the shit that already reached to his neck.

4

"So, what's it going to be now? Do you know the woman or not?" The inspector was growing impatient. For hours now he had been sitting there with this nice doctor, who supposedly could not harm a fly. He was familiar with that, of course. Outwardly dapper and supercilious and internally marked by abysses of the soul. It would not be the first time. The inspector decided to place the fine gentleman under a little more pressure. A little subliminal brutality, a few threats, and he would fall apart.

Rafael Makord was silent. He was silent for a long time. But his silence did not mean that nothing was transpiring in his mind – quite the contrary. Each of his eighty billion nerve cells was working at full speed. All of his cognitive functions, which he had explored during many years of study, seemed occupied with conceiving torments for his tortured soul. The simplest questions became a painful program that burned its way through the convolutions of his brain in cascades of electroshocks.

Do I know this woman or don't I know her? That question was only seemingly simple. And just how could he explain to the inspector that both answers were valid?! That he thought that he knew her somehow, but on the other hand he had no idea who she was. Under the inspector's hammering questions he tried to order his thoughts. Like a mental patient who feels that he is at the mercy of dark ghosts, he tried to find real footing in the confusion of his memories, ready to defend his own reality against the world outside.

What he remembered was the following:

It was true that he had gone to bed with a woman the previous evening. He had known that woman, because she had been something like his girlfriend. He would have liked to have had her as a girlfriend and there were also the first signs that something like tender ties were beginning to develop between them. That evening, the previous evening, had been the evening of decision. They had attended a rock concert in the Linzer Posthof. After that he had invited the woman to dinner, in order to get her into the mood. After that they had gone to his place, and then it should actually have happened. The attractiveness that this woman radiated for him, the erotic fascination that he had felt since their first meeting, everything about her had magically drawn him to her. And every-

5

thing also fit together, the food, the music, the scent, the looks, the kisses. It actually should have worked.

But it did not work. In the decisive moment, when he had slipped her blouse from her body, when he had caught sight of her flawless breasts, when he had caressed her hips tenderly and believed that he was very near his goal, she had jumped up and pushed him away amid wild screams. She had gathered up her clothing, screamed "Rapist!" and had run away. And the only thing that he remembered was that he no longer understood anything anymore. He knew that she loved him. He had waited an entire lifetime for this woman, who was like his spiritual twin. And she had pushed him away like a clump of mud. She saw him as he had never wanted to see himself. Beyond that he knew that on that evening he had felt absolutely miserable and weak, and that he had tried to drown that monstrous feeling with a lot of wine and vodka. He had fallen asleep that way. The woman had been gone and the alcohol had gone to his head. And after that there had been nothing else.

From a distance, through the patches of fog in his confused perception he heard the furious voice of the police inspector: "Come on and confess now. It's quite simple. I can count it on the fingers of one hand. You invited the woman to come home with you. You wanted to have sex with her. That's still not a crime, of course, and the woman didn't look that bad at all. A bit too old perhaps for a young man like you. But that's supposed to be the modern thing. Young man, old woman – if the curves fit, there's actually nothing to say against it. And while still alive the attractiveness of that body probably left nothing to be desired. It's clear that you would have liked to fuck her. Perhaps the old woman even encouraged you, for you don't look too bad yourself. They say that an affair with a young gigolo also appeals to older women. But then for some reason it didn't work. The lady suddenly no longer wanted to do it. Perhaps she rejected you somewhat insultingly. For some reason that is not quite explainable to me, something snapped in your mind then. You felt rejected. You couldn't stand the humiliation. A young man like you – and an older lady rejects you. That really does go too far."

Inspector Wimmer paused meaningfully.

"I gather from your statements that you're a specialist. Just what would a psychologist be likely to diagnose in your case? Mother complex perhaps? Perhaps your mama was not so kind to you in your childhood? Perhaps you've already been rejected often before? Perhaps you've piled up the rejections over several decades – in your subconscious or whatever you call such shit. In any case, the sexual rejection set something in motion in the depths of your soul. I'm not an expert in those things, but the psychiatrists of the Wagner-Jauregg Hospital will clear that all up. The hatred of your dominant mother that has lasted for years, the rejection by many women, all of it was embodied in that woman that night. And suddenly you had to pay them back. Once and for all they had to make good what they had entered into your deficit account. Somebody finally had to pay for all the evil things that wives do to their husbands and mothers to their sons. And then you reached for the knife. That's the way it was. Admit it!"

The young man's eyes stared into emptiness. Perhaps it was easier to say farewell and enter the world of the insane. And just how was he supposed to explain to the inspector that the woman whom he had met did look like the dead woman, but was about twenty years younger than the corpse. If the dead woman were his girlfriend, then she would have aged twenty years in the process of dying. And if that was true, then his consciousness had probably strayed into a paranoid vision.

2

Krumau, September 1941

Told from the point of view of Hermann Markosky

The town on the Moldau River sparkled in the soft glow of late summer. Its inhabitants lined the streets to pay reverence as the new era marched in. Soon the men of the SS and the SA would march past in full regalia, with the black laurel leaves on their lapels, with steel helmets, polished boots, and everything that belonged there. The German Reich stood at the apex of its power. German troops controlled Europe from Hammerfest to Benghazi, from Biarritz to Kiev. The *Führer* was the man of the hour; he had won all the battles, and now his soldiers were getting ready to slay the Russian bear.

Hermann Markosky basked in the light of that wonderful day. He had already bet on the right card years ago and sensed what was in the little speaker from Braunau. That power would change the world. Hermann had read *Mein Kampf* and had known that this was also his struggle. Making amends for the injustice that had been done to the Germans in the Versailles treaties was exactly what he wanted. The German essence would heal the world and Hitler was the prophet of this new era. Markosky had known it, and now it was reality.

The SS unit marched into the city from the south, past old buildings that had once inspired Egon Schiele to create epochal paintings. They continued on across the Moldau bridge, up to the fortress, and across the covered bridge into the castle gardens, where they were gathering for the parade. With their hands on their carbines, the men listened to the speeches of the officers and Party functionaries who praised the deeds of the *Führer* in bombastic tones. For two years Hitler's formative hand had lain over the Sudetenland, the Bohemian Forest, and Czechoslovakia. The injustice of the past was expiated. The Germans from Bohemia had been led home into the Reich, just as had the Austrians, the Alsatians, the Carniolans, and the citizens of Danzig. The concentrated power of the Aryans could no longer be stopped, and that was obvious to the entire world.

Even for Markosky himself it was a special day. First of all, as an SS storm trooper leader he was permitted to lead his own unit. He was now a decision maker in a position for which he had strived for years. In that respect the years of harsh drills, the Party training, and the review of his racial origins had paid off. Hermann Markosky belonged to the elite, and he was proud of it. He was also happy for his family, which came from Krumau. They had eventful times behind them. Twenty-three years ago they had still been members of the national population of the Danube Monarchy. Then the Treaty of St. Germain had awarded them to Czechoslovakia and in so doing had denied the German Austrians, of all people, the right of self-determination, which had been used as an excuse for the destruction of the Royal and Imperial Monarchy. That much injustice had to be punished, of course. Hitler had corrected that injustice and the Sudeten Germans were somebody again. The arrogance of the Czechs, who had oppressed the Germans in the interwar period, was now being paid back with interest.

Markosky was most happy about the fact that this repayment was now the nucleus of his assignment. His unit had been assigned to the Protectorate of Bohemia and Moravia in order to insure peace and order here. And every Sudeten German and especially every Czech could figure out for himself what that meant. Being jovial was over with now. Every Czech nationalist, every dissident, and in general everyone who was suspected of participating in resistance to National Socialism was taken into custody. Off to the labor camp; there they would begin to think differently. It was a special pleasure for Markosky to bring justice to all of the snobbish neighbors who had humiliated him as a child. A brief hint to the Gestapo was sufficient, and things took their course. Everything that they had done to his family in recent years was noted down in the book of justice and now led to unavoidable consequences.

Yes, yes, they should not have gotten into a fight with us, the stupid Czechs, thought Hermann grimly. *For a hundred years they spared no effort to destroy the Habsburg Monarchy, a state that was not all that bad and in which the subhuman Slavs were taught German culture. That is the natural order of things. The strong govern the weak. But the Czechs wanted to turn that natural order upside down, and in 1918 they had reached their goal be-*

9

cause the idiotic Americans gave credence to their crazy arguments. That crack-brained idealist Woodrow Wilson, who had no idea about European conditions. Why did he have to get involved? And then the Czechs became cocky. They actually believed that the weak could govern the strong. But they deceived themselves, deceived themselves very much. And now the bill will be presented to them.

When the parade was over, the soldiers distributed themselves among the city's taverns. Markosky and his friends met in a small bar in the vicinity of the Moldau weir below the fortress hill. From the tavern garden Markosky could watch the play of the water in the loop of the stream that meandered through Krumau. He had loved this place in his hometown since his childhood. Here you saw the fishermen, the birds, the people who were out for a stroll, and the fortress hill; it was the most beautiful and peaceful place in the world. From the water rose a coolness that calmed the mind, especially on hot summer days. Here a person could live comfortably, and that was how it should remain. The intermezzo of the Czechs was over.

Then Markosky saw a familiar face.

"Adi, you old fox, come join us and drink with us. Waiter, another beer, and hurry up!"

Hermann Markosky waved at a young man who stuck out from the crowd with his cold blue eyes and high forehead. *Looks good, that boy, the Aryan has been carved into his face,* thought Markosky. *He really does look good, but no wonder, he's also my brother, of course.*

Adolf Markosky sat down with the men at the table.

"That was a great day for you. The Czechs made long faces," said Adolf. "You could really see how bitterly they clamped their teeth together because they are now no longer the masters in the country."

"He's right," roared the other SS men, "for today Bohemia belongs to us, and tomorrow it will be the whole world."

"It could also have been your day, Adi," said Hermann Markosky insistently. "Join us. Come to the SS and you'll belong to the elite of the Reich."

"I don't know, Hermann. I'm not a political man. Hitler has accomplished some great things, sure, but I really don't have any idea about those things. And besides that, first I must finish my education, and that can take a while yet. If I'm not drafted into the army before then. I received a postponement once, of course, because medicine is a science that is important for the war, and fully trained doctors are more useful to the army than half-trained ones. But a postponement won't work a second time. That's why I sit over my books day and night, for who knows how much time I have left?"

"Adi, you're such a moron. You really have no idea." Hermann Markosky's fascist soul became impatient. "It's precisely with the SS that all doors will be open to you. Come to us and Heinrich Himmler will arrange everything for you. You want to finish your studies? Do it! As an SS man you'll have your doctorate in nothing flat. True Aryans receive special treatment at the universities. No, don't be afraid, not the special treatment that we have planned for subhuman people and weaklings. You'll be channeled through all the examinations at a rapid pace. No professor will dare to let you fail, because we need fully trained doctors on the front as quickly as possible.

"Or don't you want to go to the front and risk your life for the German cause? No problem either. Nobody will accuse you of cowardice. That's completely out of the question with an SS man. We also need you doctors for other tasks. In the many labor camps where we put the Czechs, the Socialists, and the Christian Democrats, you'll have to look after the health of the inmates, so that they finally learn how to work, ha, ha. In that regard I recently heard a lecture given by an SS doctor. They have all kinds of research projects running with regard to genetics, racial purity, and refinement of the Aryan race. They're authentic visionaries. And the best part is, in the labor camps they have all kinds of human research material at their disposal, material that can't protest, ha, ha, ha." Hermann doubled up with laughter.

Adolf felt somewhat uncomfortable in this group. He turned the conversation to other topics, because he still did not want to become a part of this machinery that was invading all of Europe with fame and glory. He was simply a scientist and wanted to enter the field of medical research. While he was drinking his third beer, however, Hermann's arguments began to eat their way slowly into Adi's mind. Research projects with unlimited human material? That could lead to revolutionary results. For centuries ecclesiastical morality had retarded the research enthusiasm of modern medicine. In

11

the beginning physicians had to be careful that they did not wind up being burned at the stake as desecrators of dead bodies. Semmelweis still had to struggle with pseudo-religious ideas about the "genius of the illness," when he discovered the pathogen for childbed fever. Because it did not suit the people in power that he took the field against superstition and ignorance, they finally put him in an insane asylum. How far along medicine could already be if it had not been constantly slowed down by lack of faith and antiquated notions of morality!

Hermann was right about one thing: Ideas of morality were foreign to the Nazis. They were prepared to ignore all taboos, if it served their beliefs. Weren't they like the first anatomists in that regard, the ones who took the corpses from the graves in order to be able to explore the human body at last? Didn't Hitler behave like a surgeon when he spoke of the fact that the rotten ulcers had to be cut out of the body of the German people, in order to lead the latter to health?

Unlimited research possibilities, a quick finish to his studies. That actually sounded seductive. Genetics had always interested Adolf. He was convinced that genetics would dramatically change the future of humanity. But for now he pushed the thought aside again and let himself become infected by the mood of his brother, who was becoming more and more beer-happy and nostalgic.

"Do you remember, Adi, how we played by the weir as boys, even though the stupid Czech police prohibited it? We fished, hunted ducks, and built dams. Those were the days. Once Navratil, the stupid janitor from across the way, discovered us and furiously took us to task. You were so startled that you fell in the water and were about to drown on me, if I hadn't caught you by the collar. And then you wouldn't have become such a great medicine student, would you?"

"Yes, Hermann, back then you probably saved my life, because the current was so swift on account of the melting snow. Since then I've only felt safe when you're in my vicinity. What would I do without you? You're the older one and have always been the stronger one. It does fit that you in particular became a soldier, because you've always supported others and protected people. God knows, that was necessary when the band of Czechs lay in wait for us after school to beat us up."

12

"Today nobody beats us up anymore. Today we're the ones who dish it out. But you're right. We brothers must stick together, like the entire German nation, a united nation of brothers."

"Hermann, stop politicizing everything. I mean that quite personally. If the two of us hadn't stuck together, who knows what would have become of us? We couldn't necessarily count on our parents, of course."

"Are you referring to our melancholy father, that cowardly dog who swallowed everything they threw at him?" Hermann's voice suddenly sounded aggressive.

"Hermann, now you're being unjust. You should understand our father's situation. He was a man who had been destroyed by fate. He always measured himself against Grandfather, and in so doing he had to see himself as a total failure."

"For failures, Adi, for failures we National Socialists have no sympathy. He would have had the chance to make something of his life. But he simply had no guts. He was such a depressive soft-boiled egg. He wasn't a man at all."

"So, how would you feel, if your father were a famous and respected man, a delegate in the imperial parliament in Vienna, president of the Bohemian Chamber of Commerce, and a successful businessman besides, and you yourself wound up as a little hired butcher in the butcher shop that had once belonged to your family? And then for years you could listen to the lament of your father, who didn't forgive you until his dying day for the fact that you squandered the family fortune, as Grandfather used to say."

"Father should simply have fought and offered resistance to his opponents. He could have explained to Grandfather, of course, that all of that wasn't his fault at all. What could Father do about the fact that he had to take over the slaughter house in the middle of the World War, because Grandfather became ill? What could he do about the fact that in 1918 there was no meat left that he could have sold? What could he do about the fact that after the war there was suddenly that stupid border and our traditional customers in Linz looked for other slaughter houses? That was all fate, and he could have overcome it like a man."

Hermann slowly went into a rage: "But what I'll never forgive him for, that abysmal simpleton, that gullible humanitarian, are the mistakes that he made then. He really should have noticed what

13

was going on, when the Czech guild master in Prague turned against him. He should have become suspicious when incidentally no Czech business was prepared to buy his products. That was a big plot, and they didn't intend to hit Father at all, but Grandfather, the all-too-powerful commerce counselor. Those narrow-minded Czechs simply wanted to get their revenge for the fact that the Markosky family had been successful for decades. Out of pure envy they destroyed us, and after 1918 they had the power to do it. The economic depression of 1929 was then only the dot over the *i*. When bankruptcy became unavoidable, those narrow-minded men rubbed their hands together and bought our business. To culminate the humiliation they then offered Father a small job as a butcher in the branch in Krumau. Since everyone else rejected him, he had to take the job and let the old neighbors grin derisively at him every day. 'Well, how are you doing today, Mr. Counselor of Commerce?' 'On your high horse it was probably too windy, wasn't it?' Every one of those statements was a stab in the heart, and it still pains me every time I think of that humiliation."

"And then he simply became depressive and drank. From a medical point of view that's a very normal reaction," Adolf said, trying to placate his brother.

"From a medical point of view, from a medical point of view, get off my back with that shit. They pushed him to death, that band of murderers. And I had to cut him down from the ceiling beam, I, at the age of fifteen, because nobody else was there. Nobody helped me even with that." Suddenly Hermann's entire body was shaking; he wept and buried his face in the table top.

Adi put his arm around his brother to comfort him. He, too, had tears in his eyes when he thought of his father, whose death was so incomprehensible in spite of all the explanations. They had still needed him anyway, they would have had so much to catch up on, where he had never had time throughout their childhood, always occupied with the possibility of still being able to avert the bankruptcy after all. Once again the brothers sensed how much they needed each other, how much sharing their mourning helped them to survive.

Then a comrade butted in and said, "Now he's gotten to the morality thing again. It's always that way after the sixth beer. Now stop crying. Only Jews and laundry women do that."

14

The brothers quickly regained their composure as if they had been caught doing something that was forbidden.

"You're right, buddy." Hermann was apparently in a good mood again. "If the Czechs see us like that, then they've won. Not on your life, another wind is blowing now. What doesn't kill us makes us harder. And it's hardness, after all, that the Czechs need now, isn't it, comrades?!" Hermann's voice was drowned out by the loud yelling of the SS men.

Hermann and Adi made every effort to become cheerful again. Power through joy – that, too, was a command of the *Führer*, which they were supposed to follow. The sadness that had flamed up briefly seeped back down into the subconscious; there it transformed itself slowly into hate again. After several hours of drinking the entire world seemed to be merry and the happy soldiers marched merrily through the Soviet Union, and merrily onward to China, and merrily fell on the necks of the Japanese, and continued to drink happily with them in a victory celebration that never wanted to end.

Hermann could probably have continued to drink himself into unconsciousness in order to deaden the sharp pain in his heart. Then suddenly he was shaken from his grogginess by an army courier. The courier pressed a dispatch into his hands. Hermann read the brief lines that were written in an army staccato and was suddenly wide awake:

"Brother, I don't believe it. Do you know what this is? It's a call-up order to report to the central office of the Reich Protectorate of Bohemia and Moravia in Prague. I've been assigned to Reich Commissioner Heydrich as his personal adjutant. Insane, I can't believe it, such things don't happen. The god Heydrich himself has requested me for special assignments. I've reached the goal of my dreams. *Heil Hitler! Heil Himmler! Heil Göring* and whatever their names all are. I must leave immediately. Adi, come with me to Prague. You'll see. Heydrich's the best. He gets things accomplished. With Heydrich we'll shake the world to its foundations!"

Hermann jumped up on the table and did a dance of joy there, applauded by his comrades. He waved the beer mug in his hand and boisterously poured the contents over the astonished Adi's head. Then the latter was also wide awake and did not know whether he should laugh or cry with his brother.

15

3

November 2, 1991

"You can come out, Makord." The prison warden opened the door of the jail cell in which the young man had spent the night. "You're lucky. Some bigwig did everything in his power to get you out of here, including a telephone call to the police commissioner. When the powerful people use their connections, we little officials get shit on for doing our work. It's a shitty world. So get out of my sight before I change my mind."

Behind the policeman Makord caught sight of a serious figure in a gray suit, whose facial expression betrayed a certain native cunning behind a hard façade.

"May I introduce myself? Wegener is my name, Dr. Wegener. Your father has sent me. He has instructed me to take over your legal representation. I can guarantee you that I'll settle this case as well, just as much to the satisfaction of you and your father as I have settled all of the previous cases in which I have been permitted to be of service to your father."

Wegener, my father's lawyer, thought Makord bitterly. *Now I've really sunk to the depths, if I'm dependent upon the knowledge of this shyster and my father's help.* Makord was torn. On the one hand he had sworn to himself that he would not take anything from his father ever again, no advice, no money, and especially not what his father called support. They had carried on so many discussions with one another, discussions that had always ended in conflict and bitterness. The old Makord, the rotten fascist!

If his father had anything like principles, then they had probably been whispered to him by the devil or by Hitler in person. Father and son were about as similar to one another as fire and water, as heaven and hell, as jungle and desert. Makord had been so happy to have finally escaped from the old man's rigid world. And now this! The old fogy actually imagined that his wayward son was once more in need of Big Daddy's powerful arm.

On the other hand, Makord had to admit that he was in no position to reject offers of support. And the old man *was* powerful, had extended his influence in all directions over the course of decades. The old Makord's word could intimidate officials, cause doctors in the rotation to tremble, and move nurses to tears of impotent rage.

Even if the old man had now retired as chief physician, he had still been skillful enough to continue to cultivate his influential connections. Placed before the choice of either rotting in prison or resuming the militant contact with his father again, which consisted of a mixture of dependency, loathing, and contempt, Makord gritted his teeth and chose the latter. After all, fathers are there to help their sons. Papa will take care of it – that had been drummed into his head from childhood on. Authority and leadership move the world. Even if Makord had ceased to believe in such imbecility fifteen years earlier, the time had now apparently come when even the greatest idiocy could prove to be true. Sons need fathers, at least in order to be released from prison.

Dr. Wegener led Makord to his car. "We'll drive to your father's villa now and there everything else will take the proper direction." The lawyer's jovial eloquence hammered a staccato at Makord's strained nerves. "We'll clarify all of the legal questions. We'll file a complaint against the police. We'll prove that all of this can't be true at all, that you have an alibi, etc. etc. Don't worry at all. Wegener will take care of everything."

For a moment it seemed to Makord as if he were a spinet from the baroque period. His strained nerves were the strings that Wegener sensuously tightened in order to pluck them like a virtuoso, in order to bring forth a furioso composed of different notes. The furioso, however, did not consist of well-tempered piano notes, but of cascades of pain in Makord's head, comparable to the atonal dissonance series of an avant-garde composer.

Makord wished longingly that Wegener would be struck by an acute paralysis of speech.

But that did not help at all; the lawyer continued to address Makord and to bombard him with items of legal terminology. With that he prepared the ground to a certain extent for what awaited Makord when they arrived in front of his father's villa. When they had been led into his father's study by the housekeeper, father and son initially remained silent as they looked at each other.

Makord was familiar with that silence. His father's face looked as if it were petrified – ice cold and yet glowing. Somewhere Ma-

17

kord had read something about cold nuclear fusion, i.e. extreme energy at low temperature. That seemed to him to describe his father's radiance accurately.

There was also something disdainful and dissatisfied. The father had never gotten over the fact that his son had become a weakling, an emotional person – a psychologist, where in the world of medicine door after door would have been opened to him. As Makord endured his father's gaze, he noticed how the coldness radiated back from his own face as well. He, too, had only contempt left for his father. He did not think highly of his world; he condemned it. In their frosty aloofness father and son were equals.

The attorney attempted to break the ice with his superficial eloquence. "We will, of course, file a plea of nullity, in an emergency an appeal. We'll prove that the accusations against your son are absolutely ridiculous. The son of an honorable chief physician – that would be even better. And he doesn't know the woman in question at all, and they don't even know who the corpse is…"

Makord felt as if the lawyer's words were immersing him in the impenetrable clouds of vapor that make any orientation impossible on November days in Linz. A no-win situation that usually ends in a crash while driving on the highway. That diffuse sensation was ended abruptly by his father's striking voice:

"You've made a mess again, my son! But that was to be anticipated from your way of life."

Makord felt a burning rage rise within him, quick as a flash and hot, like glowing magma in the throat of a volcano shortly before the eruption. *That miserable pig, disparage and despise, that's all he can do,* he thought to himself, and then he blurted out, "Just don't think that you finally have me in your grasp or that I give a tinker's damn about your opinions. Fine, you got me out of jail and I should probably be grateful to you for that. But that's purely routine for you, because you old Nazis have all kinds of experience in how to avoid a just prison sentence."

"I forbid you to use that tone with me, my son. I would have sunk into the ground if I had spoken to my father that way. Now you see where you wind up, if you spit on all the values that have made us Germans great. You with your maudlin sentimentality. Without discipline, your drives run away with you. No wonder they think they can make a science out of drives, like that Jew Sigmund

18

Freud. It's all unscientific drivel, this so-called depth psychology that you have devoted yourself to. And where has it taken you, your doctrine of the ambivalence of feeling, that so-called theory of the love-and-death drive? You kill the woman you love like in a cheap crime novel, bah!"

Makord had that old familiar feeling that a lid weighing tons was placed over his anger. The magma flow receded back inside his body and sought out the weakest tissues to unload its destructive power there. Simultaneously Makord's attention jumped into the most rational corner of his mind, where he analyzed his situation like a detached observer. The lid that his father placed upon him again and again had, to be precise, three facets:

First there was the total disdain with respect to other people. Next to the old Makord, the true Aryan, the orthodox, all-knowing physician, nobody else could hold his own. With that poisonous dart of contempt, his father put a leak in all the fuel tanks from which the feeling of self-worth normally feeds, and a person very quickly felt weak, incapable, and guilty.

Second, there was the complete ignorance with regard to the feelings of other people, where empathy would have been appropriate. This act of "not even ignoring" caused the son's world of experience to collapse in a flash, as if his own perceptions were denied their right to exist.

And third, there was the claim to absoluteness of the father's dogmas that caused his son's system of thought to waver again and again, as if the logic of his own mind were abnormal, deformed, and by definition false. After every conversation with his father, the son felt incapable of exercising his will, of feeling and of thinking, like a monstrosity that was to be disposed of as unworthy of life. It was therefore an act of long-standing self-defense that caused Makord to avoid contact with his father.

"Wegener, once again we can't do anything with the boy," the father said caustically. "I suggest that you take care of the matter."

"Very well, Professor, the matter is in good hands with me," Wegener responded solicitously.

The matter, the matter, Makord cursed silently. *Why must they always talk of matters, when it's about people?* Always remain nice and objective — how often he had heard that. Objects have no feelings; objectified people can be mistreated, ignored, cut up, killed, and

19

recycled. Makord had never yet had the desire to remain objective where objectivity was misused as a disguise for power structures. And for as long as he could remember, his father's offer of contact had been a violent one – dominating, manipulating, and ignorant. For that reason he now had no objection to the fact that the conversation with his father came quickly to an end. After all, it was senseless to argue with an old fascist, for that generation did not want to change.

4

Prague, August 1968

The masses on Wenzelsplatz chanted the same words resolutely again and again: "Dubcek, Swoboda, Dubcek, Swoboda, Dubcek, Swoboda." They screamed them at the Russian tanks that occupied their country. The people did not want to accept the fact that now, for the fourth time in this century, they were supposed to endure a foreign occupation force. First the Austrians, then the Germans, then the Russians, and now the Russians again. They did not want to believe that the freedom of the Prague Spring was over. For a whole year the general secretary of the Party, Alexander Dubcek, had given them hope of a humane form of communism, and the Czechoslovakian president, Swoboda, had supported that development. It could not be, it must not be that the invasion of the Russians and the other "brother countries" put an end to those hopes.

Mara marched in the front ranks and waved her transparency "Down with Stalinism." She encouraged the people around her to offer nonviolent resistance to the Russian soldiers. She had learned from her earliest youth that violence could not be tolerated; violence was the illness of Europe; violence had made the Czechs unhappy. Violence must be resisted. Her mother had impressed that upon her so often: We are the victims; we must not forgive the perpetrators, for that would excuse their deeds. We must resist them by pointing out a new path, a path of humaneness, a nonviolent path. That was exactly what Dubcek was preaching to his countrymen, the thing with which he moved them to enthusiasm, even now, after the invasion of the Russians. No violence! We are walking a new path. We will stop the tanks with flowers.

How right he was. How astonished and helpless the Russian soldiers were when the demonstrators put flowers in their hands and stuck flowers in the barrels of the tank guns. How were they supposed to fight against peaceful demonstrators? Mara trusted Dubcek and she trusted her mother's words. She was certain that she was on the right side. The Czech flower revolution would win.

21

Although they were surrounded by innumerable people, the tanks moved slowly forward. They were on the way to the government buildings, to the radio station, and to the Czech Communist Party headquarters, and they would not let themselves be stopped by a few unarmed demonstrators. At least that was what their orders said. The people in the front ranks had to jump aside in order not to be crushed by the tanks.

Mara wrinkled her forehead. They must not be permitted to get through. They must not be permitted to arrest Dubcek. They must not be permitted to remove the Czech government. That had to be prevented.

Then an idea occurred to her: "We'll stop the tanks with our bodies!" she shouted loudly and lay down on the ground. Others took up the cry: "We'll stop the tanks with our bodies!" And soon dozens of people were lying on the street. The tanks stopped. To crush defenseless people in a time of peace – even hard-trained tank commanders did not have the heart to do that.

The strategy worked. The tanks were able to move forward only a centimeter at a time, and the people did not slide aside until the very last moment. It went back and forth that way a few times, and finally the progress of the tanks came to a stop.

It remained that way until into the night. The people sat on the street, and the tank commanders looked helplessly down at them from their turrets. A good mood spread.

Antonin, who sat next to Mara, raved about the victory that they had won that day over the Russians: "We'll drive them out of the country with our bare hands. They can't defeat a united nation, not in 1968, not in a civilized world. They would make total fools of themselves if they put down this reform movement with brutality. They'll see that. They must see that."

"Let's wait and see," Mara tempered her fellow student's euphoria. "The Russians have never shied away before, from sacrificing a few people in order to safeguard their power. Have you forgotten the millions of victims of Stalinism, the purges in the Party and the army, the dead kulaks, the political prisoners in the gulags? No, the Russians have always been difficult to get along with."

"This time we'll be successful. The violence of the past could only be successful as a political implement on the basis of suppression and palliation. Stalin was able to liquidate millions and in spite of that persuade the people through his propaganda apparatus that he was their nice little father who protected everyone. But now there's television that immediately makes every act of violence visible to the entire world. Don't you see the many journalists with their cameras in our ranks? Peaceful demonstrators crushed by tanks – just how would that look in the evening news? The people of India have already used that to get rid of the English, and the Vietnamese are doing exactly the same thing with the Americans. You can't win wars that way anymore. The Russians are brutal, to be sure, but they're not stupid. They won't dare act against us and depose our elected politicians."

"I hope you're right." Mara became more optimistic again. "By the way, do you know that the Russians also want to prohibit the steamrollers now?"

"Why? Do they want to prevent the Czechs from driving cars?"

"No, no, they are irritated by the loud noises from the machines because they constantly hiss Dub – cek, Dub – cek, and that drives the Russians crazy."

Antonin laughed at the little joke, and they kept themselves awake all night with jokes about the Russians and discussions about the future of the gentle revolution.

The next morning, the Russians turned to a new strategy. Infantrymen moved up and began to carry away the sitting demonstrators. In the beginning that did not help much because new demonstrators sat down on the ground in place of those who had been carried away. In spite of that the Russians kept to their strategy, and thus it soon came to scuffles between soldiers and Czechs. The rumor made the rounds that the Russians were not only carrying the people away but had already begun making arrests. Some people became afraid and withdrew. The determined ones remained sitting there.

Mara was suddenly in the middle of the tumult. Around her there was a tangle of bodies that stretched and twisted themselves in order to escape the clinging arms of the soldiers and the men in uniform all around, who forced themselves between the bodies in order to clear them out of the way.

Mara was grabbed by two soldiers. She resisted and screamed, "You can't arrest me! This is a free country! You're treading on the idea of communism with your feet. Stop! Put yourselves on our side!" But it did not help at all. She was dragged across the street to an army truck, and they roughly shoved her into it. The vehicle was soon full of people. Russians with machineguns ready to fire held them threateningly in check.

The truck drove to the outskirts of the city and stopped in front of a building that had apparently been remodeled into a provisional prison. The Russians led the people into the building and locked them by tens in small rooms whose windows were barred. Mara sat down in a corner and looked around her. *A former boarding school*, she thought to herself. *They put in the bars so that the pupils could not run away and go home. So now the Russians want to keep their eye on us. That can be trouble yet.* But she thought to herself that they would let them go again in a short time.

Just what could they object to in her case? That she supported her people just like all the other Czechs? Then they would have to arrest all of Czechoslovakia, and they would not find that many boarding schools in the entire country. No, the Russians just wanted to achieve their objectives, and for that they had to get the people off the streets. Then they would want to have peace and quiet, the peace and quiet of a cemetery, to be sure, but peace and quiet nonetheless. Thousands of innocent detainees would only further heat up the mood in the country, they knew that. They would soon send them home again.

The next few days confirmed Mara's estimation of the situation. Gradually her roommates were set free. New demonstrators moved into their places and were put in the room with Mara. It was only a matter of hours until it was Mara's turn. They needed space.

Many days passed. Mara had already been in the provisional prison for a week. The room had already been filled and emptied again several times. Every time she wanted to go free with her comrades, the military guard turned her back.

They seemed to have forgotten Mara.

Slowly she began to worry.

*

At the same time, a few doors down, in the office of the watch commander, a momentous discussion took place.

Alexander Kyusnov, the watch commander, saw himself confronted by an unfriendly figure who had sat down in front of his desk. The man across from him sat there in a stiff pose and a flawless uniform and presented himself as being very Russian. But somehow his face did not look Slavic, and his Russian had an accent that Kyusnov unfortunately could not identify.

The visitor raised his eyes threateningly: "You don't have to look at me so skeptically, Comrade Kyusnov. You know who and what I am."

Kyusnov did not want to know it that precisely and therefore remained defiantly silent.

Then the weird visitor became clearer: "So, to refresh your memory, everything once more: My name is Mayinski and I represent the KGB here. I therefore don't have to emphasize that my assignment came from the highest level, and that there can be no discussion about carrying out the necessary measures."

Kyusnov actually did not feel like discussing things, as much as the behavior of the arrogant stranger disgusted him.

The latter seemed accustomed to not having people contradict him, and so he continued his monolog: "So I suggest that you again quietly look through the list of the detainees that I gave you days ago and determine whether or not they're all able to be moved. I mean, I don't know, of course, how intensive and with what means they were 'questioned.' In the case of grave injuries you will see to the appropriate medical care. In two days, let's say Saturday at one p.m., the deportation will occur."

Now Kyusnov's resistance stirred after all. He could not understand what was required of him there: "I don't intend to question the appropriateness of your order, of course, I simply don't quite understand. Do you really intend to transport Czech citizens away to Russia? After all, they're only simple workers and students who protest against our invasion. They'll quiet down in a few weeks anyway, when they see that they have no chance against us. And then we'll have pacified Czechoslovakia and freed it of counterrevolutionary elements as designed in the plan of the Soviet International."

25

Kyusnov had hoped to be able to pacify the man across from him with the memorized cadre slogans. When Mayinski did not betray the least emotion, the watch commander had to state things more plainly: "If we now cause people to disappear, that will only stir up the people to new demonstrations. That really doesn't make any sense. We want to have our cause appear in a just light before the eyes of the world. Deportations would be water on the mills of our opponents."

"The matter is closed, and in your own interest you should stop asking such questions."

"Why do you specifically want these two dozen people, when we've already released hundreds of others? Let's take this Mara K. or this Antonin N. – they're certainly not counterrevolutionaries or agents. They're young students who permitted themselves to be incited."

Mayinski's face showed no emotion and Kyusnov slowly became despondent: "The mothers and fathers of those students will go to the barricades if they don't get their children back. I don't see what your deportation is supposed to accomplish, aside from the fact that reports about it will be smuggled to foreign countries and the media will present us once more as the empire of evil. That can't serve the communist idea. Freeing Czechoslovakia of counterrevolutionary elements, yes, but I consider unnecessarily severe measures to be counterproductive."

Mayinski became impatient. He put on his fanatical expression: "Comrade, you're risking your military rank if you don't immediately end this discussion. I can't tolerate this insubordination. It's undoubtedly clear to you that I must report this to my superior, and that can have unforeseeable consequences for you personally. So be reasonable and carry out my orders!"

The threat worked. Kyusnov became afraid. Or perhaps it was only the usual insight into the reality that nothing can be done against the power apparatus.

"Very well, Comrade Colonel, the prisoners will be ready to march away on Saturday at one o'clock. They're all in flawless condition, since no severe hearings took place. Long live the international revolution!"

*

26

When Mara was finally led from her cell, she breathed a sigh of relief. They had not forgotten her after all. She had known it. It had only been a question of time until they set her free. When she was shoved into the military truck again, however, she had an uneasy feeling. When the vehicle full of prisoners left Prague and headed east, Mara's fear changed to panic. In her despair she screamed at the guards: "Where are you taking us? I didn't do anything. You can't lock me up! I have a little daughter in Prague. I have to go to her. She needs her mother. She doesn't know where I am and she will already be in the depths of despair."

The Russian soldier showed no emotion.

Mara jumped up agitatedly: "What are you doing with us? Why are you doing it? This can't be true!"

But the soldier silently shoved the barrel of his machinegun toward her and motioned for her to sit down again.

Mara wept. It suddenly became clear to her that she would perhaps never see her child again. She pleaded once more for sympathy: "You have a mother, too. What would it be like for her, if she never saw her child again? Could you do that to your mother? My daughter is still so small, only three years old. And she doesn't have a father. What will become of her without me? You just can't do that!"

"Orders," the soldier growled in Russian, but his voice had a placating, even apologetic tone. He actually felt sorry for the young woman.

Mara looked out at the fields of the Czech plain. Perhaps for the last time. What would become of her little girl? Sure, Mama would take care of her. But how could Mara bear to live without knowing how her daughter was doing? She could not do it. She would not be able to stand it. It would drive her crazy.

Unimpressed, the Russians continued to drive eastward.

5

November 3, 1991

"So now tell me very calmly what happened that night. You can tell me everything. You must tell me everything, no matter how abysmally despicable it might be, for I'm your lawyer." Wegener's murmuring voice made its way into Makord's inner ear and evoked there a sensation similar to the whistling tinnitus that had tormented many of his patients for years. This disgusting man didn't really expect him to spread out his deepest motivations openly before him, did he? As a psychologist Makord was accustomed, to be sure, to gazing into the depths of other people. But he also knew a lot about the façades that most people erect to hide their inner lives from the outside world. So it was also an easy thing for him to let a conversation partner run up against such a façade: "I already told the police inspector. I really have no idea what happened that night. I was drunk, and I had never before seen the woman who was lying on my bed in the morning."

"Now do stop trying to fool me," Wegener growled, "and tell me the whole story once and for all. Otherwise I can't do anything for you."

The whole story! What was the whole story? If Makord had learned one thing during his course of study, then it was the knowledge of how difficult it is to obtain the whole story, no matter what it was about. Human perception has infinitely many facets, and what we think we know usually coincides with only a part of reality. Health and illness differ from one another above all in the degree to which perception and reality coincide. To make it even more complicated, it could be determined that health and normality were a matter of pure convention. If a person's perception corresponded to what the majority of his fellow human beings considered to be reality, then the person was healthy. The belief in witches, devils, and demons was absolutely in order during the Middle Ages, but in the 20th century a sign of insanity, even though in that particular century so many demonic things happened to the people.

28

While Makord refused to enter into a dialogue with the repulsive lawyer, his thoughts wandered to the student years that had formed him to such an extent. Father, of course, had de facto declared him to be insane when he wanted to study psychology. Psychology, an unprofitable science, how was one ever supposed to earn money with that? Father had been thoroughly flabbergasted when Makord began to grow interested in depth psychology, in the subconscious, in the carnal motivations of human beings, in the innermost secrets of the soul, in the dark past, the apparently rational acts that were distorted by irrational motives.

For a long time Makord had not understood what horrified his father so much about Freud, Adler, Jung, and Reich. No – Makord had to correct himself – Father acknowledged C. G. Jung more than the others, strange. Finally Makord discovered that all except C. G. Jung were of Jewish descent, and that all of psychoanalysis had been rejected and de facto exterminated by the fascists as a Jewish science. Hitler had driven all the psychoanalysts, apart from a few Aryan exceptions, from Vienna. They had never returned and had also never been asked to return. Then it had suddenly become clear to Makord: With his interest in depth psychology he had penetrated into the darkest shadows of his father's soul. As critical sons often do, he was able to provoke his father most with that field which the latter least wanted to see: unconscious feelings and motivations, even motivations in general – they were what the fascists suppressed most, the things that had no place in their biological view of the world, the things they intended to exterminate completely in order to become hard Aryans. So that was what drove the father to white-hot anger with regard to his emotional son.

"So, once more from the beginning," Wegener murmured on, and the whistling in Makord's head swelled to the roar of a five-ton truck. "Try to remember what happened that night." Reluctantly Makord began his description: "So, in the evening I went out with my girlfriend. At least I thought that Vera could become my girlfriend. We had become acquainted a few weeks earlier and seemed to understand each other well. Our thoughts and feelings were somehow similar. The one seemed to grasp immediately what the other one was saying."

"And did you have a sexual relationship?" A voyeuristic glow flashed briefly in Wegener's eyes.

29

"It didn't go that far, or rather, on that evening it should have gone that far. We went to a romantic restaurant for dinner. Waiter and candle light, everything fit together. Then we went back to my place and continued to drink that delicious *Vino Tinto* from Andalusia that I have stored at home. I put on Bruckner's third symphony. We embraced and began to undress each other. When we were standing naked in front of one another and I wanted to take her very firmly in my arms, she suddenly pushed me away from her, hit me in the face, and cursed me as a rapist. Before I could recover from my astonishment, she had gathered up her clothes and stormed out of the apartment, and in the process she continued to scream imprecations at me from the stairwell."

"Can you explain that to yourself somehow?" the astonished lawyer interjected.

"Of course not! What would you think, if the woman that you had just fallen in love with dealt with you in that manner?"

"Did you perhaps get involved with an insane woman?" Wegener's voice had an ironic undertone.

"That's naturally always the simplest explanation," Makord lectured with the face of a psychologist. "If you don't understand something about the person facing you, you declare him or her to be insane. Usually you only express with that the fact that you know nothing about the other person. No, Vera wasn't insane, but on that evening something snapped within her. And what that was, I simply don't grasp."

"And what happened after that?"

"I was naturally deeply crushed, sad, and depressed. I finished drinking the remaining bottles of the *Vino Tinto* alone to deaden my sorrow. And then I fell deeply and completely asleep. When I awoke the next morning the dead woman was lying next to me."

"Couldn't it be that you forgot something there? Perhaps you didn't tolerate the rejection and the insult. Perhaps the woman did come back? It came to a scuffle and you reached for the knife. Perhaps you didn't want to kill her at all, but only to injure her, the way that you yourself had been injured in your masculine pride. It could have been that way. When you saw what you had done, something snapped in your mind because of the shock. Retrograde amnesia, we're familiar with that, of course. The famous suppression that you psychologists make so much fuss about struck you yourself this time."

"But all that doesn't fit together. Above all, it wasn't the same woman. The dead woman isn't my girlfriend!"

"You can tell that fairytale to your grandmother." Wegener became impatient. "You already described for me earlier, during our ride in the car, exactly how your girlfriend looks: Small, petite, black hair, brown eyes, curved hips – and that's exactly how the woman looks, whom I was earlier allowed to view in the morgue."

The attorney was about to place his dirty fingers on the sorest point of the story. Actually Makord was not certain himself. Purely externally it could have been the same woman. It would mean, however, at the same time, that Makord was insane or had gotten into a nightmare that he could not understand. If, however, he did not want to doubt his own sanity, then it could not be the same woman, and specifically for a very definite reason: "The dead woman is twenty years too old to be my girlfriend." Makord forced the words out in torment.

"Well, we won't get anywhere with it in front of the court, if we enter a plea of non compos mentis because the girlfriend was too old for you. It's said to be modern these days for young men to take older women. Oedipus complex and so on. On the contrary, that is, of course, the best motive for murder! First you need them, and when they become too old for you, you want to get rid of them again – an act committed in the heat of passion, murder. With that explanation we'll deliver you right into the prosecutor's hands."

"No, you don't understand anything at all. The dead woman does look like my girlfriend, but she is approximately twenty years older than the woman that I was with."

For a brief moment, for which Makord was infinitely grateful, Wegener was speechless. For a few minutes of silence no further questions occurred to him. Finally that roguish, cunning expression flitted across his face again: "Just what did you put in the good woman's wine? Have you perhaps changed sides and joined the chemists? These days, of course, biochemistry can produce almost everything. Why shouldn't there be substances that exorbitantly accelerate the process of aging when combined with alcohol? Per-

31

haps you wanted to make the lady cooperative with some little tablet and in the process you overlooked a substantial side effect?"

Makord felt how the kettle of his pent-up anger slowly began to boil again: "You don't believe that yourself. We're not in a science fiction novel in which people can age twenty years overnight."

Again Makord's mind wandered. He remembered the film *Zardoz*, in which rapid aging was used as a punishment for disorderly fellow beings. In another film Mel Gibson had aged decades within hours, after he had spent the previous years cryogenically frozen. In those films it seemed absolutely real that people suddenly became old. In reality as well there are experiences where people under stress become old and gray within hours. If his girlfriend felt that she had been treated badly and indecently by him, then that was probably such a stress.

Wegener did not relent: "What biochemistry and genetic technology accomplish these days is really very impressive. So, who can say that in the laboratories of our chemists there have not been substances for a long time that can steer the aging process? I just read that there is a certain gene that is responsible for the velocity of aging in the different species. Perhaps you psychologists are not at all as harmless as you act? Perhaps there's an illicit field test running secretly here? Patients receive a tranquilizer and in reality a pill is being tested that influences the aging process. Any pharmaceutical firm would do anything to find the pill of eternal youth. But if the experiment goes wrong, then the pendulum swings in the wrong direction and the person becomes older instead of younger – bad luck. That's why these experiments must be conducted in secret, of course, because with such a risk you would never receive a license for the tablets. It would not be the first time, of course, that doctors have lent themselves to such things, if it results in a lot of money. And in this situation it's probably a matter of a lot of money that a little, poorly paid psychologist could really use."

Makord's nervous system was on the point of collapse. His mind felt as if the cogwheels of his thought mechanisms were gradually blocking each other. What Wegener prattled on so sloppily about corresponded exactly to the criticism that Makord had to level against modern medicine and biotechnology. It was actually conceivable that the study of genes, neurotransmitters, and enzymes was being abused to manipulate human beings. It was possible to turn the physical and mental structure of human beings upside down by means of chemicals. This could definitely happen without the knowledge of the affected person, as was customary and even scientifically necessary in the so-called double blind studies, in which neither the physician nor the patient know which medicine is administered. That had also often occurred in the history of medicine. There was, for example, a seriously discussed theory that the AIDS epidemic in Africa was started by an unauthorized polio vaccination program, without the Africans knowing what was happening to them. Makord lived in a time when Aldous Huxley's horror visions in *Brave New World* were gradually becoming reality. The progress of biotechnology had become so rapid that nothing seemed impossible anymore. So, why couldn't a young woman become an old one overnight on the basis of a poisoning? Anything is possible if the feral pack of unscrupulous researchers is turned loose on humanity.

But it seemed unthinkable that Makord in particular would get involved with the devils of that biological research. After all, he had turned away from his father's world of medicine for the very reason that he detested all of the effects of modern research so much. Because that one-sided biologism was deeply repulsive to him, he had decided in favor of the study of the mind. Specifically because he had no interest at all in biochemistry and genetic engineering, he would never in his life have gotten involved with one of those pharmaceutical companies that were his archenemies. Only in a state of mental derangement would he use such substances and put them in his girlfriend's wine.

With that Makord had arrived once more at his central question: Was he mentally deranged? Was the common opinion true, that psychologists are themselves insane? Did he perhaps have a split personality that in its conscious part rejected everything that came from his father's world, but in its shadowy unconscious part continued his father's work and secretly opened doors and gates into human minds for biotechnology, without the conscious part noticing it? Did he perhaps, in his unconscious mind, want to obtain his father's recognition by secretly carrying out experiments similar to the ones his father had performed as a young physician? Everything was conceivable in a world composed of insane phenomena.

33

Once again Makord was confronted by the deep self-doubts that suggested that perhaps something was wrong with himself. For years he had sensed that there were shadows in his past that were dark and threatening but inaccessible to his consciousness. At that point of his thought process a red warning lamp always flashed, which moved Makord to walk no further along that path of self-knowledge: "You're now entering the taboo zone. If you cross that boundary you'll be shot," something seemed to scream loudly inside him. Makord knew that he had to take that warning seriously, if he wanted to keep his five senses together. He therefore abruptly terminated the conversation with the attorney, turned around, and walked out the door.

A somewhat astonished Dr. Wegener remained behind.

6

Prague, June 1942

Told from the perspective of Adolf Markosky

"Well, didn't I tell you that the SS has something to offer? In that uniform even your wretched figure looks quite decent." Hermann exuberantly boxed his brother's shoulder. "You finally came to your senses and joined us. But now tell me, how are you doing with your new duty?"

The two brothers had met in a coffee house in the vicinity of the Karlsbrücke. Adi looked thoughtfully out over the buildings in the old part of the city to the Hradčany Castle, and his eyes stopped at the St. Vitus Cathedral. Hermann's boisterousness tore him away from his dismal thoughts once more.

"Oh, well, not bad, I mean, there are worse things. My work in Terezin isn't uninteresting, but it's only medical routine. Listening to lungs, measuring blood pressure, reporting on the health condition of the prisoners, and so on and so forth."

"Nothing worse, now listen." Hermann's spirit, which had been hardened in many Party training sessions, knew no pardon for his sensitive brother. "Didn't everything work out super? You obtained your doctor's degree in record time, under the wings of invisible patrons, of course, that's clear. A little note from Heydrich was sufficient and your path was as smooth as the German Autobahn. And now you already have your first position as a camp doctor. What more do you want? Yes, yes, I tell you, the war is promoting your career. Brother, we're going to go a long way yet. All over the East capable men will be needed, military people, organizers, and naturally doctors as well. We're going to transform entire countries. Together we'll clean up the trash and the sloppiness. The two of us, Brother, you and I, we're going to land right at the top. We'll outdo our old grandfather in houses, and the name Markosky will glow like it did in the old days. Although, since we're talking about it right now, Markosky needs to be polished up a little, doesn't sound German enough. Perhaps when we have an opportunity we should Aryanize the name a bit."

"Hermann, now you're taking off again. We really don't need to change our name. It's good enough. And what's that supposed to mean? Do you really intend to claim that I owe my success only to Heydrich?"

"No, no, it wasn't meant that way. Of course it's first and foremost your success. If you weren't such a smart guy, you would certainly not already have your medical doctorate in your pocket at the age of twenty-two. But a little help from friends can't hurt, can it? Let's say that the SS accelerated your unavoidable success somewhat and perhaps saved you two or three semesters, so that everything was finished before you were inducted for duty that was important for the war. And you do have to admit that it's much more enjoyable to spend the war as a doctor with the rank of lieutenant, than to spend it as a medical orderly bandaging screaming wounded men."

"Yes, that's certainly true. And I'm also really proud of my final examination. You know, success is a great thing, and quick success is marvelous and screams for more. I just can't wait to be called up for really important assignments. You know, medicine really can change the world. Through hygiene, vaccination, and eugenics we can totally revolutionize ailing old Europe and put it on healthy legs. I already have my own ideas about how that will work."

"You see, old boy, I like you like this." Hermann became intoxicated with the delusions of grandeur that he had fostered for a long time. "Now you've grasped the trend of the new era. That very thing is what we National Socialists want, too. To put the ailing Europe on healthy legs. You could say that we're the medicine that the sick Europe needs. What's good in medicine must be right in politics. If we want to bring Aryan man into full bloom, then we must exterminate the European plagues. You can't negotiate with plague and cholera, you have to destroy them. We're the immune system that destroys the bacteria. For that reason we must smoke out the rat holes, cut out the puss pockets, and destroy the vermin through disinfection."

"Just a minute, I'm the doctor. Where did you suddenly get such a medical way of saying things?" protested Adi with a laugh.

"I can't do anything about it. I have it all from Heydrich. I tell you, the man is efficient. What he takes hold of has substance. You

36

should listen to him sometime when he comes with his visions for the East: a thoroughly cleansed land, totally plowed up, the ground fruitfully prepared for Aryanization. The world won't recognize those countries!"

"Hermann, but now you're exaggerating!" Adolf protested. "One could think that you were talking about Siegfried from Wagner's *Ring des Nibelungen.*"

"That's what I'm doing, that's what I'm doing! The man is really a figure of light, a true Aryan. Even Adolf Hitler can't compete with him. In his views he's as clear as glass, immediately knows what has to be done, and in the implementation he's ice cold, I tell you. He doesn't let himself be stopped by any scruples, once he has recognized the importance of a thing. I could listen to him for hours. You know, there's finally someone there whom I can really approve, who's even above me. All during my childhood I had to decide on my own, and now there's somebody here who knows the way. And how! He has all the maps in his head, from Prague to Vladivostok."

"But just what is he actually planning to do?" Hermann's enthusiasm for Heydrich made Adolf very uneasy. "After all, he can't exterminate all the Russians and replace them with Germans. And he can't lock up all the Poles that are against Hitler in camps. We can't build camps that big at all. You know, in my work as a camp doctor doubts come to me, too. Must we really imprison so many people and treat them so brutally? With many of the people I examine, I find clear signs of torture and then have to write something stupid in the report like 'fell down the stairs.' And then again and again there are executions without a trial, and then they call it 'shot while trying to flee.' Is that the new era that you're always talking about?"

"Oh, Adi, now you're the old simpleton again. You're going to become a gullible philanthropist like your father yet. Did you think that the construction of a new world would take place entirely without sacrifices? Where things are smoothed with a plane, shavings fall, and in the war there are those who fall. That was the case in Caesar's time, with Charlemagne, and with Genghis Khan. Do you know how many dead people those great military leaders have on their consciences? And does that diminish at all their place in history? On the contrary! It's just the opposite. The more dead

37

bodies a leader leaves on the field of battle, the more famous he becomes. That's the magic of power. Death in the battle establishes the fame of the victor. Without dead people, no fame, it's very simple."

"The losses in battle I can understand, but the civilians in Poland and Russia…"

"Not the Poles, not the Russians," said Hermann interrupting his brother, "Heydrich wasn't aiming at them at all. The Slav is, to be sure, subhuman and inferior in his heritage. But in the final analysis he's definitely related to the German and also comes, if you want to put it that way, from the original Aryan race. That means, through eugenic breeding the Slavic nations are thoroughly capable of ennoblement. The victorious soldiers will impregnate the women of the defeated peoples and in so doing they will proliferate the race of the victor. That's the oldest form of eugenic breeding, as old as humanity. We'll let the Poles and the Russians live. They will simply be Aryanized.

"No, what Heydrich has in mind is the real pest that is poisoning our race. Genetically it's the Jews of the world who already control the economy and the financial markets of this world. And spiritually it's the Bolsheviks of the world who are undermining and contaminating the strength of the individual with that crazy idea of communism.

"In communism nobody has to exert himself, for the others do everything anyway. That leads directly to decadence and is the exact opposite of the Aryan superman. Hitler has now recognized that world Jewry and the Bolsheviks of the world have joined forces to begin dominating the world together. That's a struggle of good against evil, superman against the subhuman, light against darkness. There can be no compromises there."

Everything went black for Adi. He slowly began to grasp the extent of what Hitler and Heydrich, the SS and the SA were really planning. And he was not sure what he should think of that vision, whether he should admire that genetic revolution or whether its effect on people should make him shudder. For a few moments he was totally speechless.

"That flabbergasts you, doesn't it? That's what I've been telling you. Heydrich doesn't leave anyone unimpressed, not even if you've never seen him with your own eyes. He who is not for me is

38

against me – that was recognized already two thousand years ago by a man who would change the world. And now you're one of us. You're marching with us. Together we'll enter the light of the new Valhalla, and the new Odin will lead us."

Adi was still speechless. Hermann was once again in the other dimension from which it was so difficult to bring him back into reality.

"Well, Brother, it's already late! I have to go back to my work." Hermann was still totally euphoric. "Heydrich is having a public reception now. He needs me there. You know, propaganda and so forth. Next time you can tell me more about your work in the camp, alright?"

Adolf followed his brother with his eyes for a long time. When the latter walked across the Karlsbrücke, his form slowly grew smaller and finally disappeared in the direction of the Hradčany Castle where the reception was supposed to take place in the state-rooms. When he was sitting alone in the coffeehouse, he lapsed once more into the brooding that had already plagued him all his life. For or against, who was supposed to know that? "Don't ponder things so much, boy," his mother had often said to him. "You can't change the course of things. Do like your brother. He simply storms off and takes hold of the thing. He's much happier than you are."

But Adolf could not do things differently. He had to look at every situation first from all sides, weigh the advantages against the disadvantages, and assess the dangers. Only when he was quite sure that the advantages outweighed the disadvantages and that a thing had to be done, only then did he make his decision. Then, however, he uncompromisingly followed through with it to the last consequence. He would never change a decision once it had been reached and wrested from his pondering.

Eugenics, racial renewal, medical progress, the new man, health of the entire nation, success for all Germans – different thoughts and theories danced though Adolf's head. The thoughts whirled and gave him no peace. Adi knew from experience that this storm of thoughts always took place when a new theory crystallized out in his mind. Those were often important turning points in his life, and for that reason he let his thoughts run freely. At some point he noticed that the empty coffee cups were piling up on his table. So he must have already given free play to his thoughts for some time. *Doesn't matter*, thought Adi and enjoyed this leisure that accompanied extreme mental activity.

Suddenly there was great turmoil outside on the streets. Sirens howled, policemen and soldiers were running around, all in the direction of the Hradčany Castle. With a dark premonition Adolf ran out into the street and asked a soldier what was happening.

"They murdered Heydrich. The Czech criminals simply blew him up. Before the eyes of the German army and the police. That simply can't be true."

Adolf could not breathe: "Heydrich alone, or somebody else as well?"

"His adjutant threw himself in front of him to protect him. His name is Markwitz or something like that. But it didn't do any good. Now both of them are dead."

Adolf was numb. He felt again the piercing pain in his breast that had tormented him since his father's suicide. As with a minor heart attack, when a part of the heart muscle dies and hardens, Adolf made his own diagnosis. Medically his heart was completely in order, and it would also be that way this time. But spiritually his heart was now dead and petrified for all time. He was now alone. He would never again love anyone as much as he had loved his brother.

In that deepest loneliness, Adi's soul saved itself through a magical ritual. Adi melted together internally with his dead brother. Hermann's spirit jumped over into him, and his brother's legacy would continue to live through him. Adi accepted Hermann's characteristics into himself: the determination, the boldness, and the uncritical devotion to the plan that had once been decided upon.

In his pain regarding his dead brother, Adolf took on his racist ideas: Hermann was right. There was good and evil and there was the battle between light and darkness. The time of pondering was past. It was time to fight against the darkness. After taking his father from him, the Czechs had also taken his brother. The Czechs were the evil and the darkness. As in the holy battles, Adi reached for the flag that had slipped out of his fallen brother's hands and raised it on high, so that it fluttered in the wind, visible for a long distance.

It was the flag of revenge – and Adi looked upward at the bloody inscription: Counted, paid, and repeatedly avenged.

7

November 4, 1991

There it was again, the siren that howled in his ears. In Makord's nightmare it announced the approaching air raid. The American bomber squadrons came at night to raze the *Führer's* home town to the ground. In panic the people rushed into the air raid shelters, Makord in the middle of them. In the stairwell he stumbled, fell headlong, and the crowd trampled over him and stepped on his head. It was suddenly nothing but soldiers' boots that were shattering his skull.

He woke up bathed in perspiration. The sirens of the air raid became weaker and turned out to be the ringing of the doorbell. When Makord opened the door, weary and crestfallen, Wegener stood at the entrance.

"If the mountain doesn't come to the prophet, the prophet must probably come to the mountain," trumpeted the lawyer cheerfully. "You disappeared from my office so quickly yesterday that I couldn't make heads or tails of your behavior. I therefore thought that we should continue our nice conversation of yesterday."

Makord was too tired to protest. *What difference does it make,* he thought, *somehow I do need him, of course. Somebody has to help me out of my miserable situation.*

Wegener looked around the psychologist's apartment and whistled appreciatively through his teeth: "Well, well, you have it quite nice here. To be sure, it doesn't compare at all to the period pieces in your father's villa, but on the other hand it's quite witty."

His gaze swept across the hodgepodge of Ikea shelves, Thonet chairs, late nineteenth century desks, and different small souvenirs from various countries. On the walls were abstract paintings that Makord fabricated in his spare time when he wanted diversion from the problems of his clients. It was a bachelor apartment, where dirty dishes and unwashed laundry contributed to the supplemental background of the picture as a whole.

"So, where did we leave off yesterday?" Wegener began cheerfully. "We were talking about clarifying the identity of the dead woman and additionally about clarifying the identity of your girl-friend. Yesterday we were not yet in agreement as to whether it was a matter of two different identities in this case, or of one and the same identity, right?"

Makord nodded his head miserably.

"Yesterday we concerned ourselves with the biochemical hypotheses," Wegener declared expertly. "They were, of course, thoroughly fascinating, but also somewhat complicated. Overnight a more plausible possibility occurred to me. Couldn't it be that the dead woman is a relative of your girlfriend, that is, her mother, an aunt, a cousin, or something? On the one hand that would explain the similarity, on the other the great age difference, which perhaps really can't have arisen so quickly."

"Vera has no relatives, at least not here in Austria. She grew up in Prague in her grandmother's home. Her mother has been missing for twenty years, and her father is unknown. Vera only came to Austria a year ago to study sociology for two semesters in Linz. She came here all alone and has never had any visitors. Even if a relative had come to visit, it could probably have only been her grandmother. And she's over seventy, and the dead woman would be too young for that. And the theory that I would go to bed with my girl-friend's grandmother is really stretching it. The Oedipus complex is, of course, well known; that is, men who are fond of women who could be their mothers. Men who are fond of women who could be their grandmothers are rather rare."

Although Makord actually had nothing to laugh about in his situation, a grin crossed his face at this joke. He had finally given Wegener a snappy retort.

"Hm, so not a relative," murmured the lawyer. "Perhaps a doppelganger? That's a familiar phenomenon, of course: people who look alike because they happen to be of the same type, have the same beard shape, the same hairstyle, etc. Don't laugh. It happens to me constantly that I'm confused with people that have a moustache like mine. You know Jürgen von der Lippe from German television, of course. That television moderator happens to have a beard shape that resembles mine exactly. You won't believe how often people say to me: 'Oh, Jürgen von der Lippe is here again.' You have no idea how much that gets on my nerves."

"Doppelganger or not, even if there is somebody who looks like Vera, she didn't tell me anything about associating with such a person. And even the doppelganger theory doesn't explain how such a person, assuming that she exists, wound up in my bed, of all places, during the night, of all nights, when my girlfriend left me in a very peculiar manner."

Suddenly Wegener had to laugh uproariously: "Perhaps somebody cloned your dear Vera? That's supposed to be very modern these days. Or perhaps Vera is only a clone of the real Vera who's still living in Prague? Perhaps some crazy professor is conducting an experiment with you. You're familiar, of course, with Dolly, the first cloned sheep. That sheep looks exactly like the original sheep, only it's a few years younger. If somebody were now to clone the real Vera, then the clone would look exactly like her – except for the difference in age. We would have the same person existing twice at different ages. And the crazy professor in some laboratory in the Eastern Block would now like to find out in an experiment how the test persons react in a situation that can't exist in the normal rational world. He sends you the young Vera first and then the old one and examines how you react. Perhaps you're only a guinea pig and don't even know it."

"Now stop talking nonsense." Makord didn't see anything funny at all. "If the day is long, we can paint out many humorous fantasies like that for ourselves. But remember that you're supposed to represent me as an attorney, and that I'm in a dangerous situation. I don't feel like joking, even if it's a question of gallows humor. For days we've been going around in a circle. I know neither who the woman is nor how I got into this situation."

Wegener's expression became more serious: "Well, then we must first do some detective work. Let's put together the facts that we already know. Tell me about your girlfriend. Perhaps that will give us a clearer picture. You say that Vera comes from Prague. What do you know about her history and about the history of her family?"

"Vera's an only child. She was born in Prague in 1965 and was raised by her mother during those initial years. Her mother was an activist in the Prague Spring of 1968, when it was a matter of getting rid of the Russians and creating a communism with a humane aspect. Her mother was able to become enthusiastic about that, and if Dubcek, the leader of the Czechoslovakian Communist Party at the time, had remained at the helm, then she might have gone far. As we all know, however, the Prague Spring was suppressed by the Russians, and in spite of the initial resistance of the Czech population, the Stalinists under Husak finally got the upper hand. Many of the idealists fled to the West back then, as long as that was still possible. Vera's mother wanted to stay. The fact that wasn't really broadcast very loudly by our media is that the Russians arrested some of those activists to break the resistance. When Vera was three years old, her mother was arrested by the police. She was never seen again and nobody was able to find out where she was taken. After that, little Vera was taken in by her grandmother, the only relative that she still had. Her grandmother raised her until she was an adult. Vera has no siblings, no aunts and uncles, because her grandmother, too, had only one child that she raised as a single parent."

"Hm," muttered Wegener, "a child that loses her mother and grows up with her grandmother, who doesn't know what became of her daughter. That sounds very much like a psychological history. After all, that's your specialty, Dr. Makord. Don't you psychologists always talk about the fact that such events can traumatize people? And wouldn't that be an explanation for why Vera acts so strangely? Isn't it possible that the disappearance of a person's own mother makes that person somewhat peculiar, even insane? You psychologists do like to get involved with insane people. Perhaps you also do that in your private lives? Your inclination toward the unusual brings you into contact with difficult people, so perhaps also with difficult girlfriends who suddenly do unexpected things."

"Vera's not insane. Yes, she has certainly gone through a lot. In her nature there is something fragile and sad. I sensed that from the very beginning. There's something in her gaze, as if she had experienced all the terrors of this world. From the first day of our acquaintance on, I have had the feeling that Vera needs me, that I can help her, that I must help her."

Makord's face had a soft, loving expression as he forgot his difficult situation for a few moments. "But just why am I telling you all that? That's not your concern at all."

"Yes, it is, yes, it is, I have to know that," Wegener insisted. "Only when we understand what kind of a person your girlfriend is, can we find out what motives led to the actions of that night. Trust me. I'm an expert in these things. If you're dealing with a crazy story, as we are in your case, then you have to filter out what sort of a person has a reason to behave insanely, and who has an interest in moving the parts of the puzzle apart so that nobody recognizes the relationships anymore. It's tedious detail work, but we'll put together puzzle piece after puzzle piece until we know the real content of this story."

From his mouth to God's ear, thought Makord, although he actually had no affinity for God. As a child he had sometimes played detective, but that was a long time ago. Since he had become an adult, his interest in the subtleties of police work remained within microscopic limits. His analytic mind had shifted in the direction of studying the human personality. Now he suddenly had to let a lawyer demonstrate to him that the psychology of personality is something with which attorneys deal on a daily basis. Perhaps he should change his field and become a court consultant.

8

Prague, September 1968

Olga had searched the entire city, after Mara had not come home. But she was nowhere to be found, as if she had been swallowed up by the earth. The uncertainty made Olga ill. It was terrible to lose her only child, and these days one had to assume the worst. The Russians occupied everything, the radio station and the government building. Dubcek had been arrested. Now when he appeared on television, he was permitted to say only what the Russians had dictated to him; that was clearly noticeable. All citizens were admonished to remain calm and return to their homes. *Calm, the moment I hear that,* thought Olga cynically. *There's constantly some dictator who wants to calm Europe down, and with that he only means the infinite suffering that he causes the people.* Olga had become too hardened to be fooled anymore. Hitler, Stalin, Brezhnev – they were really all the same. Crazy men who destroyed entire countries in their megalomania and hid their paranoia behind a great ideology in order to be able to sell themselves better. Olga had experienced too much – in the Second Word War, when the Germans poured hate over the whole country, after the war when the communists revolted their way into power, and now it was starting up again. The mistaken deeds of those so-called politicians could no longer shock Olga.

Nor did she let herself get involved in anything in the private sphere anymore. She had kept the identity of her child's father secret, for the shame would have been too great, if the neighbors had learned the circumstances of Mara's birth. She had never let any man get close to her again, because men were repulsive to her for good reason. Yes, she felt revulsion, if a man stared at her with an aroused look. Olga had decided to do everything herself and had devoted everything to her little daughter. She had accepted any and every job, as a switchboard operator, as a secretary, as a factory worker, in order to earn enough money for herself and the child.

It was worth it. Mara was such a dear and clever girl. She began to study, wanted to become a lawyer. Law was a good profession, for there was so much injustice in the world to stand up against.

47

Olga had told Mara everything about the violence that she herself had suffered, and about the injustice that had happened to the Czech people. Mara soaked up her mother's stories like a sponge, and she swore to her mother that she would do everything to bring to light the hushed-up crimes that Olga had told her about.

But not until she was old enough and had the means to take up the battle. The professional training would be Mara's weapon, and Olga shied away from no expense to make that education possible for her daughter. And now she had disappeared, the most important and dearest person that Olga still had.

Finally Olga learned that many of the demonstrators had been arrested and that Mara was probably among them. She also found out where they had all been taken and went to the old Catholic boarding school that had been closed by the communists because religious instruction was not compatible with the principles of the Party. Together with many other mothers, she implored the guards at the entrance to let her see her daughter, but all of them were pushed back.

So there was nothing left for her to do but to return every day, to wait and see if Mara was among those who were permitted to leave the boarding school again. Usually she held little Vera in her arms, who cried and screamed for her mama. To comfort her, Olga pointed to one of the windows of the boarding school and whispered in a calming voice: "There's Mama, behind that window. The bad men have locked her up there. But Mama will come out soon, because she didn't do anything, and the bad men can't keep her locked up. We'll wait a little longer now. Mama will come soon."

And many young Czechs actually did come out of the building, colleagues of Mara's whom she had already brought home to visit. They confirmed to Olga that Mara had been arrested with them. They also said that the confinement was bearable and that it could not be much longer before they released Mara as well.

After two weeks the last ones came out of the boarding school and were free, and then nobody else came. Finally even the Russian soldiers cleared out of the building. A sergeant approached Olga and jumped down her throat: "There's nobody else inside. Go home."

"But my daughter must still be in there. She was arrested."

"*Nyet*, nobody else there. Go home."

48

"My daughter's name is Mara Kurkova. She must have been in there. Look in your reports."

"*Nyet*, there is no knowledge of a Mara Kurkova. Go home."

Olga's face turned ashen. *They made her disappear. They deleted her name from the records, as if she had never existed. They liquidated her or carried her off, tortured her, oh God. Not that, not that again.* Dark memories raged through Olga's mind and mixed themselves with the panic of the present. Something broke within her and took away the courage that she had mustered for so long in order to fight against this world of men.

But there was still Mara's child, who now had no mother. Vera needed a mother and Olga would take her place. Something in Olga revolted. She had not been able to protect Mara; instead she would now protect Vera. Nobody would take that child away from her now.

When she got home, Russian soldiers were waiting in front of the door to her apartment. Olga flew into a fit of rage: "You bastards! You sons of whores! You took my daughter away! Don't you have enough yet?! What do you intend to do to us now? Go home to Russia and torment your own women, you brutal sadists!" Only little Vera in Olga's arms kept her from jumping at the nearest soldier and joyfully scratching his eyes out.

Two soldiers of the Red Army grabbed Olga; a third took the screaming Vera away from her. They took her to the nearest guard post, where a lieutenant was waiting for her. The lieutenant came directly to the point: "I have here an order of the Czech Welfare Service. You're housing the child of a counterrevolutionary woman in your apartment. According to the order, all children of arrested counterrevolutionaries are to be placed in a home in Prague, so that they will receive a good communist education. That order is being carried out herewith."

Olga was beside herself. It did not matter to her what they could still do to her, whether they would also lock her up, whether they would also make her disappear. She had had enough of all the misery that they were causing and had caused her. She would no longer let them gag her, not anymore. She would fight like a lioness for her young. She tore Vera back into her arms and clung to her, unwilling to ever let go of her again.

49

"You're not going to get this child, not this child. You've already imprisoned my daughter, although she didn't do anything to anyone and was a good communist. What else are you going to do to us? Do you want to make the Czech people your enemies for all time? Today you won with your tanks, but the next revolt will come and your time will run out. And what will you do then, as murderers, torturers, and kidnappers of children? Don't you Russians have any mothers at home who mourn for you? Don't you have any families? How do you think our neighbors, our countrymen will react, when they all learn that you're kidnapping our children and our grandchildren? I swear to you that I'll scream this injustice out into the whole world. You'll have to arrest me right now if you want to prevent that. I'm going home now, and I'm taking my granddaughter with me."

Vera had stopped screaming and was clinging to her grandmother's skirt with eyes full of fear. The lieutenant was somewhat confused. The matter was not proceeding as simply as he had expected. He left the room and went looking for his superior officer in the back of the building: "Comrade Major, the child was brought here as ordered, but the woman is creating difficulties. She is threatening to arouse all of her neighbors and acquaintances against us if we take the child away from her. Should we also arrest the woman?"

Before the major could answer, the elegant colonel who had been standing behind him drew attention to himself: "So, so, the woman is creating difficulties. But we're accustomed to dealing with difficulties. Major Kyusnov, I told you about the importance of this mission. The deported people and their children are of great importance for our struggle against the imperialist aggressor. We need all of them and can't let ourselves be stopped in this mission by maudlin sentimentality and sympathy. The matter will be carried out as planned.

"But we don't want to create more of a stir than is absolutely necessary. I shall therefore take the matter into my own hands. Follow me, gentlemen. I'll show you how it's done."

With the major and the lieutenant in tow, the colonel entered the interrogation room in which the grandmother and granddaughter were still clinging to one another. Vera was trembling with fear; Olga trembled with rage.

"My name is Mayinski. I represent the KGB here. You know what that means. You certainly know as well that there is no point in getting in our way. What must be done will be done, and nothing and nobody can stop us. So give up your ridiculous resistance. You're only making the matter worse with it. I wouldn't like to have you arrested, too. I assure you that nothing will happen to your granddaughter. She'll enjoy the best education that the communist movement has to offer. She'll receive every opportunity to have a career later and has a great future ahead of her. Just what can an old woman like you offer her? Do grasp the fact that our plan is the best for everyone."

"I'm supposed to trust you? If you're after my granddaughter that way, then you're also probably responsible for the disappearance of my daughter. What have you done with her? Where have you taken her? For God's sake, at least tell me what has happened to my daughter."

"Unfortunately I can't give you any information about that. We know nothing about the whereabouts of your daughter."

"You hypocrite. Of course you know that. My daughter was in the Catholic boarding school, together with all the other prisoners. She's the only one who didn't come out again. And you're apparently in command here. So don't tell me that anyone here could let out a fart without your knowledge. You've robbed me of my daughter, and now you also want my granddaughter. Why are you persecuting us this way? Just what have we done to you? Just how can you separate a little child from her mother, you monster?"

"Your daughter should have thought sooner about whether or not she should join counterrevolutionary demonstrators. I can't do anything for you there. Of course times like these also bring burdens for the populace. The placement of parentless children in a home is a generous offer of the government to minimize those burdens."

"You liar. You twist everything to suit your needs. It's abduction of children and you want to sell it as a generous offer. Over my dead body, you, you..."

As Vera began to cry loudly, Olga suddenly paused. She looked more carefully at the colonel's face. *I know that face*, she thought to herself. *I know those cold blue eyes and that crooked, wry mouth. Yes, I know you better than you would like.* Olga broke out in cynical laughter:

51

"Mayinski, yes, your name is Mayinski. Don't make me laugh. A nice Russian name, where did you get it? I know you, you monster, I know you only too well. And this isn't the first shameful deed that you've hatched, is it? It would probably be of interest to these officers to know who you really are. And if you insist on it, we can clarify that here and now. You like witnesses so much, who tell everything. Alright, I'm at your disposal. Or you can let me leave with my granddaughter, and then my memory could very quickly become as weak as is appropriate for an old woman."

Now Mayinski's face turned pale. He had overlooked something in his plan. Of course, the mother of the prisoner, of course she must know him. And it would not be good if that story made the rounds. Shit. Oh, well, sometimes you simply have to make small cutbacks, but that would not cause further damage to his cause. One human being more or less did not matter. It was now of the highest priority that this woman did not tell the major and the lieutenant any stupid stories. And she had just offered him that. A fair deal.

"Let the woman and the child go!" ordered the colonel.

Major Kyusnov was so relieved that at least this matter had ended humanely, that he dispensed with any questions so that the colonel would not change his mind.

9

Makord strolled pensively through the streets of his home town. After Wegener had shut his briefcase and murmured something about studying the documents, Makord needed fresh air. He left his apartment on Anastasius-Grün-Strasse and then walked across Blumauerplatz and along the main road in the direction of Schiller Park. He had often taken that route when he needed time to reflect, and today, as well, he continued along it, at last through the old town and up onto the castle hill to look out over the church towers and blast furnaces of his home town from above. Those spiritual and industrial monuments of his home town seemed to him to stand next to each other in peculiar harmony and to confirm that everything human strives upward, the prayers as well as the exhaust gases of the factories. But what had Father said in his infinite wisdom: "What strives upward can fall far." How true! Makord's thoughts took refuge in fantasy, as they always did when he found himself in distress. After his life had been knocked out of kilter, he clung to the only abiding fixed point. He philosophized about his home region.

Linz – Actually it was a great city, of course. The people here had experienced so much. The Celts called it Lentos after the bend in the river. In the Roman camp Lentia the legionnaires held their ground against the attacks of the Quadi, Marcomanni, and other Germanic tribes. Finally, after a defensive war that lasted four hundred years they were overrun anyway, left in the lurch by a certain Mr. Odoacer in Rome, who had decided that the era of the Roman emperors should come to an end. St. Severin gathered in the terrified survivors of the invasion of the Germanic tribes and brought them to a secure place in the remnants of the empire. From that time forth the citizens of Linz saw their place of refuge in the Catholic Church, until that trust was driven out of them again with fire and the sword by the Counterreformation. Makord remembered what he had read about that era in a school chronicle: How lively his high school must have been as a Protestant rural school, with jolly teachers, rebellious students, and pigs in the schoolyard; and how strict and boring it had then been under the Jesuits, who drove independent and rebellious thinking out of the students, because it represented a danger to those in power.

Linz had long been a small, tranquil town, too unimportant to draw famous events to itself and more inclined toward ordering its thoughts in peace. Johannes Kepler had poured his observations of the planetary orbits into eternally valid laws here; Anton Bruckner had dedicated his life to playing the organ and writing symphonies. Writers like Hermann Bahr and Adalbert Stifter had written their books, contemplative and longwinded, very much like this city's rhythm of life.

Only sometimes the powerful had retreated into this small town, and usually those were turning points in which something new came into being. Emperor Frederick III had ruled the Holy Roman Empire from Linz, when he invented the Habsburg marriage policy and in so doing founded an empire in which the sun never set. A. E. I. O. U. – The entire world is subject to Austria. In school, they had inoculated Makord with that elitist statement of past greatness. Perhaps a certain A. Hitler had also heard that statement in middle school and mixed his personal form of megalomania from it. Emperor Leopold I had also fled to Linz when the Turks were preparing to conquer the capital city of Vienna. This act of personal cowardice was later recast in fame and glory: the Turks lost and Prince Eugene established the power of the Danube Monarchy. For the next two hundred years the Slavic nations were under the patronage of the German master race – Hitler would seize that idea, too, in his striving to obtain lebensraum in the East.

Hitler – for Rafael Makord there was something remarkable about that nonentity. Officially he was never mentioned, but indirectly people constantly encountered his shadow in this city. As a little boy Makord had very cautiously crossed the streets and playgrounds of his neighborhood, always careful not to give the adults a reason to interfere. Walking on a lawn, a loud ball game, a funny creative idea – anything could be a stimulus for the aggressive lunge of an adult. The tirades of curses and hate that were then poured out on the unsuspecting children usually ended in the invocation of the diabolical master, which was, to be sure, taboo, but nevertheless constantly present: "Under Hitler there would not have been such a thing." "They would have sent you little brats to the gas chambers, too." "A little experience in a labor camp and

54

you would learn to behave." "We need a little Hitler here. He would clean things up."

A little Hitler – when saying that, the old men usually indicated the size of their thumb. When they had then calmed down somewhat, they often added long explanations that they, too, no longer wanted the big Hitler who had fought so many wars, the one who above all had lost the war and brought so much suffering and destruction with him. But the little Hitler, he had given them work; he had created order and cleaned up the scum. That man, yes, he was alright and the people could still use him in the contemporary rotten era. As a little child, Makord had believed that Hitler had appeared as a twin. The big one was the evil one; he was defeated and belonged to the past. The little one still lived on in the hearts of the adults who had once cheered for him and still ensured that his successors worked to achieve discipline and order.

The little Hitler had given the people work, homes, and automobiles. The little Hitler had survived. The citizens of Linz still lived in the Hitler buildings on the Spallerhof, small public welfare buildings from the period of fascism, and they still called them Hitler buildings. And almost all fathers drove Volkswagens on the Autobahn that had been built by Hitler. The automobile of the German people, the Volkswagen, had remained a success story. And when Makord's schoolmate was killed with his family in a Volkswagen on the Autobahn, it was like a hero's death in honor of the German nation. Only the front had changed. Instead of the Eastern Front it was the economic front on which victories were won and on which the losses and suffering were transformed into more palatable corrections of the front.

When Makord went to see his grandmother, he got on the train at the main railroad station, a model of Speer's monumental architecture, where two stone lions bore witness of the past claim to power. And the finance office, where his father paid his taxes, still resided in the bridgehead building on the Danube, where Hitler's architects had placed it. It was almost a joke of history that the New Gallery of the city of Linz was also housed there. After all, Hitler himself had seen himself as a would-be artist who wanted to transform all of Germany according to his petit bourgeois artistic taste. It was embarrassing that the New Gallery housed precisely those modern paintings that Hitler had wanted to preclude as degenerate art. Makord had once seen a plan of how Hitler wanted to transform his home town. It was supposed to become the art capital of the German Reich, and all over Europe paintings were stolen that were supposed to be brought together in an enormous museum in Linz, to the glory of the *Führer*, who wanted to be not only the greatest military leader but also the greatest patron of the arts of all time. Thank God, nothing had come of that, and the people of Linz were left with the New Gallery, which was nevertheless at least in a Hitler building.

But all of that was nothing in comparison with the Linz steel industry, the former Hermann Göring Steel Mills that had been founded by Hitler and developed into an important component of the armaments industry. Here thousands of slave laborers had to contribute to ensuring that there was no lack of weapons on the Eastern Front. And that industry was also a success story. After the war new processes for making steel were developed here, processes that went throughout the world. L-D steel, named after the steel-producing cities of Linz and Donawitz, now helped the warlords throughout the world to maintain their armament production at the latest level of technology. So nobody could say anymore that Hitler had no success. Even the serious attempt by Austrian politicians to ruin the steel industry through political muttering was only able to stall the success of the Linz steel furnaces temporarily. "As tough as leather, as swift as greyhounds, and as hard as Krupp steel." At least the last part of Hitler's vision had survived.

With all of these indeterminable witnesses of the past, Makord was amazed for a long time that the teachers, politicians, and decision makers acted as if it had all never existed. The Second World War was not treated in the schools. Before the 20th century was reached, the school year was usually over. Linz was famous as an industrial city with poor air quality; people could not talk about the original purpose of that industry. It seemed as if the workers had taken possession of this industry, and the United Austrian Iron and Steel Mills now belonged to the socialist factory committees, into whose hands they had fallen like unclaimed plunder. Austria, as the first victim of National Socialism, apparently had nothing to do with its past. It was the first country to be attacked by Hitler, whom Providence had led here to lead his homeland back into the

German Reich. It was embarrassing that not a single Austrian soldier had fired a shot to prevent it.

This Austrian schizophrenia had informed Makord's childhood. The big Hitler had haunted his nightmares, which were full of carpet bombings, concentration camps, and Gestapo raids. The little Hitler had been omnipresent in Makord's education in the form of his teachers, his relatives, and above all in the person of his father. The little Hitler was also the reason for the conflict between father and son, because Makord did not want to have the little Hitler and did not want to be raised by him. During many quiet hours when Makord was serving his sentence of house arrest in the dark cellar, because the little Hitler had once again set things in order, Makord comforted himself with the childish idea that he was not fighting against his father at all, but only the little Hitler who possessed his father like a demon. Thus he was able to love his father quietly and secretly after all, as every son would like to do, if only he were permitted to do it. When he angrily lit into his father in protest and promptly received draconian punishments, then it was only a justified resistance against a fascist dictatorship and had nothing to do with that secret love for his father.

There was, however, a point in Makord's life when the suppressed love for his father died. Makord hated his father honestly and abysmally when he had to observe how the latter dealt with his wife. Makord always had the feeling that he had to defend his mother against his father's power, and inwardly he also gave him the responsibility for her early death. Although – officially the marriage of the old Makord could not have been better, and Makord would have been declared insane if he had communicated his criticism of his parents' partnership to the neighbors. The respected chief physician with his beautiful young wife, they really were a picture-book couple. They had class and knew how to behave. At the balls in the Businessmen's Club they danced the Vienna waltzes in the first row and were respected members of the Linz citizenry. Mrs. Makord was also the kind of lady that she was supposed to be, pretty, virtuous, reserved, and friendly. She seemed to hang on every word her husband spoke and was always energetically at his side. The two of them were united. The husband led and the wife allowed herself to be led, and in the opinion of the people of Linz that was not just a good recipe for dancing waltzes.

57

The young Makord knew better. He was familiar with the melancholy in his mother's soul. Her gentleness was actually lifelessness, her calm manner in reality apathy. Her tractability was lack of spirit, for her spirit had been broken long ago.

And he knew who had broken his mother's spirit. His father's commanding manner had locked her inside a prison, compared to which his house arrest in the cellar seemed like a vacation hotel.

Mother had come to the nursing school from the mill district as a young girl, in order to become a nurse. She had soon idolized the successful doctor who obviously had a rapidly rising career in front of him. And when the great doctor proposed marriage to her, she was thrilled and had reached the goal of her dreams. Back then she honestly loved Father and saw in him a servant of humanity. That would later change.

Had Father fallen in love with the young nurse? Makord did not know the answer to that question for a long time; or better said, for a long time he did not want to admit that he knew the answer. His father did not really love his mother. What he loved was her gentleness, her subservience, her capacity for devotion and admiration. His parents' marriage was of the kind that the marriage therapist Jürg Willi had described as narcissistic collusion. Father wanted to be admired, and Mother could admire. And as long as that interplay worked, his parents' marriage also worked.

But, in accord with Jürg Willi prophesies for narcissistic marriages, his parents' marriage foundered when Mother dared to attempt to have her own opinion and to question critically many things about Father. That attempt did not last long, and it was crushed by Father with all his might, like the first beginnings of an opposition in a dictatorship. Mother obviously complied, but with that her love had died.

As a child Makord already sensed that long before his birth something had happened between his parents, something that was never talked about, something taboo and weird. No, perhaps that was only his imagination, and the reason for his parents' bad marriage was perhaps quite unspectacular. Their love had simply died, the way it did in many other marriages.

Instinctively, however, Makord knew that his feeling was correct, that there was a family secret there that he had to uncover. Perhaps he had studied psychology in the hope of tracking that secret by doing so. In any case Makord knew that his mother had already been a broken woman when he was born. She functioned as an external shell and played perfectly the role of the dear chief physician's wife. Inside, however, she was dead and empty, her soul long since dead.

Here was the foundation for Makord's deepest hatred of his father. The latter had taken his mother from him, even before he was born. The longing for a loving mother remained unfulfilled and Makord grew up like an orphan, an emotional orphan in any case.

Whatever that secret was, it was perhaps the reason why Mother did not have a child for a long time, and Makord appeared as a late-born child of old parents, when nobody expected a pregnancy anymore. And it was perhaps also the reason why at the age of eighteen Makord lost his mother, whom he had spiritually really never possessed. Whatever that secret was, Mother never talked about it and took it with her to her grave.

Mother – Makord became as sad as he did every time he thought of her and felt the pain and the loneliness that had molded his childhood. He tried to distract himself by letting his eyes sweep across the old section of the city whose streets and squares could be viewed so well from the castle hill. Suddenly something tore him out of his pondering and electrified him like a bolt of lightning. Down below, on the square in front of the state theater, a woman was strolling along, and she looked damned similar to his Vera. Makord looked more intently at her and followed the strolling gait of the young woman with greedy eyes, as if he wanted to suck the beauty of her body into himself. Then he knew – that was Vera. She was alive!

Makord felt a feeling of happiness flow through his body. Whatever had happened, he would be able to take his beloved in his arms again. And, what counted more at the moment, Vera was the proof of his innocence. She would have to come to the police inspector's office with him and testify that he had not killed anyone. He jumped up and ran down the stairs on the castle hill as fast as he could, in order to reach the square on which he had seen Vera. The problem was only that for strategic reasons the builders of the castle had selected the location such that the pathway up to the castle was crooked and difficult. It was correspondingly difficult for Makord to make the climb down from the castle before a person down on the square strolled out of the observer's field of vision. And as hastily as he leaped down the steep stairs, when he arrived in the old section of the city, Vera had disappeared. And as much as he searched for her in all the little alleyways, he could not find her.

Once again Makord did not know if he had imagined it all or if he should trust his senses.

10

Terezin, January 1943

Told from the point of view of Adolf Markosky

For weeks it was as though Adolf Markosky were numb. He carried out his medical routine like a robot that could reel off a program, once it had been learned, in endless repetitions. As a doctor he was able to function; there were no cases of typhoid or tuberculosis, and even the number of shootings remained within the normal bounds. So he had no need to reproach himself, and his superiors were satisfied with him. An SS man stands erect in every situation, and personal histories are there to be suppressed.

In Markosky's soul, however, a storm was raging. Hermann was dead, his father was dead, his mother was sitting alone and sad in Krumau. If only he had had somebody to listen to him, someone who would have understood his suffering. But there was nobody. Ass clenched tight, shoulders back, chest out, and face to the wind – that was all the SS had to offer him. Suppress, suppress, suppress, and a bottle of liquor for pharmacological support. All that could not have happened. Or perhaps it did happen? They had chased that Jew Sigmund Freud away, and the only thing that *he* could do was dig around in the wounds until things were even worse. No, that was really not the Aryan way.

If he had only been able to rid himself of the pain somehow. At least once a day Adolf choked and had to vomit. Then his heart raced so hard that he would have unconditionally diagnosed an angina pectoris for himself. But his shitty colleague confirmed to him with every examination that he had the heart of a lion and was fit for a marathon. That really could not be. If only there had been a cure for that pain. But nothing helped, no anesthetic, no sleeping pill, nothing. Markosky was going around in circles.

He tried to divert himself. And for that, after all, he had enough opportunity. Every day new human material came in. All of them Czechs. All of them murderers. Nothing but members of the ethnic group that was responsible for the deaths of his brother and father. Responsible for the fact that Markosky now sat alone in this

61

concentration camp with the heart muscle of a mummy, petrified and dead. When his longing no longer had a goal and his mourning found no listeners, Markosky transformed all of his energy of feeling into hate. And with every Czech that he had to examine, that hate became more intense. With every palpitation that belonged to the clinical routine, he pushed down somewhat more firmly until his patients screamed out in pain.

Thus hate became the motor of his activity as a physician. Thousands of Czechs were entrusted to his care. But they had already misused his trust, before they ever saw him for the first time.

With the passage of time Markosky also lost his scruples with respect to torture and shootings. Where before Hermann's death he had still had sympathy for many prisoners and had even helped some of them find relief, to the extent that it was possible for him, now he felt that the whole thing was fully in order. After all, who had sympathy for him? Who had had sympathy for Hermann? Who had had sympathy with his father? Had any stupid Czech ever thought about that? No! That was how they wanted it. They did not want to live peacefully with the other nations of the Danube Monarchy. They absolutely had to have their own state, so that they could finally oppress the Germans. And as anyone could see, in the process they would definitely stop at nothing; and for them no humiliation, no method of torture was too good to use.

They wanted it that way, so that was the way it should be: an eye for an eye, a tooth for a tooth; after all, that was even in the Bible. Vengeance is mine, said the Lord. And in Terezin Markosky was the Lord and his word was God's word. And a word of God sufficed, and destiny took its course.

The entire camp had become an instrument of his revenge. And the banner of retaliation waved above the camp, visible from far away to all Czechs, who trembled at the sight of it.

And they all came to the god of vengeance, led by the archangels of the SS. The survivors of Lidice who were chosen to be the first memorial to vengeance – they paid for Heydrich's death. And Moloch, the god of vengeance, swallowed them with a loud belch and they were gone. The cadre of Czech nationalists – all of them were brought in. Moloch chewed them longer, for he wanted to enjoy their slow death. The officers of the Czech army – there Moloch only took a little bite and spit them out again, for he was not a cannibal, you see, and they were still good enough to serve as over-seers for the prisoners. And then the delicacy, the Jewish citizens – Moloch gobbled them up like a desired dessert. He could never get enough of them.

It did not take long and Markosky felt like an archangel, and the black uniform of the SS became a robe of feathers that gave him wings. With fire and sword he would create order in a rotten time. Hadn't it always been that way? Hadn't God judged the peo-ple, when they had gotten off the right path? During the Great Flood, in Sodom, in Babylon, and in Egypt? Had the Lord even hesitated to use the instrument of vengeance to discipline his peo-ple? – No! And for that reason the god of vengeance had to disci-pline the Czechs, before he mercifully took them into his lap of Aryanization again.

Sometimes Markosky awoke as if from an evil fever dream. Once he was in the process of examining a balding, potbellied older gentleman who suddenly dropped to his knees in front of him and pleaded with him: "Adi, Adi, it really wasn't meant that way. I was just afraid that one of you children would fall in the Moldau and drown. Then I lost my temper. Yes, I was certainly too strict, but only out of fear and worry. Adi, Adi, you know me. It's me, the old custodian from across the street!"

Look here, Markosky thought to himself and came slowly awake, *old Navratil, the stinking bastard who always lay in wait for us. You, too, will not escape your just punishment.* But somehow the old man had revived Markosky's heart. No, he could not be angry with him, he really had almost drowned. So what? Sometimes the Lord lets mercy prevail, and he assigned Navratil to kitchen duty where little could happen to him.

That evening Markosky's consciousness had awakened again; for a long time he could not go to sleep, and the old doubts, the old ruminations were there again: *What are we actually doing here? We're killing people, subhuman people to be sure, but nevertheless, is this sup-posed to be the new era that Hitler promised us?*

And he suddenly felt possessed by an evil spirit, Hermann's spirit, which found no rest and dug its claws into the back of Adi's neck and slowly ate up his brain.

I can't participate in that any longer. I'll quit serving in the camp and have myself transferred to the front. That's at least an honest fight that I don't

63

have to be ashamed about. But Adolf had hardly fallen asleep when the nightmares came again, and this one was the worst one of all: He saw millions of Germans, Sudeten Germans, driven out by the Czechs, their fathers slain, their houses pillaged, authorized by a decree of the president. And when he awoke covered with perspiration, he knew that the Czechs would do that very thing, if they were ever allowed to come into power again. They would draw the angel of vengeance to their side, and that could never be permitted to happen. Markosky was not here by chance; it was his mission to repress the Czechs once and for all, so that they could never again do to German women and children what they had done to Adi's family.

An insidious change had taken place in Adolf's personality. The old brooding individual had disappeared. The angel of vengeance had breathed a new feeling of self-worth into him. The fearful boy, who had needed his brother as a protector, was past history. He was now the protector himself. He watched over everything that moved in the camp. The highly visible megalomania that had sometimes frightened him in Hermann had passed over to him. Greatness or destruction, Valhalla or the twilight of the gods, it was all one and the same thing. And when the first reports from the encirclement at Stalingrad came in, and it slowly became clear that the boys would never come home to Germany, he knew that this was all a part of the great plan. Moloch demanded new sacrifices; he drank German blood, too, and he had to be fed. The more sacrifices were made, the mightier Moloch became and the further the wings of the angels of vengeance would reach. *Better Czech blood than German*, Adolf thought, and he filled out the lists of the dead.

At some point it was enough. The thirst for revenge had been slaked. The angel of vengeance folded his wings together and landed on the gallows above the cemetery to rest. One should not awaken him, for his claws were still sharp.

The angel had hardly fallen asleep when the pain in Adi's heart reawakened. That unbearable pain, the sting in his breast that tormented him day and night – when would it finally stop? Why did medicine have no remedy available for it? Aspirin, Alka Selzer, all garbage, nothing helped.

And a last spark of reason kept Adi from reaching for morphine, for he did not want to throw away his mind as well, after he had already lost his morality. His mind – he still needed that.

If he was going to use an addictive substance, then it should be a legal addictive substance. The legal drug alcohol offered itself, but it was not sufficient; after a brief anesthetization the sobering pain was quickly there again. Then Adolf discovered that he had long since reached for the addictive substance that had been offered to him with a comradely grin the entire time: "Here, go ahead and take it. It's free, doesn't cost a thing. You'll see. It tastes delicious and you'll never want to be without it again." Hermann had been the first seducer; then he had still hesitated. But meanwhile he had become severely dependent, dependent upon the feeling of power. He needed the fact that the camp inmates trembled before him, crept away in the dust knowing with panicky certainty that Markosky's thumb decided between life and death. Yes, that really was a good feeling. When pain moved the blade in his heart, then Markosky swallowed power like a pinch of opium.

At some point the hunger for self-awareness was also satisfied. With the regular level of power-opium in his blood, Marlowsky was sure of himself. He was now important, important to the war, and nobody could get past him. Nobody would ever again dare to laugh about him or not to take him seriously.

But the pain was still there, and there was no cure in sight.

Finally Markosky remembered his strongest weapon, the one that he had never let go of and that had never left him in the lurch. That was his power of reason, his mind, his intelligence. Aryans are more intelligent than all the others, and physicians are the most intelligent Aryans. His mind had to find the solution. His medical mind would find the cure and release him from the tyranny of his feelings.

11

Linz, November 6, 1991

Makord was depressed. For days he had been running back and forth through his home town in search of Vera. He was certain that he had seen her. Or had he seen only what he wanted to see? He was familiar with that, of course, from perceptual psychology. The observer projects his wish image into reality, until he believes that this image really exists. In any case, the police inspector would not believe him if he babbled something about a living Vera.

Speaking of the inspector, he was once again on his back and would not let it rest. He was certainly having him watched, even if he was not permitted to lock him up. That did not matter either. But there were also still Dr. Wegener and his father. They all wanted answers from him; they all took him to task. What he had been thinking of when he did it and so on. Shit on it.

There they were again. Makord felt persecuted. No, it was not his imagination; there actually was a car following him. It crept slowly along behind him like a shadow. *But now I've had enough*, he thought furiously. *If the police inspector wants to know something about me, then he should simply ask me, man to man. There's no sense in constantly running away.*

He walked toward the car and looked through the windshield. And there he could also now see – the hard visage of his father. *Him I really don't need right now*, Makord thought crossly and abruptly turned around. The car rolled slowly onward, and his father called after him through the open side window, "Son, get in now. I have to talk to you."

Makord only walked faster.

"You stubborn fool, come on, I'm worried about you."

The idea of worry caught like a fishhook in Makord's soul, and as much as he fought against it, an invisible line drew him backward. *Father is worried, how nice*, Makord growled to himself. *He's never done that before.* But as if drawn in by an unseen line, he finally landed on the passenger seat in the old man's Mercedes.

"And what do you want?" Makord barked.

"So, you really could show a little more gratitude. After all, without me you would be sitting in jail and would not be taking a pleasant stroll here through the beautiful Gugl."

The Gugl, the Linz city park, ran from the center of town up in the direction of Freinberg and actually was beautiful. With walks through the Gugl, Makord was able to relieve stress. His father's words, however, brought him abruptly from zero to a hundred again.

"Thanks, that's enough again," Makord grumbled and got out.

"Good God!" the old Makord cursed. "Can't I even talk with my son in peace? You're all I have." The fishing line pulled powerfully backward, while his father parked the car and hastened after his son.

You're all I have, Makord thought with a grin. *That could also have occurred to him sooner.* But the old longing of the little boy, that someday his father could approach him without little Hitler, timidly raised its head.

"So, what do you want?" Makord growled anew.

"My God, I simply want to know what's going on. Don't let me die ignorant. I'm your father and I have a right to information."

"A right to information, yes, a right to information, yes!!! – you miserable hypocrite." Makord began to shriek hysterically, and the longing boy had transformed himself as quick as a flash into a raging panther who wanted to scratch his father's eyes out. "That's something new, alright. When were you ever interested in the truth, you façade king? A perfect show and behind a sea of lies the rotten eggs that nobody is permitted to smell – that's your specialty. When did you ever tell me the truth about you and Mother? Why don't you tell me the truth sometime about your dehumanizing dealings with women? Why don't you tell me the truth about your time in the war? The nice surgeon at the front who patches poor soldiers together. That's a likely story!

"Why don't you tell me the truth about how you got away at the end of the war and didn't land in prison as a Nazi? And why in the fifties you advanced so rapidly in your career, as if nothing had ever happened. A powerful Nazi before and a powerful Nazi afterward. Let somebody try to imitate that. During my entire childhood I had to play the hypocrite, too, and look up to Papi in gratitude, to the physician and humanitarian who ensures that the dear little children come into the world. In comparison with that, the story of the stork can well be imagined. Isn't it rather the truth that it was fun for you to serially cut out the women's uteruses and ovaries, to castrate all of them under the guise of cancer prophylaxis? If you knew how many of your patients sit in my office and cry bucketfuls of tears because they can't have any children, and my dear Papi is responsible for that? Every time I could sink into the earth with shame and it's your fault. You make me sick!"

Makord was startled at himself, at the fact that he had suddenly dared to pose all of the questions that were so taboo and yet had already occupied his mind for so long. His legs instinctively began to move faster and were obviously of the opinion that it was time to flee, before his father's revenge caught up with him. Astonishingly enough, his father did not flip out this time, but continued to run after him.

"Yes, should I have let all those women die, just because that suits my son? You're talking about things that you know nothing about. Do you know how miserably a woman perishes with a uterine carcinoma? Twenty years ago surgery was simply the only prophylaxis there was. And nevertheless I invented an operation that is gentler than anything that was there before. That's the truth. You, with your endless fantasies about what all could lie behind things. Everything is being reinterpreted, given a different meaning. You constantly suspect evil intentions behind the deeds of people. You have a persecution complex. That's the truth!"

"Delusion comes from imagining, and that means sensing, suspecting. You can't prove everything that you sense scientifically. But if my profession has taught me anything, then it has taught me this: that man's ability to sense things usually points in the right direction, no matter how crazy it might seem. Fine, I know nothing about medicine, and perhaps I do you an injustice and your motives were clean and pure. In spite of that, I sense this pile of rotten eggs in you, eggs that stink to high heaven, ostrich eggs, dinosaur eggs, an entire clutch of dinosaur eggs, stuff for paleontologists. And why do you avoid my questions about the past again, huh? Were you really a man without qualities, to loosely quote Robert Musil, during the entire period of the war?"

68

"I was a doctor on the front and tried to save the wounded, to ease the wounds of the horrible war. There's nothing bad about that, and I don't have to be ashamed of it."

Makord would have liked so much to believe his father. It would have been balsam on his wounds to imagine his father in a field hospital on the front, the proof that he was a healer and not a warrior. But it was not true. Makord sensed precisely that his father was lying.

"Then tell me now, inform me now about the sections of the front that you were assigned to, which battles you survived. Give me a few pieces of information that can be investigated. Were you in Stalingrad, in Kursk, in Kuban or where, talk, inform me. As your son I have a right to information."

"I was with the Southern Army Group for the entire way to Stalingrad and back. I've already told you that a hundred times."

"Stalingrad and back. So then you were with the six thousand survivors of the Sixth Army. Six thousand of 200,000 prisoners survived, and you of all people were among them. So, a little miracle. The real miracle, however, is that the prisoners continued to die wretchedly in Siberia for years, while you were very properly doing your rotation in Linz. I believe a lot of things, but that the Holy Ghost had a hand in what happened in Stalingrad – that would be news to me."

"I escaped from the trap at the last moment, with the last plane, when we flew the wounded out. But what's the point of all this? We're not in the Nuremberg trials here. I'm not the accused, but you are. I just want to help you to get free of your murder charge. Whether you did it or not, we'll get you out of it."

"So you think that I'm capable of it. You actually believe that I could kill a woman. You know me that well. Or should I say, you know yourself that well. The rogue acts the way he thinks. For a Nazi a murder is something natural, as long as it's expedient."

Now the old Makord finally began to shriek hysterically. The son had finally brought the father to that point. He was almost ashamed of it, and yet he gloated inside. His father was completely his old self again. Dr. Albert Makord had had his pride injured, and now he did not take that very well: "You spoiled brat, you, with your bright ideas that all those who participated in the war are criminals. Just what did we do? Defended our homeland, protected our wives and children from the Russians. You wouldn't be in the world at all, if we hadn't risked our lives. I've worked hard all my life, so that you would have it better someday, and this is the thanks I get. Bah!"

The old man almost succeeded in getting sympathy and guilt feelings to take possession of his son. But sadistic rage and righteous anger were quicker. This time the old man had taken the bait. Makord could feel it. This time he would draw him out of his reticence.

"During the war you didn't have a wife yet or a child that you could have defended. You had only your career to think about. And for a career back then you had to be a Nazi. There was no other way. Even if not out of conviction, then at least with a Party book, so finally admit it."

"Were you perhaps there? Did you perhaps experience that era, Doctor Know-it-all? Do you have any idea what it means to save your own hide in a dictatorship? Perhaps we should have risen up and shot Hitler, is that what you think? Many tried to do that, and they were dead before they knew it. I wasn't born for that kind of heroics and neither were you, especially not you."

Rafael Makord became uncertain. No, it would not have been any easier for him either. He, too, would have been a nominal Party member, too cowardly to risk his own hide. He could also have lived with a cowardly fellow traveler as his father. But Makord sensed that his father was still lying.

"Fine, perhaps you didn't commit any war crimes. The crimes of the army never took place. The actual crime is that today they put up exhibitions that are all a pack of lies, or so you would have us believe. When the army exhibition was shown in Salzburg, an SS colleague of yours simultaneously presented an exhibit of poor soldiers who were the actual mistreated people. That's how you see it, and I can't prove to you that it was otherwise.

"But there remains something else, specifically the collaboration of the medical profession with the Nazis. As a doctor you must have felt very comfortable in those surroundings. After all, Hitler opened the doors and gates for organ specialists. It was only the psychologists that he persecuted and murdered, because they were all Jews. That's why I'm a thorn in your flesh, because psychoanalysis is something that is so absolutely un-Aryan, isn't it?

And that's also why I became a psychoanalyst, because I simply have to know what provokes your subconscious so much about it.

"But a surgeon, an internist, even a genetic researcher – back then those were respected people. It was a militarily important profession. They needed the surgeons to keep the soldiers able to fight for as long as possible. They needed the psychiatrists to diagnose resistance as garbage and confine it. And the genetic researchers, well, they were the crème de la crème, the high priests of National Socialism. They could produce the scientific evidence for the existence of the Aryan superman. And let's look at your area of specialization. You earned your money as a gynecologist, but your scientific reputation is based in human genetics. You wrote all of your papers in that field. Human genetics, such a beautiful phrase, is completely modern again these days. The discovery of the human genome will change the world, they say. And what did they call it fifty years ago? The doctrine of heredity, and that led directly to eugenics and euthanasia. You were a genetic researcher then, and you have remained one to this day. Genetics is your bible, is for you the only true science. You see nothing to the right or to the left of it. And just as you euthanized – more bluntly: killed – cripples back then, today you will abort, euthanize, kill a mongoloid fetus without hesitation after examining the amniotic fluid. Well, just what is actually the difference?"

That provocation hit home. Now Rafael Makord had drawn not only his father's honor, but also the reputation of the entire medical profession through the mud. Now his father had to come out of hiding. Makord sensed that. And suddenly his father's voice broke into dissonant, shrill overtones, as if he intended to imitate the baroque countertenors without having ever practiced it: "You ignoramus! You unscientific pseudo-academician! You probably don't read any medical books on principle?! How much more overwhelming proof do you want? Everything is established in the genes, the constitution, the personality, yes, even the destiny of the individual. They've done research with identical twins that grew up separately, and both suffered the same strokes of fate at the same age. They had the same patterns of movement and the same quirks, although their upbringing was different."

He has never heard anything about astrological twins, Rafael thought scornfully.

"Or let's take ethnology: Why are the Sioux and the Maasai tribes larger than all of the tribes around them? Perhaps because they hunt buffalo and drink the blood of cattle?"

He has never heard anything about shamanistic rituals and spiritual traditions, thought Rafael complacently.

"And do you really want to wipe the successes of genetic research from the table: the fact that we are in the process of finding the corresponding gene for every illness, for every character trait?"

He doesn't even read the relevant studies, Rafael thought with a diabolical grin, *otherwise he would know that the genes are only letters, and they have discovered only a salad of letters without having the slightest idea of how the semantics and the grammar of the genetic code function.*

"Take for example obesity, being overweight, a scourge of modern humanity. We have more and more overweight adults and children. That's slowly becoming a medical prime risk factor with respect to both cancer and heart and circulatory system illnesses. The obesity gene has long since been identified, and with gene therapy we'll soon have obesity under control."

Just strange that this gene did not manifest itself during the last hundred thousand years when all of our ancestors looked like skin and bones, sneered Rafael inwardly.

"Or let's take the aggressively violent. The aggressiveness gene has also been isolated. Through gene therapy we'll soon be able to eliminate violence and aggression once and for all."

Okay, I'm convinced. I'll become a gene surgeon and cut all the genes out of you Nazis.

"And in psychiatry there has been enough evidence for a long time that psychiatric symptoms are passed on from generation to generation."

The poor man has never heard anything about family patterns. It's also strange that we sons of Nazis don't have anything at all in common with Nazi violence. Perhaps it's a recessive gene that will come through again in the grandchildren. — Hello, Grandpa, can I introduce you to your murderer grandson? He has it all from you.

"Through gene therapy we'll soon have endogenous depression and schizophrenia under control."

For God's sake, a united nation of Aryan supermen who have forgotten how to feel and imagine, no thanks.

"You see, my son, science does not make mistakes. We were on the right track back then, as we are today. Everything can be placed on a rational, biological basis, and that basis simply lies in evolution, in natural selection, in which the stronger eradicates the weaker."

Have you heard anything about the comet that destroyed even the most superior dinosaurs?

"And you're one of the strong. You're my son. You have the best talents. You could go a long way, if you would only finally accept my help."

But I don't give a damn about your murderer gene. I don't want it.

"Follow in my footsteps, and the world of science will lie at your feet. Anything is possible there, right up to the Nobel Prize. Damn it, there's also genetic-physiologically based psychology. You could become a university professor in that in Vienna."

Good old Papa. With connections anything can be arranged in Austria, even a professorship.

"Recognize it at last. Join us. Become a true scientist. What do you get from interpreting dreams, from that carnival magic that can be used to read anything from coffee grounds, the phases of the moon, and the flight of birds, but offers nothing tangible? Renounce the superstition and believe your old father just once!"

The old man had talked himself hoarse, and slowly he ran out of words. He was happy about the fact that his son had listened to him for so long without contradicting him. Perhaps if he were to listen to him more often there was still hope that he would become a real researcher who worthily continued his father's work.

But Rafael Makord knew enough. He had his father where he wanted him. He needed no further proof. Albert Makord was a fascist, a genetic researcher, a eugenics scientist. He had been stuck in the spiritual corset of National Socialism for fifty years. He still believed in the pure Aryan superman; only the tools had become more modern. Instead of racial extinction there was now genetic extinction. Rafael was finally certain that his perception was correct, that where he imagined fascism to be, there really was fascism.

Rafael was relieved, almost joyful: "Bye, Papa! We'll see each other in court." He said it, got up, and left.

A somewhat perplexed Albert Makord remained behind.

73

12

Bergen-Belsen, February 1943

Told from the point of view of Adolf Markosky

"Dear colleagues, I am pleased that you were able to take the time to come to Bergen-Belsen in order to cultivate intellectual exchange and hold the banner of science high in spite of this difficult time. For a medical convention, the framework here is certainly modest. Nor would anyone understand, if we were to have sumptuous festivities right at the time when the Sixth Army is being led off from Stalingrad into captivity. May Providence protect them from the worst. *Heil Hitler!*

"Nevertheless it is of special importance that almost all of the camp doctors of the SS have gathered here to exchange ideas. Unfortunately, I must excuse Doctor Mengele from Auschwitz. Right now he can't keep up with the selections at the ramp. But since his specific research is so important, he sent Doctor Paulsen to us as his representative."

SS Medical Corps Colonel Ritter slowly began to move along with his speech. "Gentlemen, I've come directly from the headquarters of the *Führer*, and I am pleased to be able to give you from the most competent source the latest guidelines for building the thousand-year Reich. As you will see shortly, your cooperation in that effort will be of the greatest importance. Gentlemen, in his godlike greatness the *Führer* has created an enormous Reich, and in the process has come further than Napoleon, than Caesar, yes, even than Alexander the Great. Soon he will be named in the same breath with those luminaries throughout the world.

"But the *Führer* can't do everything by himself. It was to be expected that the incomparable energy of our beloved *Führer* would give rise to resistance and provoke our enemies throughout the world, who do not want to recognize the benefits of our movement. On all the borders they are now arming themselves in order to force Germany to its knees. The *Führer* anticipated that and now puts the second part of the plan of Providence in force. The *Führer* trusts not only the German soldier and the German worker, who together carried our tanks and cannons into the far reaches of the Russian steppes. Above all he trusts the superior genius of the German scientist. The *Führer* knows that the Aryan spirit will produce accomplishments that the world as yet doesn't even suspect. Just as during recent decades all of the famous discoveries were owed to the German intellect, it will also be that way in the coming years. At this very moment, when the enemies are sharpening their knives, that fact will be decisive. The *Führer* is counting on Providence to place the miracle weapon in his hands in time to win the final victory, in spite of the tremendous superior strength of our enemies. The *Führer* now needs you, Gentlemen, to create that miracle weapon for him.

"You think that the miracle weapon is the business of the nuclear physicists and the rocket technicians, of Wernher von Braun, who will soon shoot his V1 rocket into the jaws of the English? Certainly, that rocket weapon, with its enormous explosive power, will be a part of this plan, and the engineers in Peenemünde are responsible for that. But what is the greatest weapon that has decided all wars?

"The greatest weapon is the human being, and the greatest weapon of all time will be the Aryan warrior. And the *Führer* needs you, Gentlemen, to exalt the Aryan man to the status of the miracle weapon."

Ritter made a meaningful pause, and an excited murmuring went through the audience. That was the reason for this meeting; that was why they had hauled all of the SS camp physicians away from their work, although the work increased with every passing day, and nobody wanted to think about a vacation. The doctors hung on the words of the colonel, who drove his speech toward its climax: "Just why did we cover the whole Reich with camps and place them under the supervision of our best men, the SS warriors? Out of sadism and cruelty, as enemy propaganda is trying to convince the people? No, Gentlemen. You and I, we know better. The camps are places of concentration; they are workshops from which the new human being will emerge. The old is being ground into pulp, so that the new can be born. Just as nature brought forth all species through selection and selective breeding, in these shrines of National Socialism we will create the human beings of the future.

75

The breeder kills the weak and multiplies the strong. That has been the case since the beginning of life.

"I know, Gentlemen, that you have long since grasped the importance of this assignment. I know that the elite of the German medical profession have already begun innumerable research projects in the camps. I know that all of you are using the auspiciousness of the hour to achieve the best through unbounded research on human beings. And now I challenge you here today: Focus this strength. Exchange views without small-minded consideration of copyrights and similar Jewish nonsense. We need the Aryan superman here and now. A German soldier must be stronger than ten of his enemies. Tough, agile, hard, enduring to the last, insensitive to pain, ready to stab the bear in the heart with his last breath. Then we will be victorious. *Heil Hitler!*'

Markosky was impressed. This man Ritter understood how to sweep the people along. Suddenly Markosky, too, was sure of himself again: Yes, the whole thing made sense. With all of the necessary severity in the camps, with often seemingly cruel necessities, it was about the birth of a new era, about the creation of a new human being. Death is the most important tool of life. Hadn't the dinosaurs been swept away in a powerful catastrophe to make room for the mammals? Hadn't the Neanderthals died out to make room for homo sapiens? Hadn't God himself drowned the bad in the Flood in order to breed a new race? He who walks in God's footsteps cannot shy away from a small Flood. The nation that falls away from God will be drowned. *Now it's being burned, because it still hasn't understood anything*, Markosky thought with a cynical grin. Water, fire, gas – every judgment of God has its element of destruction.

What had Ritter said? ...*insensitive to pain*...That was an interesting point for Markosky. After all, he had been searching for a long time for a medicine against pain that could silence the unending torment of humanity at last. Man was a biological mistake. The brain was constantly tyrannized by pain signals of some kind. A hand placed on the top of the stove, and a person was already rendered lame for days. A little gunshot wound and the soldier already forgot his strength. A little stroke of fate and the person immediately fell into depression. Yes, that human sensitivity to pain, which at some time had perhaps had a biological purpose, had long since become a hindrance. It hat to be eradicated.

But how?

While Markosky was lost in thought, he caught sight of Paulsen at one of the neighboring tables. Paulsen, Mengele's representative – that could be interesting! Markosky moved over to the other table and introduced himself: "Allow me, Markosky, I represent the Terezin camp. I'm extremely interested in your research plans. I've heard that Mengele has amazing things going on. No wonder, from a statistical point of view he also has the most material at his disposal, of course."

Dr. Paulsen felt flattered: "Yes, yes, Auschwitz really is something special. Nowhere else do we have so much opportunity to analyze the genesis of the subhuman Jewish race. I am convinced that we have meanwhile had 50% of the Jewish population in our hands. 50%! That's no longer a small sample; that's almost the entire goddamned Jewish reality. Mengele is great. He works like a berserker. He writes everything down. He also doesn't let a single person escape; that's why he makes every selection personally. Sometimes I'm almost insulted because he doesn't think that I'm capable of doing that. But viewed intellectually it's completely clear to me that the man wants a comprehensive survey. How were the inferior Jewish genes able to pollute the superior Aryan culture of Europe and in the process even gain the upper hand? That question justifies any sacrifice. And the more statistical material comes together in one man's hands, the sooner we'll find the answer.

"But – you'll laugh – the Jewish question isn't the most important thing for Mengele at all. The solution of the Jewish problem is, to a certain extent, only a side effect. The problem of why the garbage arises is only important if we want to create perfection. Mengele's central problem is the creation of the superman. As tough as leather, as agile as a greyhound, and as hard as Krupp steel – you're familiar with that. Mengele is convinced that in a short time he'll deliver the result to the *Führer*."

"Which result do you mean?" Markosky gasped.

"You've surely heard which experiments we're conducting in Auschwitz. We operate on living people without anesthetic. We conduct shock experiments – cold shock, insulin shock, heat shock, electroshock. Mengele wants to plumb the limits of human

77

physical stress. He is convinced that this frontier is the constituent element of Aryan superiority. If we succeed in losing the fear of that frontier, then the Aryan warrior will be born.

"And now comes the most important thing. By what means will we overcome that fear of the frontiers? Think about it! What's the essence of medical doctrine?"

"The doctrine of heredity?" whispered Markosky hesitantly.

"Precisely, a German medical man can simply not be hoodwinked. You've grasped it. The doctrine of heredity is the golden path to the goal."

"Does that mean that Mengele is planning a certain kind of selection, a kind of breeding?" Markosky was electrified.

"Yes, you smart aleck, you're on the right track. Just why do you think that he takes on the work and stands at the ramp every day, no matter what the weather is? He's looking for a certain group of people who are suitable for his experiments. People who have very specific characteristics that are written all over their faces. He filters those out of the crowd. He also lets them live, for their genes are still needed."

"Which genes?"

"Well, Ritter just proclaimed it. The genes of the superman."

"And Mengele wants to find them among the subhuman people? That doesn't fit."

"That's a valid objection. Subhuman man as a species needs to be exterminated. That's right, for most of his genes are rotten. That doesn't mean, however, that individual genes in certain groups aren't precisely what is still missing in individuals of the master race, thereby preventing them from becoming supermen. It's something like the case of the lion and the snake. Let's imagine that somebody could decide to be either a lion or a snake. What would he choose? The lion, of course. But now the snake's poison is the only thing that can really become dangerous for the lion. Let's imagine that in addition to his strength we could now fit the lion with the poisonous fangs of the snake. First of all, he would be invulnerable, for the poison that's already in his body could not have any further effect on him. And second, his power would double, for he could then kill not only powerfully, but also very quickly. So before we stomp the snake to death, we must analyze its poison and make it useful for ourselves."

78

"And just exactly what is Mengele looking for?"

"Invulnerable, strong, insensitive to pain – isn't that how we would construct the perfect warrior, if we could? If we could breed a troop of perfect fighting machines, who would then still be able to stop us Germans?"

"Nobody!" Markosky shuddered.

"Now Mengele came up with the following idea: Among the people who have survived extreme stress for generations, in individual cases it has possibly reached the point of genetic adaptations that facilitate surviving extreme dangers. Life can adapt to almost everything, if it has enough time for it. There is life in extreme heat and cold, life under the enormous pressure of the deep sea; lizards can amputate their own limbs; salamanders can re-grow limbs, etc., etc. Even human beings can adapt to both the polar ice and the desert. Thus, if we were to concentrate all of those characteristics in the Aryan warrior, we would win. For that, however, we must first find the corresponding genes, and that comes only by way of breeding isolated populations in which a certain desired gene appears in high concentration. Once we've found such a population, then we can also crossbreed the gene into Aryan man.

"If we are looking for a gene that makes man invulnerable and extremely loadable, where would we be more likely to find it than in that very group of people that have survived the most extreme stresses, perhaps for generations already? Think of the bacteria: Through chemical poisons we can exterminate 90%. The 10% that survive are resistant to the poison. Do you understand the analogy now?"

"The Jews who...?"

"Precisely. For two thousand years Aryan culture has been defending itself against Judaism. There have constantly been expulsions, pogroms, and killings. The Jews who are alive today are the descendants of those who survived all that. Must not certain genes build up there? And those who survive the hell of our extermination camps, assuming that any of them succeed at all, won't they be the hardest of the hard? And next comes the scientific test. That consists of Mengele's pain experiments. Normal human beings do not survive them. Those who survive the experiments must bear the decisive gene. And Mengele protects them like the apple of his eye; he lets nothing happen to them."

79

Markosky shivered: "But what does he intend to do with them? After all, mixing the races is strictly prohibited."

"Well, I don't know where it goes from there either. But that's how it is with basic research. First you must clarify the mechanism. Only then does the application become apparent. I don't know either how Mengele envisions the result. Perhaps a certain amount of crossbreeding is permitted after all in breeding the fighting machines. Even the Turks made use of Christian children to breed the Janissary battle troops, and for all practical purposes they let their victories be won by the descendants of the infidels. And that would be no problem, of course, for instead of destruction through labor or destruction through Zyklon B, destruction simply takes place in battle. Or someday we may learn to cut out and transplant individual genes, who knows? Those questions are being dealt with by our colleagues in the Lebensborn Project. We deliver the genetic material to them as a basis."

Markosky was quite dizzy with excitement. The Jewish question basically did not matter to him. He was not a politician but a scientist. What interested him were the scientific possibilities that actually seemed limitless to him after this discussion. Yes, that was how it had to work. Perhaps Mengele really was a genius. The isolation and breeding of human groups that apparently bore a certain gene material in them. That had always worked before. Through breeding, man had made killer machines from harmless little dogs. Through breeding, one could also create the killer human being.

But even that did not really interest Markosky. Mengele's theory concentrated on a certain point, on a discovery that would be a blessing for humanity no matter how the war ended. Human beings who had survived extreme pain perhaps bore the gene in them that made them insensitive to pain. An anti-pain-gene, so to speak. And that was what Markosky wanted to find.

Then you could breed human beings *without pain*. And then those unbearable pains would be gone at last.

13

Linz, November 8, 1991

Makord was really tired. He could not find anything that would have relieved him. He had once again been in a lengthy interrogation with the police inspector, who would have preferred to have locked him up again immediately, because the evidence against him was becoming more and more solid. Nor was Dr. Wegener any real help. Those many legal snares, the ifs and buts, the coulds and shoulds, all of that lawyer talk would not help Makord in a trial. Makord knew that, and his despair increased accordingly.

When nothing at all helped anymore, then he holed up in his apartment like a wounded animal in its burrow. Today it had reached that point again. He put a bottle of whisky next to his bed, put Bruckner's *5th Symphony* on the phonograph, and as the sounds of the stringed instruments swelled to a powerful crescendo, he lay down and pulled the covers over his head. Today he did not want to hear anything but the comforting tones of his neurotic favorite composer, who had recorded his fears with bombastic power a hundred years earlier.

But peace did not come. Makord had hardly dozed off into dreamland when the doorbell rang.

"Can't I ever have any peace?" Makord cursed to himself and jumped up.

When he opened the door, he could not believe his eyes, for she was standing there – young, beautiful, and shy, the way he loved her.

Makord's mouth dropped open, but not a sound came from it.

*

"May I come in?" Vera asked softly, and Makord quickly stepped to the side.

Where have you been?
Why did you run away?
What do you have against me?
Do you know what difficulties you've gotten me into?

81

What actually happened that night?

The symphony was just beginning the furioso with grandeur, and the questions trumpeted through Makord's mind. But his mouth was still dry and speechless.

Vera stood in the vestibule. Makord stood as if rooted to the ground. The flood of sound went up and down like a fire siren.

"I came back," whispered Vera.

"Why?" stammered Makord.

"I don't know."

The music became too loud for Makord, and he silenced the pathetic fanfares of the symphony with the press of a button.

Then there was silence.

And there it was again, that silence between the two of them, which seemed to speak in many colors that had not taken any form. That let them feel so much that could not be conceptualized. That was full of attraction and full of taboos. Rafael Makord wanted so much to embrace Vera, but that was forbidden. He was drawn to her heart, which seemed simultaneously near and miles away.

Rafael sought for an innocuous question: "Are you doing well?"

"Yes, I'm doing fine. Or no, I don't know. I have no idea."

"What happened to you?" Rafael finally found his way into his normal conversational rhythm.

"I wandered around for days. It was as if I were in a trance, without a destination. I'm still quite dazed, as if something stopped working in my head."

"Why did you run away?"

"I don't know. Don't ask me. I have no idea."

Silence again.

Silence. Protracted, nerve-racking, and yet full of tenderness. There was no answer to Rafael's questions and he stopped asking them. But he sensed the loving gaze that streamed from his eyes, and that was enough for him.

As if to provide a diversion, he poured two glasses of whisky. When they were sitting next to each other on the sofa like old friends, at first Vera looked around the room like a frightened animal, as if she wanted to determine if there was a hidden danger lurking somewhere. Then she slowly relaxed.

82

Finally she began to talk: "That evening was simply horrible, you know. No, it's not your fault. It was also beautiful, of course. I did want to be with you. I even wanted to be with you completely, but that wasn't possible. It was so terrible."

A peculiar declaration of love, thought Makord to himself, and slowly his macabre sense of humor reawakened.

"I wanted to be very close to you, and in the beginning it was even beautiful. The music at the concert and our conversation at dinner, they were wonderful. I wanted to let go of myself with you, but then, when you undressed me, something came over me. It was so horrible, and now that I'm sitting next to you, I feel it again." Her entire body trembled.

"Perhaps you can't understand that. I don't understand it myself. There was suddenly this terrible feeling of violence in the room. Everything was so revolting. You were behaving like a rapist who wanted to force something that couldn't be done. Just as if it didn't matter at all to you what I felt. I wouldn't have had any opportunity to say no. You had that insane look in your eyes, as if you were wildly determined to take me hard, like a prey that falls into the hunter's hands. And I felt that you would bore through me with your penis, with knives, with all the weapons that fell into your hands. You would torture me, hit me, make me bleed, and my sufferings would be fun for you. It was so terrible. It is so terrible. I can't stand it." Vera's entire body was shaking.

"Vera, I love you. I wouldn't do anything that you didn't want." Rafael was completely perplexed. "Yes, I wanted you, and I still do. I thought that you wanted it, too. But you're mistaken about me. I wouldn't do anything to anyone, and especially not to the woman I loved. But it's normal for a man to want to sleep with the woman he loves."

"Yes, I thought that, too. But this feeling inside me is so bad and tells me something completely different. I know that you love me, but my feelings tell me that you're a rapist and that you're only hiding your true feelings. That you're only waiting for the opportunity to get me in your grasp, when I can't defend myself because nobody can hear me."

"But Vera, that's a totally absurd idea. Have I given you the slightest reason to see me that way?"

"Yes, you're right. It's crazy. And nevertheless I feel that way."

"You know, that evening I really didn't understand the world anymore. I thought you liked me. I thought that you would be the right woman for me. And then you accused me in a way that no woman had ever done before."

"Rafael, I don't understand it myself. Something snapped inside me. It was as if something shot into my mind that didn't belong to me, as if something from another time took control of my actions. And then it was quite real again. At that moment I saw you as a violent man. I could feel that you would do something to me."

"But Vera…," Rafael tried to say reassuringly, but he did not get far.

"After all, how am I supposed to know what's true?" Vera asked agitatedly. "Now you say that you're a considerate man. I can believe that of you or not. Is the truth what you say or what I felt that evening? Who knows? If I hadn't run away, then perhaps something would have happened after all."

"I dearly wished that something would happen, but something quite normal," Rafael pouted. "I would have liked so much to have felt you, your breath, your skin, your hair. I was so much in love with you and simply wanted to be happy with you. And then you pushed me away. Don't you think that your behavior was very insulting?"

"Yes, of course, I know that. I didn't want to hurt you." Vera tried to appease him. "Actually I wanted to sleep with you, too. But then I couldn't. My God, don't you understand? Sometimes irrational, ambivalent things happen and you simply don't know what is the matter with you."

"Yes, yes, I understand you. I understand you only too well. Ambivalence of feelings. That happens to all of us. You love somebody and then you injure him. You want to be close and then you push the other person away again. It happens so often that it's now almost normal again. I understand only too well what's taking place inside you. You simply can't really decide what you want from me. And that's the very thing that hurts me."

"You don't understand anything at all!" Vera responded sourly. "You psychologists always think you know what takes place inside people. You have a term for everything, an interpretation, a drawer, and you place our feelings inside it, and with that you think that the matter is resolved. I'm not ambivalent toward you. I know that I

84

like you. I just can't sleep with you. That's something completely different. And I'd really like to know for myself why that is."

Now Rafael was torn. On the one hand his psychologist's mind began to work busily. The concepts and the theories actually did just tumble out of him, and the interpretations of Vera's behavior and attitude almost tripped over each other. As a professional counselor, he actually did have all kinds of possible explanations for Vera's behavior, and that caused him to assume a loving and understanding attitude. But as a lover Rafael was deeply hurt and felt more like taunting and striking out. He had to be careful that the resulting product was not a mixture of aggressive understanding.

"Not to be able to stand a lover physically is really a very unambiguous form of rejection. You simply don't really love me. Perhaps you feel that I'm quite nice, as a friend or comrade, but as a man you don't find me attractive. You can say it quite openly."

"Rafael, you're such an idiot, and you're destroying everything. Don't you understand that it has nothing to do with you, but with something else entirely? Something is happening inside me, something that I myself don't understand, and it probably has nothing at all to do with you."

"I can see that, of course, the fact that the whole thing has nothing to do with me." Rafael had ultimately reached the point of taunting her. "Perhaps it has something to do with another man. Perhaps I'm only a fill-in, an adventure that suddenly became too hot for you. First you make me eager, get me going full bore, and then you say, oh, that was probably nothing. And after all that I'm supposed to understand everything."

"Rafael, you, you…" Vera's words became a hysterical scream. She jumped up and stormed out of the room.

After a few minutes Rafael went into a panic at the thought that Vera could run away again and disappear this time once and for all. He ran after her and found her outside on the balcony of the small apartment. He approached her very cautiously, placed his hands gently on her shoulders, and whispered in her ear, "I'm sorry. I didn't want to hurt you."

"Rafael, do you believe that I'm going insane?" Vera sobbed, as she rubbed her face, which was red from crying. "Am I having hallucinations? Do I hear voices? Or am I simply incapable of love? Tell me very honestly what you think of me."

"I think that you perhaps had a very strong memory of something that you experienced in the past."

"It wasn't a memory. It was real. You were the culprit, the rapist. I felt that. If I'm not insane, then what I sensed is true. If it's not true, then I'm insane."

"There's an explanation for your behavior, which does not require that we declare you to be insane. We psychologists call it transference."

"What's that supposed to mean?"

Rafael retreated into lecturing, which he always did when the emotions of the person with whom he was talking became too dangerous for him: "Transference works as follows: Let's assume for the moment that you actually did have a very negative experience with a man sometime, a man who severely injured you, who mistreated or raped you. That experience was perhaps so bad that you never wanted to think of it again. The experience was suppressed and stored in your subconscious. Your wish to forget the whole thing was realized, until the point when you were in a similar situation again, when I wanted to go to bed with you. Then the entirely suppressed memory shot into your mind again. In the process you transferred your negative memories of the violent man to me. That is, you projected the image of that man onto me, as if I were he. But I functioned only as the screen onto which the image of another man was projected. That means, it's not I who am the violent man, but that man from your past."

Vera looked up briefly and then stared off into space for a long time, as if she were far away. Perhaps she examined the many storage spaces of her memory to see if that mysterious culprit was hiding there anywhere.

Finally she shook her head. "That's a stupid theory. I've experienced hardly anything with men, especially not an episode like that. And if it were a memory, I would have to know who or what it was about."

"That's the very thing that's unbelievable about the subconscious: Experiences are suppressed so strongly that we no longer have the slightest intimation of them. And it doesn't have to be a memory from your adulthood at all. Mistreatment often happens in childhood, and there suppression works especially well and has many years to erase the traces of the injurious event. Yes, I even know patients who remember something that they themselves did not experience at all."

"Now what's that supposed to mean?"

"Sometimes children take on memories and feelings from their parents." Rafael continued with his lecture. "That occurs especially when the parents had to suppress something so firmly that they did not confront themselves with it again during their entire lifetime. The traumatic experience is then like a mailed package that remains lying there well packed and is not picked up by anyone. Sometimes a curious child then discovers that package and unpacks it. When parents totally suppress something painful, that pain appears again in the experience of one of their children."

Vera became sarcastic: "So, if I may be permitted to get to the point: You believe that I believe that you are a rapist, because I experienced a rape that I can't remember, or because my mother was raped, who likewise can no longer remember it. The problem with that is that I don't even remember my mother anymore. Then how am I supposed to remember something that my mother experienced? That's all nonsense."

"Of course that's all only a theory. I don't know either what really caused your feeling that evening. I'm only certain that I didn't want to do anything bad to you." Makord paused for a moment. "When did you actually see your mother for the last time?"

"I was three when my mother was arrested. So, I can also hardly have taken over anything from her. After all, she no longer had any time to raise me or to communicate anything to me. I remember only a pretty face with glowing hair that looked at me lovingly. And now all that's left is the pain of her disappearance." Vera had tears in her eyes.

"Sometimes it's the pain that inseparably links people to each other." Rafael tried to be comforting, but he did not really succeed. What Vera had experienced was too sad. For that reason he simply put his arm around her and held her tight. Now he knew once more that this young woman needed him and that he wanted to be there for her, no matter what happened as a result. And he felt Vera's muscles, which were tense in the beginning, slowly relax.

87

14

Moscow, August 1991

The female patient's eyes flickered restively. She looked around her like a hunted animal. They would soon come again and hurt her. The men in the white coats would grab her and inflict violence on her. That had been happening for years, and she could not do anything about it.

She fled from the patient's room to avoid the visit. Before the nurses could give her the next injection that would incapacitate her again for days, she intended to use the precious minutes when she was completely conscious. If the minutes became hours, she could perhaps order the thoughts in her mind, gather information, and at some time develop a plan by which she could escape from her prison. And this clinic, the Moscow Psychiatric Clinic, was a prison. They had put her here years ago. In a dark corner of her memory she knew that she did not belong here, that they had abducted her. Or was she only imagining all that? Was she really insane, paranoid, as the psychiatrists always told her? It did not matter. Whatever the case was, she knew that she had to get out of here, that she could not stand it here for another day. She had to get away to freedom, go back to her homeland, or to what she thought was her homeland. And even if her homeland was a fantasy construct of her delusions, she at least had to find out what reality was – her memories, or the opinion of the doctors that she was only hallucinating everything.

She had gotten to this point again and again. But before she could take the next step and gather indicators and information, she was knocked out by the nurses with another injection. As if the doctors were able to calculate exactly how long the medications deadened her consciousness and when she needed the next narcosis in order to degenerate into a vegetable. That was a perfidious, underhanded force, more disgusting than everything else that the patient had experienced in her life. Brutal force could break your arm, but it would heal again. A rape took away a woman's honor, but somehow you could survive that. The psychiatrists of the Moscow Psychiatric Clinic took your mind, and that destroyed you for all time.

But this time she would escape from them. During all those years she had never given up believing that she could escape. And lately the attentiveness of the prison guards had diminished somewhat. They were more and more occupied with reading the newspaper and watching television. They discussed politics, glasnost, republics, communism, and similar things, and appeared to be worrying a great deal about their future. In the process, more and more often they overlooked the strict security regulations by which they were supposed to guard the patients who were under psychiatric treatment for political reasons. Sometimes they even left discarded newspapers lying around or thoughtlessly threw them in the wastebasket. That was how even the woman patient obtained information from the outside world. She was able to figure out that the era of Stalinism was slowly coming to an end. Glasnost, that meant openness, freedom. And for years freedom was what she had longed for.

During her flight through the corridors the woman passed the room of the physician on duty. Since he now had to be making his rounds, the room was probably empty. The woman slipped inside and turned on the little television set that the doctors used to pass the time during the long nightshifts. She was lucky, because there was a news broadcast right then. Or rather there was a special report. The woman's entire body trembled. What she saw pierced her to the quick, as if she already knew what was coming toward her. The psychiatrists called it déjà vu, a certainty of having already experienced something that one could never have seen before. Fine, so she was experiencing déjà vu, but what of it? What was being shown on television was impressive even if it had never happened before:

Tanks were moving up toward the Moscow inner city. Soldiers were occupying the capital city of the Soviet Union. Gorbachev had been placed under house arrest at his dacha in the Crimea. The hardliners in the Communist Party of the Soviet Union had apparently staged a coup. Glasnost was over. Stalinism was raising its head, which they had wanted to cut off.

Gorbachev was faded in. He seemed to approve of the measures of those who had participated in the uprising and to welcome them as the salvation of the Soviet Union. But what else could one expect from a man who probably had some Kalashnikovs pointed at him, so that they were not visible on television, of course. So that was it. Goodbye glasnost. You were a beautiful dream, but Stalinism is stronger. That is why every dream of a life without Stalinism is probably a paranoid hallucination. The doctors were right after all.

Just as the woman was about to yield to her fate and accept her life as a schizophrenic, like a good girl (*What's the use? Perhaps dreaming is more beautiful than life anyway*) new images appeared on the television screen. Yeltsin confronted the tanks with a megaphone in his hand, climbed up onto one of them, declared the advance to be illegal, and look at that, they actually stopped. Again the woman had a déjà vu experience. She was familiar with that. Stopping tanks was the most normal thing in the world. She had done that a thousand times already. But perhaps only in her fantasies; and in her fantasies it had always turned out badly. Perhaps it does make a difference whether it is a president who climbs up onto a tank or a normal mortal. The tanks simply knocked down normal citizens; the woman also seemed to know that from somewhere. But with a president the tank drivers had a more difficult time; there the blind obedience that had been drilled into them had too great an effect. Whatever the case was, the tanks stopped, and the president of the Russian Socialist Federative Soviet Republic succeeded in turning the tables and placing those who had participated in the uprising on the defensive. Perhaps there was still a chance and glasnost was not quite dead.

While the opportunity for perestroika hesitantly opened up, the small window of freedom closed for the confused woman. The attendants had tracked her down; they grabbed her in a practiced grip, and even before she could protest, they jabbed the syringe of narcotic into her hip, which led her away into her accustomed stupor of pleasant indifference. Yeltsin, Gorbachev, coup participants, it did not matter at all; let them play with their tanks as long as they wanted. What did it matter to the woman, as long as she had the right dose of her legal drug under her belt?

It took days before the patient awakened from her induced stupor again. Actually she did not know at all how much time had passed. She only concluded from years of experience that it had probably taken weeks for the effect of the injection to wear off. In the beginning she was quite reluctant. She did not want to leave the land of her hallucinations. Like a sleeper who only wakes up reluctantly when a beautiful dream is not going to come to an end, she refused to immerse herself again in the hard reality of the Soviet Union. Or was it still the Soviet Union at all? Had she perhaps awakened at a different point in the space-time continuum? Had she made a journey in time? Had she fallen into a wormhole and reappeared in a parallel universe? She had to look into that immediately. During the few waking hours that remained to her before her next injection, she had to gather indicators of what reality was: The feeling in her dreams that the tanks had gone home again, or the opinion of the doctors that she was only imagining everything. The Stalinists' belief in the harsh realities of power, or the people's dream of freedom.

What was reality? The woman did not know that. But who did know it anyway?! Just who was not imprisoned in the illusions of his imagination? Didn't the communists dream just as much of unrealistic fantasies as those in the opposition to whom they imputed schizophrenia? Just who did know the truth?

The confused woman suddenly had to laugh. It was a hysterical, displaced laugh that her psychiatrists would have immediately recorded as further evidence of her illness, if they could have recorded it. But thank God they were not there at the moment.

The woman remembered the room with the television set and immediately headed for it. Again she found the news broadcast and was now really confused about what she saw and heard. The Communist Party was no longer in power and was to be prohibited. And it was said that the Soviet Union would also soon no longer exist. Yeltsin spoke of a CIS, a community of independent states. Now what the devil was that? Perhaps the doctors had given her a new cocktail of medications that now rendered her insane once and for all. Perhaps she was still hallucinating, although she felt sober. That would then be the perfect medication, one that deluded a person with the subjective feeling of normality, although it destroyed the perception of reality once and for all. A Russia without a Soviet Union and communism – that could not be; that was a fantasy. Not a single inhabitant of the glorious soviet repub-

91

lics would believe in that, even in their dreams. Too often it had already turned out to be sentimental dreaming.

No, she must really be insane. And then she also would not find a way back to her homeland. Suddenly the confused woman had tears in her eyes. And even that was again evidence of her illness. The doctors called it emotional incontinence. And perhaps they were right. She was a schizophrenic and should accept that fact.

Suddenly she heard voices. The doctors were apparently on the way to their office. The woman quickly hid in the clothes closet, for she no longer had time to leave the room and she was afraid of the next injection. In that uncomfortable situation the woman received a surprising opportunity to examine reality, one that she had not expected at all. Specifically, she was able to overhear the conversation between the two doctors who had made themselves comfortable in their office. And thus for the first time she learned what these men really thought, and not what they feigned as reality to their patients.

"Just what should we do if Yeltsin really does do away with the Communist Party?" the first one began. "Then the party book that we have used up until now to further our careers in medicine will no longer have any value. Then no stone will remain unturned!"

"Yes, you're right, Yuri. Then we won't be able to count on anything anymore. Then the archive will possibly be opened, too, and then everything will come out. And the two of us will then be sitting in the wringer."

"What do you mean, sitting in the wringer? We do live in a country that guarantees the right to work. In the Soviet Union there are no firings."

"Firings, firings – that will then be the least of our worries. As a physician you can always find work. No, the whole dirty mess will come out. All of the shit that we had to take care of for the Party will then be in the newspaper. What do you believe the journalists meant, when they picked up the torch of glasnost so enthusiastically? They meant us, the doctors of psychiatry, the servants of the Party. And if the Party no longer exists to protect us, they will openly rip us apart."

"But Pyotr, we're just harmless doctors who do our jobs. What are they going to reproach us with? The fact that we help poor, confused schizophrenics to bear their illness? That is certainly not a crime!"

"My God, Yuri, have you been living on the moon? Haven't you grasped anything at all about what we're doing here?"

"Well, just what are we doing? We're directing a psychiatric department. We treat psychotics. That's what we were trained for. That's our job, and that's why we're given the title of specialists."

"Yuri, you really don't get it. Haven't you noticed anything at all about our patients? Their constitutional strength, their high intelligence, the high degree of education? Do you really believe that we've gathered together here a selection of our country's weakest and sickest citizens?"

"Well, genius and insanity are simply closely parallel. And educated insane people are especially dangerous to the Party, and for that reason they need special treatment. We learned all that in our training. We have to prevent paranoid ideas from spreading to the working people and poisoning our nation."

"Now we're getting closer to the truth. We protect the Party from the encroachment of paranoid ideas that could stir up the people. And by definition, any idea that contradicts the dictatorship of the proletariat is an insane idea. All the people who are in opposition to the Communist Party must be insane – that's the prevailing doctrine of the Communist Party of the Soviet Union."

"You mean…"

"Yes, I mean. Our psychiatric station is in reality a disguised punishment camp for people of the opposition. Our nervous system medications serve to render people vocally dead, whose statements would still be too dangerous, even in a trial. Our injections protect the Party from the public discussion of critical ideas that cannot be permitted in a communist country. God have mercy on us if the anti-communists come to power and find that out. They will throw us to the mob, and nobody will be at all interested in the fact that we were only powerless individuals who followed orders, who could not act any differently. For, first and foremost we were subject to the Hippocratic oath to protect people and help them."

"Shit, Pyotr, what are we supposed to do now?"

"Keep the lid on it, make sure that not one of our patients is released and is able to tell his story. Or quickly flee to the West, what do I know?"

The woman in the clothes closet trembled all over. But she was no longer confused. She finally knew the truth. Her perceptions were reality. She was not insane, but had only been declared insane. They had tried to destroy her mind, and that was not paranoia but reality.

All that had happened because she was dangerous. But not dangerous because of her illness or because she would harm herself or others. She was dangerous because of her political views.

Finally she was certain.

She was an interned dissident. The psychiatric ward was only a perfectly disguised prison. The attendants were disguised prison guards. And the medications were her chains, chemical chains, more dangerous than any other chains.

And in such a game of confusion, one should not go insane.

15

Police Inspector Wimmer was basically a man with a sense of humor. Or, better said, he had once been a man with a sense of humor. His many years of service in the Linz police department, however, had hardened him. He had seen everything: corpses hacked into pieces, men who shot their wives and children, gang wars, genteel crooks against whom there was no evidence, but who audaciously committed their crimes right in front of the police, the pimp scene, the Fuego case, and many others who, despite the strongest evidence, simply did not want to confess their guilt. It was sometimes more than the strongest stomach could stand. It would have been normal at times like these to develop a stomach ulcer, but Wimmer's constitution was too robust for that. So he simply had that constant heartburn in his throat, which spoiled the taste of the best foods for him. But when he took his beloved coffee from the machine during one of his few leisurely breaks, and a surge of stomach acid rose in his throat after the first swallow, he really became peeved. Sometimes he did swallow the antacid tablets that his family doctor had prescribed for him for such cases, but they really did not help either.

There were simply many reasons to become irritated, and after all, he had not become a policeman because he had expected a bed of roses. No, he had chosen this job because he wanted to lock them all up, those criminals, put them behind bars, and put things in order – that was the justification for his existence. It pained him all the more, when he did not have enough evidence to catch a scoundrel.

Let's take the case of that young snot, thought Wimmer on that gray November morning, while drinking his second cup of coffee, which burned in his throat. *This Makord does claim openly that he had nothing to do with the dead woman. Although he woke up next to her holding the murder weapon in his hand, dead drunk, of course. What other evidence does the prosecuting attorney want – perhaps a video tape with the murder on it from every angle?*

Sometimes it really was not fun to do this job. Usually you groped around in the dark, and many cases were never solved at all. Some came to an indictment, but the criminal was acquitted on the basis of the weakness of the evidence, although anyone could see that he was the culprit. And then there were these fortunate cases where everything was right at hand, where you only had to add up two and two and present the elegant report to the prosecutor. *And then a scoundrel like that has a powerful father who knows the chief of police, and not even the bloody murder weapon is sufficient evidence, and dear Mr. Wimmer is left to investigate further. In a case like that you have to boil over.* Wimmer had read about animals that kill their prey by spitting corrosive saliva on them. He liked that hunting method very much.

There had once been a time in the Linz police department when the work of the police had been very much simpler. A well-founded suspicion of crime was sufficient, and the case could be turned over to the Gestapo, which took care of the rest. That was certainly not a constitutional method, but it was efficient, very efficient. The riffraff were off the streets very quickly. Sometimes Wimmer caught himself wistfully thinking about that time, one that his older colleagues had told him about, when he was a young policeman. On the other hand, Austria was now a democracy, and that was a good thing. The very severe methods could simply no longer be used, for this was not a banana republic, of course, even if Amnesty International sometimes presented it that way. Police who beat people! – that was ridiculous. You should still be able to press a scoundrel a little bit. That was the only thing that was left to you anyway on the tedious path of argumentation that was prescribed by the legal system. The funny thing was that this modern path of constitutionality was really the hard one, but it was simply only hard for the policeman who could toil away for an eternity in order to have at least a little success here and there.

While Wimmer was thinking about his murder case, a trace of his missing sense of humor did return to him. That Makord, he had something; he sensed that very clearly. He was some kind of smart operator, a man with chutzpa or whatever the Jews called it. Sleeps with a woman who is easily fifteen years older than he is. What might bring a young man into that kind of sexual alley? Wimmer wanted to know that. Probably a guy like the young man from the famous Hitchcock thriller. Just what was its title? Oh, yes, *Psycho*, with that lanky actor who kills his mother and all the other women besides.

Something similar must probably have taken place in the sick mind of dear Mr. Makord. Oh, well, he would find out what the man had done. He was sure of that. This was the kind of case that Wimmer liked; it had its amusing sides. It would be a lot of fun yet to penetrate the perverse convolutions of that sucker's mind in order to get the decisive evidence out of him.

And in general, that matter of the telephone call to the police chief. So he was dealing with a respected family. That really provoked Wimmer. Many enemies, much honor. To outfox the powerful people of this city – that would really be a special pleasure. Even if on the surface the father and son defiantly stuck together, Wimmer had a gut feeling that the thing stank to high heaven. A conservative chief surgeon and a flipped-out psychologist – that absolutely did not fit together. It would be a laugh, if he could not find the crack where the two of them would angrily attack and contradict each other in their statements. Wimmer would break down that phalanx, as if it were nothing, and walk off the field victorious. The two of them should not feel that they were any too secure.

While Wimmer was pursuing his fantasies with a contented smirk, the telephone rang. Puchner was on the line, the coroner: "Oh, Inspector, I find this somewhat embarrassing, but we overlooked something in our examination."

"What do you mean? Are you suddenly of the opinion that the dead woman did not die of the stab wounds that you cited in your autopsy report as the cause of death?"

"No, no, that's an unalterable fact and our medical report is also correct. We simply left something unnoticed that…how should I put it?…did not become apparent until the body was being put into storage. The corpse had something in it…"

"Well, that's my opinion, too, that the woman had something inside her. Otherwise she would not have driven the poor young man crazy that way. You're not telling me anything new there," Wimmer said, interrupting the pathologist with a grin. The case began to amuse him.

"No, you don't understand. The woman had something in her throat."

"I hardly think that she is still going to go to a doctor because of a cold." Wimmer laughed bitingly into the telephone.

97

"So, Inspector, I don't understand how you can make fun of such a serious matter. The best thing for you to do would simply be to come by and look at the whole thing for yourself."

Reluctantly Wimmer got up from his desk. Right then he wanted to get his third cup of coffee from the dispenser. That would have given his acidic saliva killer quality for the day. But it was also fun to be caustic with words, and for that Puchner was the right victim. So he drove to the pathology department at the hospital to learn how matters stood.

Puchner led him into the autopsy room, where the corpse of the murdered woman lay on a metal table. He pushed back the linen cloth and pointed to the woman's mouth. "It was because of the rigor mortis. At the time of our examination the jaw was firmly closed and we had seen no reason to examine the mucous membrane of the throat, since poisoning had already been eliminated as a cause of death. Yesterday, when my assistant wanted to lift the corpse back into the refrigeration box, he was a little awkward, and it slipped out of his hands, turned as it fell, and landed on its belly. That led to the opening of the jaw. During the second attempt to lift the corpse into the refrigeration box, my assistant saw something flash in the open mouth, something that had probably slipped from the throat into the mouth cavity as a result of the fall. This is the object in question, which the woman must have swallowed before her death and which got caught in her throat." With those words the pathologist handed Wimmer a key.

"What's this supposed to be?" Wimmer was astonished. "That looks like, like... – well, like the key to a baggage locker. Oh yes, the number is also there on it. That can really only be a locker at the main railway station, at least if the key is from here in Linz. We'll see about that immediately. Thank you, Doctor. You've helped me a great deal. Perhaps this story is becoming more exciting than I thought."

Wimmer paid no further attention to the painfully tense facial expression of the polite pathologist. He stormed out of the hospital and raced as quickly as he could through the inner city to the railway station. He very hastily scanned the numbers of the lockers and finally found the right one. Wimmer held his breath before he opened the locker. What kind of evidence would he find here for his case?

In the locker there was a valise. When the police commissioner opened it, he saw all kinds of documents and on top of them a piece of paper with a hastily written note. Wimmer read the note and ran his eyes over the papers. It was all somewhat confusing and initially made no sense. At least Wimmer could not make anything of it because the information in the documents was not in his field of specialization. What Wimmer did understand, however, was the fact that his case had suddenly become much more complicated than he had originally thought. His simple theory of a sexual murder committed by a man with a mother fixation was perhaps not as great as he had conjectured after all. In his naïve stupidity the prosecuting attorney had finally put him on the right track. He actually did have to begin researching from the beginning and organize his evidence in a totally different way. The contents of this valise would be the key to it.

Thoughtfully Wimmer read the message on the piece of paper again: *I am being followed. This man has been following me for days. He will kill me to get the valise. I have therefore put it in a locker in order to perhaps have a chance of surviving. Please give the valise to the police.*

Well, that was taken care of now, of course. The documents were now a case for the police. They seemed to have been very important to the dead woman and obviously to her murderer as well. But why had she not gone to the police with them immediately? If the woman had such dangerous material in her hands, then we could have protected her. *Please give* – that sounded very personal, as though the addressee of this message were somebody whom the dead woman had known. Had she wanted to give the key to somebody? But then why had she swallowed it? Had she wanted to prevent the murderer from finding the key? And what did the young snot have to do with the whole thing? Wimmer would have to find the answer to all of those questions.

The matter promised to become exciting. At least for today Wimmer had found the way back to his good mood.

16

Terezin, May 1943

Told from the point of view of Adolf Markosky

Even with all the brutality, life in the camp also had its pleasant sides for Markosky. Included among those was the fact that there were also many young Czech women in his care. They, too, had to strip to the skin in front of him and were probed and thoroughly examined. Even if he hated the Czech women just as much as he did all the other Czechs, he did have to admit that many of them were built pretty as a picture. Slender figures, graceful, and really very feminine, striking, esthetic faces. *Actually not that Slavic at all*, he thought to himself. Well, they had been surrounded by Germans for a thousand years and for that reason had probably imperceptibly become Aryanized long ago. And the product of this Slavic-Germanic mixing did not look all that bad, quite the contrary. Markosky felt a pleasant stirring in his lower torso. This daily vivid association with his female enemies gradually led to a very ambiguous relationship to these women. Intellectually he despised them, but physically he began to desire them more and more.

Women – in his life up to now Markosky had not thought much about them. At first women had not interested him because he was constantly occupied with his family's problems. How was he supposed to fall in love, when he had just seen his father dangling from a rope? After that, he had transformed his pain into ambition and had devoted himself completely to his studies. There, too, there was hardly any more room for women than for a cervix study in an anatomical atlas. When he had completed his course of study, events completely overwhelmed him. Before he knew it, he was in this camp, a camp into which no respectable German girl would ever stray. With whom should he then have fallen in love – a Czech woman perhaps, a communist woman, or even a Jewess? Completely out of the question.

On the other hand, Markosky had long since reached the age in which the drives demand their due with ever increasing urgency.

That was intensified even more by his social environment, which had written the culture of the naked body on its banners. One could reproach National Socialism with many things, but by God, or, should we say, by Hitler, it was not hostile toward sexuality. The Aryan man's body was a cult object, as if made for the purpose of procreating itself and planting its virility in the fruitful soil of the Germanic woman. Markosky's abstinent attitude was gradually being viewed with suspicion. One could interpret it as a rejection of the healthy German sense of nationality or, even worse, suspect him of certain inclinations of a different kind, which were not worthy of an SS man.

So he had to do something. The simplest way to prove his masculinity was to join his comrades, when they visited the brothels together. That was a popular way to let off steam and to release tension between your legs. And as a result of the numerous field campaigns of the German army, the pertinent establishments were filled to overflowing. Overflowing in every respect. For the raids in the East caused many subhuman women to view it as advisable to choose service to the German man over any service in the camp. The pleasure houses were therefore full of fresh human material. On the other hand, the plump curves of the eastern women were not at all repulsive to the German soldier, but rather arousing, and they stimulated rapid discharge. Even Markosky had no problems with that. In with his penis, thrust firmly, and the matter was quickly taken care of. But that did not give him real satisfaction. There was hardly any feeling in it; it was more like a mechanical discharge. It was production of pleasure and semen with the eroticism of a cider press. Ten milliliters of Aryan genotype, produced in one evening, to be put into test tubes for the Lebensborn Project, graded 1a for genetic research purposes. That is about how one could have described Markosky's feelings on those evenings. Thus they were not a real approach to the feminine world.

Sometimes Markosky gave thought to why he had never fallen in love. Perhaps it was related to his distant relationship with his mother. His mother was now his last relative, and yet he had no desire to visit her. There was no trace of the cozy feeling with which German propaganda described the relationship of the German soldier to his mother and his homeland. No, he did not feel at home with his mother; rather he despised her. He could not forgive

101

her for the weakness that she had exhibited during all the years when things had gone so badly for his father. His father had needed a strong wife, a fighter, who would have motivated him and dragged him along. But his mother was weak and forbearing; she accepted and said yes and amen to everything. She did not inveigh against her fate; she did not confront her husband; nor did she fire him up and support him. She simply let things happen. She left her husband hanging, and when he finally hung from the rafter she was even too weak to perform the final service for him. After that, when her sons could have used a strong support, she also left them hanging. She dissolved into self-pity. Hermann had to be the strong one. And both brothers learned that women could not be depended upon.

Markosky had never admitted to himself that behind his contempt for women there was a deep longing to be held and to be able to lean on a strong body. Like every small boy, he had needed somebody who could have given him safety, security, and devotion. A soft breast on which he could have cried his eyes out – his mother could have been that, but she was not. His mother herself had sought for a strong male breast to lean on, and she had apparently found it in the son of the powerful commerce counselor Markosky. She had always remained the little girl who wanted to be led by a male hand. That was what she had seen with her father; that was what she had learned in the patriarchal world of her childhood. Men lead the world; women let themselves be led, are patient, demure, and nice. When her husband sank more and more beneath the weight of his economic problems and could not keep his promise of strength, his mother visibly declined. She developed what the doctors called masked depression. Externally everything was in order, and his mother functioned, did not complain, and apparently bore her fate with composure in conformity with the prevailing female image. But internally she was hollow and silent, slowly died, and ceased to be the mother that her sons needed. They resisted by refusing to give her childlike love, and by depending only on themselves anymore. After their father's death, Hermann and Adolf behaved like two orphans who could now only lean on each other for support. The brothers were mother and father to each other, and their mother had long since ceased to play a role in their lives. That is why Hermann's death had such a horrible effect on Adolf, for it meant that he was completely alone. It never occurred to him to mourn together with his mother.

So Adolf did not want to depend on any woman, because that was synonymous with being abandoned. Nor could he admire any woman, for he had never encountered an admirable woman. Even grandmothers, aunts, and female family friends belonged to the same weak feminine type, perhaps because his grandfather had not admitted anything else into his world. To that extent, Markosky did feel at home in Terezin, because there the situation was a familiar one: despicable women as far as the eye could see.

The inability to fall in love was one thing, the sexual longing something else. Even though Markosky's psyche could be termed somewhat messed up, from a biological perspective his body was quite normal. Now and then his testosterone level pushed the man to penetrate a woman and discharge his sperm. But evolution had also programmed human beings to pair off and raise children together, and that did not take place completely without feelings and mutual attraction. Even if Markosky did not admit it to himself, something inside him insisted upon fulfillment, and the bodies of the whores did not suffice for that.

With that immature mixture of feelings in his heart and his penis, Markosky continued to approach the opposite sex. The daily examination of naked women gave him a broad field for experimentation, disguised by medical routine. Some women left him cold, and he didn't even vouchsafe them so much as a single icy glance. Others interested him partially, that is, certain bodily regions held a certain erotic attraction for him. He then did subject these women to a thorough examination, for after all, probing, listening, and tapping were components of clinical examination, and when probing feminine curves something useful could be combined with something pleasant. Since the young women hardly dared to protest out of sheer fear, a probing could last so long that Markosky's penis became moist without his having to compromise himself at all.

On some days he came across female specimens that evoked more within him. It might be the swing of the hips, the black hair, a wild look, a gently rounded breast – some of the women awakened a longing for more, and in Markosky's breast there was a reaction that he could not classify. It was completely out of the question, of course, that one of these women would arouse love within him, and for that reason he immediately pushed those feelings away again. Rather he disguised them as research interest, and in that way he was able to venture forward on occasion in the field of gynecology. After all, even vaginal forms, cervixes, and fertility were scientifically relevant. For procreation, it was also important how the penis fit into the vagina, and so Markosky was happy to make his penis available to research.

In the Indian *Kama Sutra* he had read that the size relationships between the male and female sex organs could determine the sexual satisfaction of couples. That was worth a project: When a large penis encounters a small vagina, or a small penis a large vagina, what is the difference in the feeling? Markosky was in the process of finding out.

That was also how it was when Olana stood naked before him. Yes, she was a worthy subject: broadly sweeping hips, long hair, glistening eyes, and pouting lips. This subject had to be examined very thoroughly. So Markosky went directly from probing to examining her vagina, and his penis was also immediately stiff enough for the research. To his surprise, however, his test subject behaved in a somewhat unexpected manner: She resisted, when he took out his penis, pushed him away, and scratched his cheeks with all of her fingernails. For the first time, he was dealing with a strong specimen of the female species. Olana was not afraid of him, and it was that very thing that started him ticking. The longing for strong femininity broke forth in him and brought his sexual longing to a boil. He had to have this specific woman, simply because she offered resistance to him and did not immediately fall over. Where there is resistance there is also support. The little indignant boy desired that female breast, and he reached for it eagerly.

The SS man, however, could not tolerate that resistance and had to show her who was the boss. So he grabbed the woman with his strong arms and turned her around so that her magnificent bottom presented itself like a ripe fruit. Then he thrust his stiff penis deeply between her cheeks and thrust again and again like a wild bull, as if he wanted to beat her tender, bore through her, and break all her bones. She would never again dare to resist him; he would show her his strength and would take her as often and as savagely as he wanted. Olana twisted beneath his grip and tried to get away from him, but that only made Markosky all the more savage. And with a throaty, vigorous scream, he thrust himself into her as hard as he could and squirted his masculinity into her vagina.

He was strangely satisfied and felt that things were alright that way. He had found what he had not sought and had taken what was now his. It took feminine strength to awaken him, and that strength had been kept from him for too long. Now it was legitimate for this woman's strength to become his possession. For how could she have resisted him?

Olana whimpered softly to herself and moaned with her hands on her belly. Markosky's penis immediately went limp. Had he perhaps deceived himself about her after all? Was she a weak Cinderella just like all the others? Just as he was about to give her a scornful look, the savagery awakened in Olana's eyes, and she threw herself at him with all of her fingers stretched out as if she wanted to tear him to shreds on the spot. As he grabbed her wrists to deflect her furious attacks, he was reassured by the discovery that he had been right.

This was the right woman. She fascinated him. She awakened his spirits. She was worth the fight. He could wrestle with her as if wrestling for his life, and that would bring him back to life. And with every battle she would become a bit more tractable and give him a bit of her femininity as a reward of pleasure and longing. There was no doubt about that. For after all, he had the upper hand.

When Olana had to accept the fact that she could do nothing against the SS man's strength, she stopped trying to attack him. She would have liked to kill him with looks and was somewhat irritated because that disdain did not matter to him, yes, even seemed to please him. Finally she gathered up her clothes, got dressed as quickly as she could, and left the examination room.

From then on, this game was repeated daily. Markosky had Olana brought to him the way a sultan sends for a slave. He always took her savagely from behind and broke her desperate resistance with a firm clinch, until she gave up like the prey beneath the lion's paw. He enjoyed the excitement that this struggle gave him, and he enjoyed the superiority and power that left no doubts at the end of the struggle. When Olana finally submitted to his grasp with a whimper, he then had everything that he needed in order to feel

105

pleasure: the resistance, the power, the struggle, the longing, the passion, and the victory. His woman had to be first strong and then weak to please him. Since Olana offered him all that against her will, he liked her.

For Olana it was no game. She hated being defeated. She hated the penis that penetrated her. She hated this man who forced her. And between brief moments of sexual sensation, what he did to her simply hurt. The humiliation hurt. The coldness hurt. The hardness of his penis, which was employed like a weapon, was painful. The cramping of her vagina was painful, as was the boring into her belly. Just how could men believe that such a violent process had anything to do with pleasure? But what else could she expect from such a psychopathic SS man?

In time Olana's resistance became weaker. Just what point was there in resisting the man's violence like a wildcat, when the end was always the same and he forced his way into her again and took everything he wanted? She gave up her resistance, withdrew completely into her contempt, and let the act happen to her, so that it was over as quickly as possible. It did not escape her notice that this man's excitement became all the weaker, the more she gave in to his violence. The cooler and the more indifferently she let him have his way, the more rarely he had her brought to him. Thus she discovered that indifference and contempt were the forces that brought this culprit to silence. She hoped that he would soon leave her in peace entirely.

That slowly spreading relief was suddenly gone when Olana noticed that her period did not come.

17

Linz, November 9, 1991

"Fine, so this is your girlfriend." Inspector Wimmer growled the words to himself. "The fact that this young lady is standing in front of me, so healthy and vivacious, clearly proves that you didn't kill her. But that doesn't help you at all. You're still under suspicion of having killed the older woman, who, for some reason that we don't exactly know, appears to look like your girlfriend."

Rafael, Vera, and Dr. Wegener were sitting in the police station and wanted to convince Wimmer that on the basis of the latest developments in this case Rafael could not be guilty. But that did not impress Wimmer in the least. He was used to dealing with contradictory indicators. The fact that there were now different possible theories regarding the case at hand would not, under any circumstances, bring him to exonerate his main suspect of responsibility.

"But how am I supposed to have killed a woman whom I do not know and about whose existence I had no idea?" Rafael's voice sounded despondent. He had been so happy about Vera's reappearance that he had believed that his problems would resolve themselves. His girlfriend was alive. For him that was the most important thing. He had not killed anyone; he was now certain of that.

Commissioner Wimmer saw things differently: "Now I believe you, that your description of the evening in question is correct up to the point in time when your girlfriend furiously left your room. A little quarrel between lovers is nothing unusual, of course. According to your account, that was at about eleven o'clock. The coroner's report indicates that our dead woman was murdered at about midnight. In that hour a lot can have taken place. Apparently you were visited again, by a woman whose identity remains uncertain. Just who can assure me that you didn't know this lady? Perhaps you were so frustrated about the failure of your amorous adventure that you invited another girlfriend to come to your place, one who, as you knew, was fond of you, who was only waiting for the chance to be with you. The woman agreed, and from that moment on everything went like clockwork."

"But I don't know that woman. I have no idea who she is."

"Fine, then for some unknown reason an unknown woman simply forced her way into your apartment. You were already angry and drunk. Perhaps you felt threatened. There was a fight, and bang, the deed was done."

Now Dr. Wegener involved himself in the discussion: "What my client is trying to say is the following: Dr. Makord had no motive to kill this woman, since he had no connection to her of any kind whatsoever and doesn't even remember ever having met her. And you yourself know, my dear inspector, that without a conclusive motive you will accomplish nothing in court with circumstantial evidence. Just try it. It will be a pleasure for me to call you to the witness stand and rip apart your circumstantial evidence. Do you really want to do that to yourself? Do you want to make a fool of yourself in public? No, I know you better than that. Until you have more evidence in your hands, you're going to leave Dr. Makord in peace. You know, of course, that the chief of police has his eye on you!"

"The chief can kiss my ass heartily and crosswise, and you, too, you toadeater." Wimmer was slowly becoming furious. "We investigate here without regard to rank and name. So keep your empty threats. We're not to the point of filing charges yet anyway. But the fact remains that this nice young gentleman woke up next to a blood-covered corpse, holding the murder weapon in his hand. And the only fingerprints on the weapon are those of your client."

"But that doesn't prove anything at all yet. My dear inspector, you have enough experience in these things. For a professional it's obvious that you wear gloves in order not to leave any fingerprints behind. And then you look for some stupid individual onto whom you can shift the suspicion, a straw man, so to speak. You get him to pick up the weapon, and then his fingerprints are on it. With that you can do a fine job of wiping out any traces of your presence, remain undiscovered, and the wrong man sits in prison."

"Just what do you intend to suggest by that?" Wimmer grumbled angrily. The attorney had exposed the sore spot in the evidence. Secretly Wimmer had to acknowledge that he was right.

"Well, we think that somebody pulled a fast one on my client. For some still unknown reason the murderer wanted to liquidate this poor woman. That was planned well in advance. It was also part of the plan to find somebody to palm the body off on. Perhaps the murderer happened to discover the dead woman's similarity to my client's girlfriend, and for that reason he watched her. And then came the favorable opportunity: My client lay drunk in bed, completely unconscious after several bottles of wine. The dead woman was placed next to him, the knife was put in his hand, and that was it."

"Well, Dr. Wegener, now you're the one who's making himself look ridiculous. Nobody will believe your abstruse theory. That would mean, of course, that a murder is carried out as if on order, when the right opportunity occurs. Perhaps the murderer also examined the phases of the moon and the status of the constellations ahead of time, what? You don't believe that yourself. And who's supposed to act so precisely here in Linz, the Italian Mafia perhaps? We're not in Chicago, you know."

For a moment peace prevailed. The inspector and the attorney had taken their shots.

"May I say something as well?" Hesitantly Vera asked to speak.

"Yes, if it's significant for the argumentation, please do."

"I've only known Rafael Makord for a few weeks. We were in the process of falling in love. We also had our problems in that regard, but I don't think that they're anyone else's concern. I appreciate Rafael as a very lovable and sensible person. I can't imagine that he is a murderer."

"My dear woman, what you can imagine has nothing to do with the matter. It's quite normal for a woman to protect her man. The fact that you can't imagine that is likewise normal. That's the problem, of course, with sex murderers. They often remain unrecognized for years because they lead completely unobtrusive lives with their wives."

"But I haven't been leading an unobtrusive life for years with Mr. Makord. We just recently became acquainted. When men kill their wives, they've built up aggression over many years, aggression that is then suddenly released when the man runs amok. None of that fits here."

109

"It's nice that you defend your boyfriend, but that doesn't get us anywhere. And anyway, I'm asking the questions here, for it's a matter of a police investigation and not of some piece of gossip in the Jindrak Café. So, what kind of difficulties did you have with each other?"

"I was the problem. I suddenly had strange fantasies."

"You don't have to make any statement about that," Dr. Wegener said, quickly interrupting her. "Not before we have discussed that with my client."

"Counselor, let the young woman talk. You're disrupting the collection of evidence," Wimmer responded fiercely.

"I want to talk," Vera continued. "I believe that I'm responsible for everything. If I hadn't behaved so strangely and hadn't left Rafael that evening, then nothing would have happened. Then this other woman couldn't have appeared at all."

"The good old *what if* is a nice party game, but it doesn't get us anywhere. So, what were the difficulties on that evening?" Wimmer asked insistently.

"I suddenly had such a strange feeling about Rafael. But it was only my own fault. He couldn't do anything about it. Rafael and I are in agreement that this feeling comes from my past and was simply projected on him like on a movie screen."

"What kind of a feeling was it?!" Wimmer's voice became insistent and intimidating.

"There was suddenly the image of a violent man who could injure and mistreat me. But it was only my imagination. That wasn't Rafael, but only a memory."

Vera recognized that she had let herself be driven into a corner, and she tried desperately to extricate herself from Wimmer's invisible grasp. She looked over at the attorney for help, but he turned his eyes away out of sheer irritation at the fact that Vera had fallen into the inspector's trap.

"Alright, what more do we need?" Wimmer exulted. "Even the woman who loves him thinks him capable of anything. Women do have a very good intuition. You sensed the violence that radiates from this man. You were afraid of him. You sensed the pent-up aggression, the hatred toward women, and felt threatened by it. My dear woman, you're not to blame for anything. You saved your own life. Who knows, if you hadn't fled from this man, then per-

110

haps you would now be the corpse that we are debating about here."

Vera broke into tears. She had wanted to help Rafael and had only brought new suspicion upon him. Whatever she undertook in her relationship with Rafael, it made everything even worse. She no longer knew what was going on at all, neither with herself, nor with her boyfriend, nor with this murder case.

"Now see what you've done, you heartless apparatchik!" Now Wegener had become angry about the course of the interrogation. He was irritated about the naiveté of the young woman, who obviously could not assess the consequences of her words. He was even more irritated with himself, because he had not prevented the derailment of this discussion. "I shall file a complaint against you for intimidation of an important witness. It was unnecessary and unfair to invade this young woman's private life. But that's once more typical for the Linz police. No price is too high for you to bring something to a quick conclusion. Constitutional rights don't matter to you at all. That will have consequences. I swear that to you!"

"Now calm down, Counselor. Sometimes someone's bark can be worse than his bite," Wimmer said in an effort to appease. He felt sorry for the young woman, and he himself had the impression that he had gone somewhat too far. "A feeling isn't necessarily evidence, and I assure you that we won't put your client in jail because of his girlfriend's statement. We need more than that to do it. Besides that, in this case there really are various suspicious factors, and your client is not the only suspect. There is new evidence that we must process first, but which perhaps points in a different direction."

"What evidence are you talking about?"

"Documents have surfaced, which the dead woman had with her. Besides that, we know that she was afraid she was going to be killed, and that she felt that she was being followed. Look here. All of that is written here." Wimmer showed Wegener the note that the dead woman had written in her mortal panic.

"That's extremely interesting. It supports my theory that there is still an unknown person who intended to liquidate this woman. It's probably connected to the documents that were found with the woman. I demand, in accordance with my client's rights, an immediate opportunity to inspect those documents, so that I can build

111

our defense strategy on them." Now Wegener had talked himself into a rage.

"Slowly, slowly. Hold your horses," Wimmer said again soothingly. "It can't be done that fast. You can't inspect those documents at all right now, since we've given them to an expert for verification. It's a matter of some sort of scientific material, about which I myself really have no idea."

"You simply want to delay the handing over of important evidence. I must insist once more that you permit me to inspect those documents."

"And I'll do that at the proper time. But for the moment you must be patient for a while yet."

*

Rafael felt completely exhausted. Wimmer and Wegener had decided his fate without consulting him. He had not even been given the opportunity to speak, as if nobody were interested in how he was doing with respect to the impending indictment. When the hearing was over, Vera accompanied him home. The two of them did not say anything for a long time, but only cautiously held hands as if to reassure each other that they were not alone in the world in these turbulent times.

"Did I stamp you as the guilty party once and for all?" Vera finally asked hesitantly.

"Vera, don't blame yourself," said Rafael, trying to reassure her. "The truth will come to light. And Wegener's theory of the great unknown man is not bad at all and will divert suspicion from me. By the way, I didn't fail to notice how you tried to defend me. That's the most important thing for me, because it means that you trust me again."

"Does that mean that you perhaps love me a little bit?"

"It means exactly that," Rafael responded, and he took Vera into his arms.

*

Dr. Wegener drove straight to old Makord's villa to give him a report about the hearing in the inspector's office.

"There's a new development. Your son is perhaps no longer the main suspect at all. It's obvious that there's another unknown person who perhaps murdered this woman."

"How did you arrive at that conclusion?"

"The woman had scientific documents with her, for the sake of which she was probably murdered. I think there's a connection. Wimmer won't turn over the documents yet."

"Scientific documents?" Something flickered in the old man's eyes. "If it's by any chance a matter of medical documents, then I absolutely must have them!"

"I already thought something like that, and for that reason I demanded the immediate surrender of the writings as the defense's right."

"Very good, Wegener, very good. I know that I can depend on you."

18

Moscow, September 1991

The female patient sweated with fear. Perhaps also with exertion and excitement. She did not know it. She had given up brooding too much about her mental condition. For years they had stopped her from reflecting, and they had apparently only confused her in the process by trying to convince her of realities that were in contradiction to her perceptions. In the end she trusted neither her perception nor reality.

No, reflection had only made her ill. There had to be another path leading out of insanity. Since that day in the clothes closet, when she had eavesdropped on the two psychiatrists, the patient walked that other path. It was time to act. If thinking and feeling had not brought her closer to freedom, then acting would do it. Somewhere in her buried memories she thought she recognized that this had once been her maxim before. But that was probably long ago.

In recent weeks, in any case, she had plunged herself into hectic activities. At least to the extent that a stupefied, drugged schizophrenic is capable of hectic activity. It was all so difficult, like everything during the last twenty years, or however long she had already been in this institution. In any case, it seemed to her like twenty years; perhaps it was even thirty, perhaps only ten, who knew the truth?

It was so arduous, trying to find ways out of the psychic prison. The simplest steps, which are totally natural for a healthy person, became insurmountable obstacles. It would be so simple to reach for the telephone, call up her nearest relative, and loudly scream: "For God's sake, get me out of here." But when you are narcotized almost daily, you need your entire concentration to recognize that this simple statement is not the beginning, but the goal of a long chain of acts.

It began with the fact that the patients had no access to telephones at all. With such access, of course, they could have telephoned around without control and put the outside world in fear and horror with their paranoid ideas, and especially with those that were hostile to the working class. No, if at all, then only the relatives were permitted to make telephone contact with the patients, and even that only after the former had been thoroughly investigated regarding their intentions and origins, which normally meant that the KGB had to become involved. Then a few visits a year were perhaps possible, again only under supervision, of course, for the visits could have had a negative effect on the mental state of the patients, who were difficult anyway.

In the case of our female patient, none of that had happened. Nobody called, nor did anyone visit her. For that reason, she had to acquire access to the outside world on her own, and for that the first thing she needed was a telephone. Since she had decided to act, she could just as well begin with that point as with any other. To the extent that her guards permitted it, she began to wander through the ward and explore it. She used every unwatched moment and every phase in which her mind was relatively free of medication to look for telephones and telephone books. The two of them could actually only be within arm's reach of the attendants and physicians. So she began to search their rooms. It sounds simpler than it was, for the moments in which the patient was lucid and unobserved by attendants, while the rooms were also not occupied, could be counted on the fingers of one hand. Finally she discovered a telephone in an office that was empty every day at seven p.m. during the change of shifts, because the duty transfer took place in the wardroom. When the patient wanted to reach for the telephone receiver, she became painfully aware that she had no idea whom she should actually call. Or what she wanted to say to the listener who was not there.

Well, what could she have said in a plausible way? "Get me out of here." Whom were they supposed to rescue, if the patient did not even know her own identity? I, who am I? A person who is being persecuted for political reasons, who has been put in the psychiatric ward. Yes, certainly, but who would believe that without evidence? She did not even know her name, her origins; under the influence of the many shock treatments and the drug injections she had forgotten everything. To be sure, she did have a name, Nina Antonova; that was on her medical record sheet. But she was certain that this was not her real name. She had so often asked the doctors to reveal her real name, but every time during the visit the doctors had only smiled at each other complacently, as if they wanted to say: You see, my dear colleague, the paranoia has progressed to the point that she doesn't even believe us, when we tell her what her name is.

She was certain that she had once had a different name, but she simply could not remember what it was anymore. She was equally certain that the hometown that was listed on her medical record sheet was not correct. Novosibirsk. Wherever that godforsaken hole was, Novosibirsk meant absolutely nothing to Nina – as we shall call her for the time being, for lack of a better name. She had no memories at all of Novosibirsk. Although, that did not mean anything either, of course, for she also had no memories of any other city. Only blurred images of old houses, a cathedral, and many, many people on the street, who shouted and gesticulated. That could naturally also just as likely be a phantasm. But those images came again and again like a motion picture, and with them Nina had a feeling of home each time. That is why she thought that those images came from her hometown, and in any case it was not Novosibirsk. She had become convinced of that when she saw a television broadcast about the cities of Siberia.

Before Nina could reach for the receiver the next time, she therefore had to solve the puzzle of her origins. That was easier said than done. Naturally, she could ask the people in the ward. Where there were only paranoid schizophrenics, that was an experiment with extremely amusing results: "You are an Egyptian pharaoh's daughter...the baker's wife from next door...a witch who has been pursuing me for years...an agent of the KGB...a counterrevolutionary who was arrested with anticommunist agitators." Nina could choose which answer she liked best. The role of a counterrevolutionary was not bad; that would also correspond to the bits of information that she had overheard in the clothes closet. The attendants' answer was always the same: But you know that, stupid: Nina Antonova from Novosibirsk.

Nothing helped; she had to get access to the medical records where there would be more. But that, too, was a difficult undertaking. The medical records were in the office of the chief of staff, and that was occupied by two secretaries, or it was locked. Whenever Nina succeeded in reaching the office, she heard gossiping voices inside and knew that they would throw her out immediately. So she had to be patient.

Finally she learned that the secretaries liked to have a glass of Crimean champagne. If the chief of staff was in a good mood and generous, it could even be a bottle or two. One day, when she saw the two of them stagger to the toilet in a tipsy state, she seized her opportunity and darted into the office. She quickly found Nina Antonova's medical history and hastily scanned it. But she found nothing in it that was really new to her: childhood in Novosibirsk, studies in Sverdlovsk, onset of schizophrenia simplex, committal to the psychiatric clinic, worsening of her condition to paranoid schizophrenia, medications…none of that gave her anything. At last she stumbled over a small notation: *black box.* Next to it there was a foreign telephone number.

Black box, black box, just what did that mean? Black box, black container. She looked around the whole office for something black, but did not find anything. So she wrote the telephone number on a piece of paper and left the office before the secretaries could return.

Nevertheless, she now had a hint. She had to look for this black box, and she had a telephone number. She waited until seven o'clock, until she could creep unnoticed into the office with the telephone. Thank God, for weeks the attendants had been occupied with the political situation outside the clinic and for that reason were not even doing their jobs according to the regulations anymore. Some no longer came to work at all or constantly slipped away to demonstrate on the streets. Otherwise Nina's roaming around would have been discovered long ago.

Nina dialed the foreign number. A short dial tone made her panicky. The number was not correct. No, that could not be. The number was too important for that. Then it occurred to her. Foreign calls could surely only be dialed through the switchboard. Switchboard, switchboard, just where is it? Oh, yes, dial a one first. Nina dialed the one and heard a brusque woman's voice: "If you want a connection, identify yourself." Shit, as a patient she would never get a connection. Nina hung up quickly.

She had to identify herself, preferably as a doctor. Doctor, doctor, there was that nice assistant to the chief of staff, just what was her name, oh, yes, Dr. Petrova. She tried to remember Petrova's

117

voice in order to be able to imitate it. Then she dialed the one again.

"This is Dr. Petrova. I need a foreign connection," she warbled in a voice that was clear as a bell, the way she remembered Petrova's voice.

"Why do you need the foreign connection?" the gruff woman's voice growled.

"It concerns the family anamnesis of a foreign patient," Nina whispered convincingly, while thinking to herself that she had not lied about it at all.

The telephone operator accepted the explanation and put Nina through. Nina's heart missed a beat when the telephone was answered and the voice of an old woman rang out: "Who is this?" she asked in a Slavic language. It was not Russian and nevertheless Nina understood, and she heard herself answer in the same language: "I'm Nina Antonova, and I'm looking for my relatives. I could be your daughter or your niece," she added in a hesitant whisper.

"I don't know any Antonova, and my daughter has been dead for twenty years. Goodbye."

The dial tone was the painful proof that Nina's search had led to a dead end.

19

November 10, 1991

"What was actually the situation with your mother?" Vera innocently threw out the question that Rafael least wanted to answer.

"I don't want to talk about it!"

"Oh, come on, I told you everything about my family. How am I supposed to really get to know you, if you don't tell me about the important things in your life?" Vera had now become quite curious.

"There's not much to tell about my mother, except that she died early. She stood in the shadow of my father all her life, a so-called gray mouse, unobtrusive, forbearing, the way men used to want women to be."

"Rafael, don't try to fool me. You look so depressed when you say that. There's really something between you and your mother."

With her woman's intuition Vera had hit the bull's-eye. A tear rolled down Rafael's cheek. When Vera put her arm around him, he buried his face beneath her chin. "She was always so sad. Throughout my childhood I felt that sadness. I can't remember ever seeing her laugh. That was so hard to bear. I was a child, and I would have really liked to laugh. But when she looked at me with her serious eyes, then everything joyful died."

"What was the reason for it?"

"I don't know. She never told me. Whenever I asked about it, she only emphasized the fact that such stories were nothing for little children. She would tell me about it, when I was an adult. And before I grew up she had already been gone for a long time."

"What can destroy a woman like that, one who really has everything that she could dream of: a successful husband, enough money, an intelligent son...?" Vera's attempt to divert Rafael with this hidden compliment miscarried.

"I don't believe that she had everything. Perhaps she lacked the very things that were most important: love, esteem, respect." Rafael became angry. "She did have my love, but she couldn't really accept that at all anymore. I had the impression that my mother's seriousness had to do with my father's behavior. I don't know exactly, maybe he never really loved her. I'm quite certain that he never really respected her. I've always blamed my father for my mother's depressions. I imagined that there was still something there that she couldn't tell me, without incriminating my father. She didn't want to make me angry with him, but that would not have been necessary at all anymore. I was against him anyway, because I sensed that he was the guilty party. But I never learned what that guilt was, and that drove me crazy. Perhaps I'm only an ungrateful son with an Oedipus complex, and I do my father an injustice. I don't know. I seem never to know anything concerning important matters. Sometimes I feel like a complete failure."

"You're not a failure, at least not for me." She dried the tears on Rafael's face. "If you feel something, then there's something to it. You just told me that a child notices everything that concerns his mother, and that children who want to help their parents express feelings that are suppressed and concealed by them. Why should that be any different for you in particular, my noble psychologist?"

"You're right, of course, but what good does that do me, when I've already been tapping around in the dark all my life? Isn't that funny? I set out to explore the shadows of the subconscious, and what has been the result? Nothing, nothing at all, except for a few suspicions that don't distinguish me significantly from people who are insane."

Vera sensed that her boyfriend was becoming more and more mired in his self-doubt, and that each of her questions only reinforced it. So she tried to change the subject with something neutral and looked with interest at the bookcase in Rafael's living room. "You've got a lot of psychological literature there," she whispered appreciatively, for she assumed that he was at least proud of his knowledge in his specialty. She picked up one book after another and leafed through them a bit, looking for conversational material.

"This one here is already somewhat dusty and yellowed. It can't be from your student days – *Die Ärzte der Nazis* [The Nazi Doctors] – I didn't know that such a critical book would be permitted in a doctor's home."

"Father would never have read that either, but it seems to have interested Mother, for I inherited it from her. It tells substantially about the collaboration of the medical people with fascism. I ate it up and can only warmly recommend it to you. A lot of things become clear to a person who reads it."

120

"It also has an interesting cover." Vera became interested in the binding and took off the book's gray dust jacket. Then a letter fell to the floor, which had apparently been stuck between the book and the dust jacket.

Rafael quickly reached for it and turned pale. "That's my mother's handwriting. It seems that she intended to leave more to me with this volume than I was able to recognize at first glance."

He began to read the letter. And his facial expression vacillated from amazement, through being touched, to horror. Vera placed herself behind him and read with him what his mother had intended to convey to an unknown addressee. Apparently she had lacked the courage to pass the letter on, so that it now reached its goal as a hidden legacy:

My dear Husband

I would have much to tell you, if you would only listen to me. But I am certain that you do not want to hear what I have to say to you. So I am writing everything down, in order to organize my arguments and bring them to the point where you cannot brush them from the table again with your grandiose rhetoric.

Let's begin with the accustomed form of address: "My dear Husband" – I have addressed you that way since our wedding, and for many years I seriously meant it. I looked up to you and admired you. You were an example to me with your intelligence, and I revered your knowledge. When you healed sick people, I thought that you really did that out of love for the people. Meanwhile I have learned many things that have changed my image of you. You can imagine which facts I mean, and you will agree with me that the characteristic "dear" does not quite fit you, to put it mildly. For that reason it must be stricken from the way I address you.

"My Husband"

Even that form of address would be thoroughly suitable between old married people. Even if the love has grown somewhat cold, there remains the certainty of reciprocal possession, which has increased over the years. Even if not a dear husband, then at least my husband. That conveys security, and this is perhaps the reason why old couples remain together, even if they only spit at each other every day anymore. But are you really "my husband"? Are you really with me, in my vicinity? Or isn't your world a completely different one?

121

Haven't you hidden your life completely from me and lived a double life? Now, that I know the true facts about you, the facts that you have kept secret from me for twenty years, I can only scream out: You are not my husband. I do not want that which you embody to be "mine" — to belong to me. Nothing is more foreign to me than your nature as it really is. So let's also drop the word my from the form that I use to address you.

"Man"¹

That is what is left. You are a man, nobody can deny that. But a man of the most evil sort. If one scratches the veneer of your façade, then everything negative appears that the term man can embody: violence, deceit, unkindness, and death. Everything that women have suffered and endured at the hand of men is embodied within you. Man, oh man. That can really knock a person down.

Why do my words suddenly sound so bitter, you ask? Why am I no longer your loving wife, you ask? Why do I suddenly take up the cry of the evil emancipated women, you ask? Can you really not imagine what has happened? Do you believe that you can continue to deceive the whole world? Then I must probably help to jog your memory.

Documentation is really something so very important for you doctors. Everything must be written down. You cling tightly to everything, every abscess, every stinking stool sample; everything that could contain something useful for research. To be sure, you make the effort to write with especially illegible handwriting, the so-called physician's handwriting, for sometimes you also keep track of embarrassing, compromising things. And you encode your diagnoses with Latin code words that hopefully nobody understands. But sometimes the patients do understand what you write about them, and then you must figure on a revolt. Therefore the secrecy.

But every secret is uncovered sometime. And so your notes fell into my hands. Even and especially those that you perhaps did not want to show anyone, because they probably cannot be outdone for explosiveness.

I will never be able to get over what you did to those women, what you did to so many people. And then you stand there and play the benefactor of mankind and even have the audacity to believe that the past will not interest anyone,

---

¹ The German word *Mann* has two meanings: husband and man. The German original creates a wordplay based on that ambiguity (translator's note).

as long as nobody discovers it. It is, of course, even understandable that you do not make your deeds public, in order to save your hide, in order not to land in prison. If you were at least sorry for it, if you had talked with me about it openly, well, then perhaps we could have found a way to each other in spite of it. But the fact that for our entire marriage you have played the role of the apostle of morality in front of me, the fact that you have disciplined and dominated me with your oh so fine example, that beats everything, that is more than the strongest womb can bear. Like a dead, poisonous fetus, I expel you from my existence. I do not want to have to carry you anymore, endure you anymore. I do not want to be poisoned anymore by your two-facedness. And I want to be able to scream out who you really are: you murderer, you brutal criminal!

It is over between us, once and for all. I leave you to your fate. May the tortured souls that you have on your conscience fall upon you like avenging goddesses, like witches and Furies, like the demons of a long past dark age that has apparently not passed away, but rather lives on in your deeds.

Do not fare well, fare unwell, the way a monster deserves to!

Signed: a person who tried to be your wife and bloodily perished in the process.

Rafael was petrified. There it was in black and white. Everything that he had sensed, suspected, was written down there in his mother's letter. His father was a criminal; he had used violence; he had tortured women. All the pain of his childhood came to the surface; his mother was not able to love this man. Now it was clear and no longer a figment of his imagination. This newly won certainty had something calming about it. Rafael could trust his senses; his world was as he perceived it to be.

On the other hand, his mother still left him uncertain. As if the old fear of his father's power had continued to work within her, his mother had not dared, even in the moment of her greatest anger, to become specific. She did not state what the horrible thing was that she reproached his father for. So once again Rafael had no evidence in his hands, with which he could have confronted his father. He already knew how the latter would skillfully extricate himself from the situation: An emotional outburst by his wife, an attack of hysteria, put on paper in a moment of anger, but without any concrete meaning. My God, there are arguments in every marriage, where people throw words at each other, which they then take back because they did not mean it that way. And after all, his wife had remained with him to the very end, because she did love him, and that demonstrated the baseless nature of all these accusations.

Once again Rafael felt that powerlessness in arguing with his father, who brushed off all the arguments and did not let himself be impressed by feelings in any way. There was absolutely no point in confronting him with this letter. His father would simply tear it apart and only soil the memory of Rafael's mother after the fact. It was probably also that same powerlessness that had prevented his mother from turning the intentions expressed in this letter into deeds. There was no point in inveighing openly against Albert Makord; he was too cunning and too intimidating for that. One could only deny oneself to him and withdraw from him through resignation. So his mother had chosen the only weapon that could reach his father's sore point. Through her own death she brought into play again the dead women that his father had on his conscience. Every female relationship with Dr. Albert Makord was a fatal one; that was his mother's legacy. And Rafael had felt committed to that legacy long before he held this letter in his hands. Where, why, and whatever had happened, Rafael would find out about it.

20

Terezin, October 1943

Told from the point of view of Adolf Markosky

Markosky discovered with regret that his desire was not a lasting one. He had liked the wild hours with Olana very much. For a while they had torn him away from his misery and drowned out the pain in his heart. In the same way that he had not permitted himself to mourn, he now refused to admit the affection that he had felt for Olana. Even if it was improbable on the basis of such a violent beginning, his affection could have grown into a feeling that would have carried Markosky beyond his blatant sexual desire. This way, however, he sought desperately to renew the sexual savagery before the feeling died out in him again.

Since, on the basis of his childhood experiences, he interpreted Olana's declining resistance as weakness and yet longed so much for strength, he had to provoke her somehow, in order to unleash the accustomed battle of sexual forces. And since he did not really concern himself with Olana's spirit, he also did not notice that the situation was the exact opposite of what he thought, and that her cold calmness was more a sign of concentrated power than anything else. He paid for his rejection of involvement with the fact that what had been close enough to touch escaped him. Instead of understanding Olana's nature and taking it gently in hand in order to perhaps win her over, he had to bore into her sadistically in order to find a response that made his loneliness bearable.

In this striving to find an answer that only had to be sought because it had just been ignored, he hit upon a mental trick. There had to be someplace where she was vulnerable. If he poked around in it, she would become furious again. He was sure of that. So after he stopped raping her as often, he began to question her thoroughly, about her family, her childhood, her life. This questioning was carried out in the form of an interrogation, with surgical incisions that cut straight across her personality, and without regard for feelings and sensibilities, so as not to let the impression develop, of course, that there was any real interest, sympathy, or understanding here. The anamnestic questioning about symptoms, genesis, and therapy possibilities offered the right framework for this unconnected form of discussion. So he could insidiously present himself as a physician, where he acted as a rapist who hid his feelings behind his violence.

But Olana was too strong to fall into his trap. She sensed the intention behind what appeared to be a newly arisen objective friendliness. She sensed that the interest was only feigned in order to penetrate into her soul, to find her sore spots, in order to disarm her completely at last. No, she would not do this culprit the favor of letting him finally have her defenseless and hysterical at his feet. She had heard stories that women in the concentration camps gave up to the point that they finally saw their salvation in the support of their rapists. As if in a survival mechanism, they fell in love with their tormenters and began to revere the SS men. That would not happen to Olana.

So she remained very terse in her answers or refused to answer at all. She gave Markosky the brush-off, as if she were an iron wall that he could not penetrate.

Yes, she was from Czechoslovakia and had grown up here.

No, her parents were not from here. They had fled from Galicia after the First World War.

Yes, she was a Czech nationalist and hated the Germans.

No, she had no siblings. Her only brother had been murdered in 1938.

Yes, the Nazis were suspected of having responsibility for her brother's death.

No, nothing could be proven.

Whether she had ever been in love was none of his business.

Whether she had ever been raped before...

Suddenly something resonated in her. Her mouth distorted scornfully. Her gaze became so frosty that her eyelashes seemed frozen to her face. Markosky had found the spot and Olana was ready to cross swords with him:

"You men, you always think that you were the first ones. You long for virgin soil, and even when you rape, the girls are supposed to lie ready for you untouched. You want to be the first and invent everything all over again. What business is it of yours, you pig, how many stinking cocks have already penetrated me? You could possi-

126

bly infect yourself with some Czech's gonorrhea or some Pole's syphilis or get the dirty bacteria of some Russian on your very noble penis. You're probably afraid of that, and it would serve you right, you violent pig. It's none of your business whether I've already loved a man or not, or who it perhaps was. In any case, you're certainly not the one who makes my heart beat faster. When you're inside of me I feel more like shitting. And that matches the brown color of your uniforms well. It wouldn't be noticed at all. Perhaps your uniforms are so brown because so many women have already shit on them, who knows? I'm sure that Hitler is coprophilic. He only gets it up when his Eva turns him on, and even then brown would be a practical color for clothing.[2]

"No, my love life is really none of your business. You don't have the slightest thing to do with that, for even when you thrust into me, I feel nothing more that I do when an insect bites me. And I'm waiting for the day when you pigs are squashed like lice. It will be a special pleasure for me to kick your teeth in, when the Red Army throws you back across the Elbe. And that day will come. I swear it to you.

"But at least you want to be unique in history. The SS men as the inventers of the greatest murder system of all time. That's really something, after all. Even if you lose the war, nobody can take that record from you, or so you probably think. If you're not deceiving yourselves. Do you really believe that the European nations aren't familiar enough with that? Don't you think that we've had it up to here for a long time with this eternal macho behavior? Do you really believe that we women haven't had all kinds of experience with all of these atrocities?

"Now I'm going to tell you something that not everybody knows, so that you don't imagine in that slow-witted mind of yours that any of your acts are something new. When the Russian army marched into Galicia in 1914, the Czarist soldiers behaved exactly the same way that you Germans are behaving today. They raped anyone they got their hands on. My mother was one of their victims, and she became pregnant from it. I don't even know who my father was, since my mother couldn't keep the many candidates

---

[2] In the German original, the word *Braun* (brown) refers not only to the color, but also to Eva Braun, Hitler's mistress (translator's note).

separate. She could have gotten rid of me through an abortion, but she loved me too much for that. She endured it, the rejection of her husband and the others in the village, because she was a strong woman. By God, we learned to live with that shame, and it made us hard. You can no longer get to me. You'd have to get up earlier in the morning to do that."

Olana had talked herself into a rage, into a kind of holy anger that then broke forth from her. Those pigs, those bestial men – they tried again and again to misuse the women for their purposes. And then they even believed that it was the right of the victor to attack any woman who got in front of their cocks. The right of the victor, what an insult! How could violence ever be a right that you claimed? But for the men, what they could accomplish by force had always been their right. In that respect these Nazis were following an established tradition.

She looked at her tormenter with such scorn, that the latter's physical desire suddenly left him. He had just been exultant because his penis was twitching as hard as concrete in his pants. Olana's fury had excited him as never before. There she was again, his wild and strong woman, who was inviting him to the next battle that would end in a lustful climax. The mood changed when Olana told about the rape of her mother, when it became clear that Olana was the result of that violence. Behind the scorn Markosky sensed despair, the panic of the changeling that nobody wanted. The enemy's child was despised until she wore the contempt as a second skin that hardened into armor. Olana loathed men in order to shelter herself from the injuries that they had inflicted upon her since her birth. There was something familiar about that kind of injury, something that awakened the pain in Markosky's breast like a sleeping dragon. And the physical desire was gone.

He had Olana led away. The fun had come to an end for him. He would not assault this woman again. She had ended her service as the object of his desire. She had committed the greatest offence that a victim could commit. She had reminded him of his pain. Perhaps he should ensure that he would never have to see that face again.

During the night Markosky was plagued by terrible nightmares. He saw the bloated face of his father, who was dangling from the rope. He was naked, and blood flowed from a wound on his left side. From the stiff penis of the hanged man hung a second rope that was strangling Hermann. The latter was gasping for breath and reached his hands out toward Adolf, as if he were calling for help. Adolf wanted to go to him, but he could not move from the spot because his hips felt like they were nailed to the floor. He looked down and saw that his penis was in the vagina of a woman whose face was distorted with rage. No matter how hard he pulled, he could not free himself. The woman held him tightly with the strength of her pelvis and looked at him scornfully as she did so. While his penis hurt beneath the vaginal cramp but did not get any smaller, he had to watch while his brother strangled to death.

Adolf woke up, wet with cold sweat. Although he was wide awake, he did not stop seeing that horrible dream image in front of his eyes. It was like an idol of his fears, fears that pursued him, but that he stared at in fascination. Death, power, and sexuality, wedged together as in a painting of hell by Hieronymus Bosch. He was most terrified by the dream woman who had seized power for herself. He thought about the conversation with Olana, who did have to be the inferior woman, the victim. Somehow the women seemed able to reverse the helplessness of the victim and direct it against the culprits. The dream image and Olana's scornful face merged together and drove fearful thoughts through Adolf's mind.

He finally fell asleep, as if numbed by this straining of mind and heart. He slept the sleep of exhaustion and dreamed only of the hope that the terrible image would not come again. A shaman drummed a gentle rhythm and whispered a magic spell: be silent, mind, be silent, heart, be still. And the sleeping man lulled himself in that silence.

Suddenly Adolf sat up straight as a ramrod in bed. He was wide awake and completely lucid. He slapped himself on the head and cursed at himself. Just how could he have been so stupid? The solution was obvious, had been readily available all along, and he had heedlessly passed it by.

Hermann had not appeared to him in a dream for no reason, and he had also not died in vain. Perhaps his death was a plan of Providence to open Adi's eyes. His big brother had given him the answer. Hermann had always known it: the right of the victor, the law of natural selection, Aryanization, the oldest form of eugenics – they were all parts of a grand plan that was supposed to open his,

Adolf's eyes to his revolutionary discovery. Against her will, the stubborn Olana had helped with it. Adi knew now how he would find his cure for the scourge of humanity.

In the morning Adi was in his examination room early, and in feverish haste he rummaged through the medical reports. When his assistant appeared for work at the usual hour, Adi snapped at him in an unusually imperious manner: "Where have you been for so long? We have things to do. Find me the documents for all of the raped women who are still alive, at once."

When Maier looked at him somewhat blankly and in the process was unable to suppress a conspiratorial wink, Markosky became more agitated: "Don't grin at me, you moron, I'm totally serious. I want you to document every rape that has taken place in this camp. And it doesn't matter to me whether it was committed by an officer, a messenger, or a prisoners' detail leader. I need data. And you will also ascertain every rape in the past; I want the complete family histories for them, and I want them immediately."

Maier could not stifle his smirk. "Do you perhaps believe that rape is hereditary, since you're so interested in those facts? Well, well, perhaps we could then breed the ideal victims. Not a bad idea at all!"

In his hectic activity Adolf only became angrier: "Maier, you don't understand anything at all. You probably parked your cock in your brain and in so doing threw your neurons into complete confusion. Simply do what you're assigned and spare me your nerve-racking questions."

With a shake of his head, Maier started to work. "The boss is slowly losing his mind. He needs a woman, a German woman, a loving German woman, not a pest like those here in the camp. Then he'll get back on his feet again."

And the thought of pretty legs put Maier in such a good mood that he quickly forgave Markosky for his gaffe. After all, in the camp there were enough legs that a man could grab at, and in his thoughts Maier selected his next prey.

21

It was quiet in the police station. Most of the people had gone home for a comfortable evening of watching television. On occasions when there was not a new corpse to examine, they had to take advantage of it to show their faces at home before their wives became uneasy.

With Wimmer it was different. He did not have a wife who could have become uneasy. His wife had already run away years ago, because she no longer thought that Wimmer's sarcasm was funny. So he could just as easily remain in his office and work on his murder case, even if his corpse was no longer quite as fresh as the dew. Ha, ha. A quiet smile helped Wimmer to get over the fact that his hot case had entered the cooled-off stage. Not only the dead woman had been frozen; the moods cooled down, too, the less current a case became. Then it became purely and simply complicated, if not boring. The tedious detail work began. The facts began to contradict each other. The investigation was in danger of petering out in the sand. And in the end an additional dead woman would be buried, whose case had disappeared into a drawer, never to be seen again.

There was nothing that Wimmer hated more than unsolved cases. Not that he would have insisted that clarity always prevail in life. The world was a chaos anyway, as he knew from long experience with love affairs, official channels, and cluttered desks. Chaos was not the problem, for after all, it justified a policeman's existence. An unsolved case meant that the murderer had gotten away with his deed without paying for it. The murderer had won, and that was unbearable.

Something reared up in Wimmer's soul and he went and got his eighth cup of coffee in order to dive into his documents with fresh strength. His stomach and his esophagus were already burning like fire, but in spite of his family doctor's warnings the heartburn filled Wimmer with satisfaction. For to Wimmer's way of thinking coffee had a great advantage. The burn of the coffee saved him from the brandy for which most of his colleagues had reached in order to bear the routine of police work. Wimmer had the pleasurable feeling of a liquor drinker in his belly, without ever being drunk. He felt intoxicated and could nevertheless maintain his sobriety. That was worth ten times more than the health risk that he took by drinking it. Just who needs an esophagus at the age of seventy-five, if he is hanging on an intravenous needle anyway.

Whenever a policeman threatened to drown in the wealth of contradictory facts, he had to try to organize the facts into a system of alternative hypotheses. That was what Wimmer had learned at the police academy. From experience he knew that only a good theory could save him from filing too many cases in drawers, which led in the end to the final assignment of unsuccessful policemen to the telephone switchboard or to similarly important activities. So Wimmer began to put in order the many notes on his desk, which he had collected regarding the Makord case. To date it was a Makord case because there was still no name for the dead woman.

In the beginning he had been certain that Makord was the murderer. Since Wimmer was no longer certain of that in the meantime, he called that thought hypothesis one. Hypothesis one was approximately as follows: Makord was a sexual deviant, a man with a mother complex, in any case an insane man, like most of those who deal with insane people, for no normal human being does that voluntarily. Makord had been rejected by his girlfriend. In his frustration he obtained the older woman as a replacement. The behavior of both women, intensified by the influence of all kinds of alcohol, caused the keg of pent-up aggression to boil over, and Makord stabbed the woman. Then he fell asleep drunk next to the corpse and was found in the morning by the cleaning woman.

Wimmer had to admit that hypothesis one was not a very elegant theory. There were too many inconsistencies. First of all they didn't even know at all who the second woman was. Secondly, there was no proof that Makord knew this woman. Thirdly, it was difficult to find arguments as to why Makord would have killed the very woman who had shown herself to be sexually willing. It would be more logical if his hatred had vented itself on the first woman who had rebuffed him. And in order to prove the whole thing about a mother complex, Wimmer would first need the affidavit of a police psychologist. Dr. Wegener would relish tearing all of those contradictions apart in court and in so doing open wide the great drawer in which everything disappears into the sand.

132

This evening, however, the thought of Wegener had something unusually cheerful about it. *I let him run nicely aground,* Wimmer grinned merrily. *And the guy even fell for it. He actually bought it, when I said that the documents from the briefcase are not available right now. One to nothing for me.* With that conciliatory thought, Wimmer took the documents from his desk drawer. He had not lied, of course. He had actually given the material to Dr. Puchner for medical certification. But before that, he had naturally made copies for himself, for he himself had to make progress in his investigation. Wimmer leafed through the material and again did not understand any of it. Complicated medical stuff – who was supposed to know anything about that?

That led him to hypothesis two, which went as follows: The unknown dead woman was being pursued because she was carrying this medical material with her, which represented a danger for some third person. The dead woman wanted to give the material to somebody whom she personally knew. That somebody was supposed to take the documents to the police. To prevent that very thing, the unknown third person killed the woman. Perhaps he even only wanted to get the documents back, but knew nothing about the locker and did not find the key that the woman had swallowed before he noticed any of it. To divert attention from himself, the murderer placed the corpse next to Makord, who was too drunk to notice anything. For a professional it was natural to wear gloves in order not to leave any fingerprints. Then he could easily place the knife in the sleeping Makord's hand, so that his fingerprints were on it.

Hypothesis two was also more than half-baked. It consisted primarily of unknowns. An unknown murderer, no known motive, no recognizable relationship between the murderer, the dead woman, and Makord. Or was Makord also the murderer in this scenario, because the documents incriminated him? But then he would not have remained lying next to the corpse, but would have tried to get rid of it.

Nothing but confusion. Wimmer felt like a gorilla in the mist. *Gorillas in the Mist* was his favorite film, perhaps because those poor apes were among the endangered species and constantly groped their way around in the mist, and that fate seemed to summarize well the work of the police. But it did not help; Wimmer had to continue his research. So he needed a psychological affidavit about Makord; he needed Puchner's statement about what was so dangerous about the documents; he had to clarify the identity of the dead woman and find out for what circle of individuals the medical material provided a motive for murder. And finally it was necessary to find the unknown third person within that circle of individuals – in short, he had a lot of work ahead of him.

While Wimmer sat thinking to himself, he heard a noise that did not fit the everyday world of the gorilla in the mist. He quickly turned out the light, drew his service weapon, and hid behind the door in order to be able to overpower an intruder quickly. There actually was somebody rummaging around in the offices, and that somebody was not a police officer, for that would have sounded different. The tentative footsteps slowly came closer and the door to the room opened hesitantly.

"Don't make a false move!" Wimmer shouted and held his pistol against the unknown man's temple. "Now put up your hands carefully and turn your face slowly toward me, so that I can see which bastard I'm arresting right now."

The unknown man followed the instruction, but Wimmer had nevertheless made a mistake, and had perhaps also underestimated his opponent. You could overpower a petty burglar that way, but not this man, who was apparently well trained and instructed. The demanded slow turn became a lightning-fast movement of the arm, with which the unknown man knocked the weapon from Wimmer's hand. Before Wimmer had found his weapon again in the dark, the man had raced away and Wimmer could only fire helplessly after him.

"Shit, what an idiot I am!" Wimmer cursed to himself. "I let myself be tricked like a beginner." At the same time he was certain that he was not dealing with a beginner here. That was a professional, obviously experienced in hand-to-hand combat.

That did bring Wimmer somewhat further along now. When he had recovered from being startled, he ordered the search: unknown male culprit, about six feet four inches tall, furrowed face, partially bald, lanky and in top condition, sixty to seventy years old, gray suit. Even though Wimmer had not been able to see the man clearly in the dark, the description would perhaps be sufficient to find a striking person who was unknown to the authorities and was a stranger to Linz, perhaps by accident, through a traffic stop or something similar. Wimmer had to hope for that at least.

Now he had his unknown third party; Wimmer felt that in his bladder. This had not been a petty burglar, for such a person would never voluntarily enter the lion's den. The man was after the documents, had probably hoped to find the police station unmanned during the night, and had not counted on Wimmer's zealousness in his work. And he was a professional; he had some kind of military or police training behind him. Wimmer smiled roguishly. It had become an interesting evening. And hypothesis two had just received a powerful boost.

22

Terezin, November 1943

Told from the point of view of Adolf Markosky

It was midnight. Markosky sat bent over his notes. Although his eyes threatened to fall shut, no fiber of his being thought of going to bed. He had been seized by the fever that a researcher feels before the important discovery occurs to him. The one that comes over a composer when he must finish a symphony. The one that grips a painter when he is completing his masterpiece. Markosky could not stop now. It was as if he were intoxicated.

During recent days the warm summer sun had invited him to devote himself to sweet idleness in streams and lakes, to let the cool water flow over his sun-tanned skin. That did not matter to Markosky. He felt neither sun nor water, neither the spice-laden air nor the warm ground of the ripe meadows. Although, as an SS man, in contrast to the camp inmates, he had complete freedom, he did not leave his office, but locked himself up, to a certain extent, in voluntary isolation. It sufficed him to be alone with his research results. He had also stopped raping women, for the statistics about the rapes were even more exciting than rape itself.

Markosky now had everything together. As ordered, Maier had delivered endless lists to him. There was a data sheet about almost every woman in the camp. Every rape was entered on it: with whom, how often the woman had had intercourse, whether it had taken place voluntarily, involuntarily, or under protest. In general, Markosky was especially interested in the reactions of the women. Had they emotionally collapsed, had they cried or taken the whole thing callously? Were they calculating and did they try to use the unavoidable act to their own advantage, in order perhaps to be treated better and survive longer? Did they plead for mercy? Did they asked to be spared, or did they even feign pleasure in order to bind the rapist to them? All of that was of burning interest to Markosky. Yes, he felt an uncontrollable pleasure in studying this data, but the pleasure had hopped to a certain extent from his penis to his mind. It was no longer a sexual pleasure, but a mental one, because Markosky sensed that all these facts brought him closer to his goal.

He would discover something totally epochal; he was sure of that. He would solve the great puzzle of humanity. Sex and violence – those were really the things that moved humanity. Weren't the novels full of those themes? Weren't the filmmakers beginning to present those taboo themes more and more unceremoniously on the screen? Why did readers and viewers lust so much after something that was supposedly loathsome? There did have to be a deeper reason for that, and Markosky believed that he knew that reason:

Sex and violence were the greatest stimuli to which the human nervous system could be subjected. The survival of the individual and the species depended on how the mind dealt with these stimuli. Sexual readiness determined the continuation of the species. Aggressive readiness determined the survival of the individual. For both of them the hormone system had developed the appropriate programs that determined the behavior of man and woman. Those programs, on the other hand, were embodied in the genetic code. The fittest survive, as Darwin determined. And the fittest were those who were sexually most active and had the greatest aggressive readiness to fight. They had the greatest opportunity to be able to pass their genes on to many descendants.

So far, so good. Those facts were known to all Aryan physicians. That was why all of the doctors of the Superman Project were doing research on those topics and seeking the genetic bases for it: Which genes predestine the individual to aggressive readiness to fight? That will generate the Aryan superman. Which genes lead to optimal sexual readiness, fertility, and hereditary quality? That will lead to the breeding of the superman in the Lebensborn Project.

All of the camp doctors had probably gotten that far in their research. Markosky's revolutionary discovery consisted of the combination of the two areas of research. If sexuality was the one medium for the creation of the superman and aggressiveness the other, then the connection of sex and violence had to lead to the decisive breakthrough. With that, rape had become the central object of Markosky's medical interest.

Why did war and rape always go hand in hand? Perhaps because man was an extremely corrupt species and soldiers were all criminals? No, it could not be that, because the Aryan soldier was the hero per se, the embodiment of the superman. So his behavior could not be against nature. If, however, nature had permitted rape for thousands of years, then that had to be a path of evolution to improve the genetic material of humanity. Then those children who were produced by rapes had to bear a special genetic substance inside them. That was quite logical, and Markosky was amazed that nobody had hit upon that point earlier. Why did it come to a fertilization at all in such a case? The rapist did not want the child, and the raped woman certainly did not want it. The midwives and witches had so many home remedies to prevent an unwanted pregnancy: blows, leaps from the stairs, poisonous herbs. The negative attitude of the woman by itself was often sufficient to condemn semen and egg cell to death. So if a fertilized egg resisted all of those negative influences, then it had to carry a strong gene in it.

And in general! The important question really was how a raped woman could have the strength to take a rape and to carry the child of an unwanted pregnancy to full term in spite of it. She had to face the culprit boldly; she had to keep the event secret from her social environment, raise the child against all obstacles, palm it off on another man, or raise it alone.

In short, such a woman had to have enormous strength and develop a very thick skin. Yes, she had to be almost unfeeling, in order not to go insane beneath such a burden. Through her behavior Olana had opened his eyes: A raped woman had to be callous, or she would fall apart under the experience of violence. And the story of Olana's mother made everything clear: A woman who carried the product of a rape to full term obviously had strong genes in her that predestined her to callousness.

That conclusively established Adolf's scientific theory: If women were raped over generations and had children from rapes for generations, the result was a massive selection pressure in the direction of insensitivity. Then those genes were passed on, which made the individual hard with respect to endurance. That was probably also the evolutionary meaning of the millennia-old fact of rape as a component of the human condition: At the end of a chain of children begotten through rape, there would be a group of human beings with genes that corresponded to Hitler's supermen: hard with respect to endurance, almost without feelings, and above all insensitive to pain. Therefore, the anti-pain gene, for which Adolf was searching so hard, had to be found in that group of rape victims. And never again in human history would such a unique opportunity to identify that gene occur. In the concentration camps, by God, enough of those tormented women were gathered to give the researcher statistically relevant data.

Adolf worked himself all the more into his mental intoxication, the more case histories he studied in the medical reports. One example after another lined up to support his theory.

There was Mrs. Claudia S.:
1939-1943: ten rapes by German occupation forces.

Daughter of a Monika M., who had been raped as a servant by her employer.

Granddaughter of a Sofia K., who, as a day laborer, was free game for the sons of the landowner from whom she earned her money.

After three years of confinement in prisons and camps, Mrs. Claudia S. was in astoundingly robust condition.

Next there was Mrs. Andrea W.:
Three rapes in the year 1943.

Daughter of a Mrs. Hermine R., who fled to Austria after she had been raped by Turks in the second Balkan War.

Granddaughter of a Ludmilla T., who had been sold to a rich pasha. – Well, what had he probably done to her?

Mrs. Andrea W. was so strong in her nature that she would have immediately been accepted into a dragoon regiment, if women had been admitted into them.

And finally there was Olana K.:
Thirty-one rapes in the year 1943.

Daughter of a Natalya K., who had been raped by innumerable Russians in Galicia in the year 1914.

Granddaughter of the kitchen maid of a prelate in Krakow, who was rumored to have many illegitimate children.

And in spite of her fate, this Olana was of such fascinating strength, to which Adolf had almost succumbed.

Adolf had dozens of similar stories lying in front of him, which all pointed in the same direction. A severe fate produced strong women, and those women were now all in Adolf's care. And according to the logic of the doctrine of heredity, the result of that selection could even be improved through purposeful breeding.

He was curious about what kind of children "his" women would probably bear. The women who had grown hard through selection crossed with SS men, who, of course, had been subjected to a severe genetic examination in their own right – didn't that have to lead to an outstanding result? Wouldn't that have to produce children, for whom the concept of pain was a foreign idea?

Apropos Olana K. It had already been a long time since he had seen her. Perhaps it was time to subject his preferred specimen to a new examination. After all, it was through the observation of Olana's behavior that he had hit upon this theory. Perhaps he would move a step further this time as well.

When the guard pushed the woman into the examination room on Adolf's order, the doctor looked at the woman with the curiosity of a scientist. He wanted to know how Olana's mental condition had further developed. Had she become even harder, or would she grow weak under the conditions in the camp after all. That would have been a pity, for then Adolf would have had one less test person. But everything appeared to be in order. Olana was as brusque and wild as ever. Adolf almost became sexually aroused because he liked that wildness so much. But he suppressed that feeling quickly, because he did not want to be diverted from his thirst for knowledge.

Or had something about Olana changed after all? As much as her character had remained the same, her body seemed to have become softer and rounder. Only then did Adolf notice how the woman's belly was beginning to arch slightly forward, and with a self-satisfied grin he registered the fact that the woman was pregnant. *Look at that*, he thought. *We left traces in the body of this woman, genetic tracks so to speak.* Without wasting the slightest thought on his own impending fatherhood, he recognized only the addition of material for his area of research. Olana would perhaps give birth to a daughter, and he could then also scientifically test his genetic theory on her.

That led him to a new idea: They should perhaps not leave it to chance as to whether or not there were pregnancies in the camp.

They should perhaps subject all of the women from Adolf's test group to a purposeful experiment. What was acceptable to any dog or horse breeder should be acceptable to the SS physician. All of the magnificent breeds of pets were the result of purposeful breeding. Only with man had eugenics been taboo on the basis of moral narrow-mindedness, but thanks to Hitler there were now no longer any limits to creativity. Now you could cross rape victims with the descendants of rape victims and compare it with the normal crossing of victims with rapists. You could also compare the descendants of Aryan rapists with the descendants of subhuman Slavs. Yes, those would all be interesting hypotheses and questions. In short, it was unavoidably necessary to examine the next generation of victims. As a consequence, that meant that the killing of the children had to be prevented.

Olana saw her tormenter's searching look and misinterpreted it. *Now he's probably thinking up a new perverse way of attacking me. Why is he starting that again, when he has left me in peace for weeks?* She had hoped that Markosky's interest had turned to a new victim, and now he was boring through her again with his lecherous gaze. All of her loathing and her entire strength reared up against it, and she was determined not to let herself be subjected to that humiliation again.

"You whoremaster, you masturbator, you bugger, you brutal beast! Did your cock fall off in the meantime? Do you have to do violence to a defenseless woman again, so that you get a hard on? Or did one of your victims infect you with syphilis, so that you no longer dare to have intercourse with the women with crab lice that you gas in the ovens? I wish that your penis would rot with leprosy, so that you could no longer do any damage with it!"

Olana had intended to drive away Adolf's desire with her vulgar curses, but the opposite thing happened. Olana's bitter aggression only served to stimulate him as it had done many times before, and he grabbed her from behind, lifted up her skirt, and thrust savagely and powerfully between her buttocks. Olana's attempts to tear herself away from his arms aroused him so much that he ejacu-

141

lated in her after only a few thrusts. Disappointed that he was left that way with the desire that had just been aroused, he decided to put his stinger in her with words.

"So, you've gotten yourself pregnant, have you? Who planted his brat in you? Are you lying at the feet of the guards now to catch their white milk? Do you think that you could put yourself in a good position with us that way? Don't you know what we do with this Jewish vermin? Do you really believe that you could carry your child to full term in this camp and possibly impress us with that?" Adolf's voice became threateningly loud.

"Oh, well, it will be best for us to take care of that right now, before you degenerate into feelings of blessed motherhood on us." He pushed Olana down onto the gynecologist's chair, summoned Dr. Maier, and had him take hold of her. Then he spread her legs and strapped them to the iron supports. He slowly began to fill a very thick syringe, with obvious enjoyment.

Olana became white as a sheet when she recognized that the Aryan pig was in the process of taking the baby from her. To prevent that she was ready to sacrifice everything, even her dignity and her pride.

"Don't take the baby from me, please, not the baby. It's all I have. After all, it's also your baby. You're the only one who has raped me. You can't kill your own child. Even you can't be that insensitive." When Adolf grinned scornfully, she thought he could do that very thing after all.

"I didn't mean it that way. I didn't want to offend you. I thought that vulgar talk turned you on, and that worked well. You had what you wanted. Please, I beg you, don't take the baby from me, not our baby. As far as I'm concerned you can take me as often as you want. Kill the babies of the other women, but not this baby."

"Well, perhaps there might be a way to save your child." Markosky slowly lowered the arm with the syringe. "But for that I expect some cooperation. If I let you go back into the camp with your belly, then you'll report to me every week. Which women are pregnant, by whom they are pregnant, how do they feel, what complaints do they have? I expect you to report every fart of a pregnant woman to me, before anyone else hears a sound. Do we understand each other clearly?"

142

Olana nodded with an intimidated look. *If he just leaves me my baby, for all I care he can abort the babies of all the others. None of that matters to me. And if I have to become a traitor, my baby will survive.* With her head hanging, she left the examination room.

Maier frowned. "Tell me, boss, why are you letting this particular brat live? It would never be recognized as your child anyway. You can't get sentimental about that."

"All of them, Maier, all of them. We're going to let them all live. All of the babies of raped women will remain alive. And you, Maier, are going to watch over them for me like the apples of your eye. Or I can give no guarantee that you will remain alive. Do we understand each other? And now get out of here!"

Markosky had already shoved the astonished Maier out the door. The latter scratched his head in disbelief: "Now the old man is finally going crazy once and for all. What does he intend to do there? A children's home in the concentration camp? Where does he think we are? People die here, they're not born. The crazy man is on the wrong track!"

143

23

Linz, November 12, 1991

The doctors at the gynecologists' convention were in a good mood. They met their colleagues, were presented with the latest research results and the most delicious sandwiches, and were incidentally able to do something for their careers and cultivate important connections. For a short time they could escape from the everyday routine of their homes and clinics and perhaps flirt with a pretty hostess. What more did they want?

Some lectures were boring, of course, but they accepted that. Cancer swabs, oviduct blockage – those old topics did not even draw beginners anymore. Then the next lecture promised more excitement. "The Woman's Constitution and Its Meaning for the Genome of the Fetus" by Dr. Albert Makord. The old pro had jumped on the bandwagon of the times once more and was delivering the most recent results from the field of human genetics, which at the time was the up-and-coming thing.

"Ladies and gentlemen, it is an honor for me to be permitted to speak a few words to you in spite of my old age and the fact that I am already retired. Nor do I plan to bore you unduly. Yes, I'm certain that my results will excite you as much as they've excited me since I began to concern myself with the questions of the female constitution."

The old Makord's sonorous voice began softly, almost cautiously, and then amplified itself slowly to a room-filling bass. Soon he would probably have even drawn the inattentive rotation doctors in the back rows under his spell, if he had not been harshly interrupted:

"Don't believe a thing he says. You don't know who this man really is. Whenever this noble physician has dealt with women, he has treated them badly. He has only made women unhappy. Here in this letter is the proof of that!" Rafael Makord triumphantly held up the letter written by his dead mother, like a bequest that he was now supposed to execute.

However, he did not get far.

"Outrageous! What's he doing here? A psychologist! What's a psychologist doing at our convention? Get him out of here!" Rafael's protest speech was drowned out by the general tumult. Some young doctors grabbed Rafael by the arms and dragged him out the door.

The old Makord had quickly regained his composure: "Ladies and Gentlemen, with that we can once again observe that somebody who concerns himself with the so-called abysses of the soul, babbles about anal shit, and fantasizes about genital urges is probably not quite responsible for his actions." Makord took advantage of the general laughter to continue his lecture quickly, as if nothing had happened.

Meanwhile Rafael paced back and forth in front of the convention hall, boiling with rage and helplessly ashamed. That incestuous gang, of course they stuck together as thick as thieves. They didn't let anything happen to one of their own. They couldn't see beyond the edge of their own plate and certainly could not tolerate criticism, those gentlemen in white. He could have expected that. But the fact that they had not even listened to him, did not even want to see his evidence – that was too much. In spite of his humiliation, Rafael was determined not to retire from the battlefield voluntarily.

When the lecture was over, the participants streamed out into the foyer. Rafael was met by poisonous looks and some people were getting ready to drive him from the building once and for all. Then the old Makord stepped in: "Gentlemen, leave this to me. I'll take care of it." His authority intimidated the hotheads, and Rafael was almost grateful to him for that. His father gestured for him to follow him, and for the first time in years Rafael actually did follow him, even if only to escape from this dangerous situation.

In front of the building the old gentleman lost his self-control: "So, my dear son, now I've had enough. Have you no respect for anything anymore? Do you want to drag our entire family into the mud? Do you want to ruin our good name, huh? Isn't it enough for you to have one foot in prison? Do you perhaps want to land in the Wagner-Jauregg Hospital, in the ward for the mentally abnormal criminals? And just what is that ominous piece of rubbish all about, which you are waving around through the neighborhood? Show it to me!"

Rafael handed him his mother's letter, and his father began to read. He became pale with horror when he recognized his wife's handwriting, and red with anger as he took note of the reproaches that were directed against him. Finally he tore the letter into a hundred little pieces before Rafael could take it again.

"Surely you don't believe that there's something to those baseless accusations. That was written by an offended wife after she had had an argument with her husband. As a psychologist you should know how that is. My God, there are such crises in every marriage. You get angry. One word leads to the next, and then you say things to each other that you didn't really mean that way. I can imagine when it was that your mother wrote that. Back then I was already very successful and had little time for her. She felt that I was not giving her enough attention and probably didn't cope well with my success either. She then became depressed. You know all that. My God, I'm sorry, too, that I wasn't able to help her. She didn't even take the anti-depressants that I prescribed for her. Do you think that I don't wish that she were still alive?"

When his father saw that Rafael still looked somber and obstinate, he continued his defense: "And anyway, what are we talking about here? She writes about some ominous facts, but doesn't state what they are. She read my research results, fine. Do you think that she understood any of it? If she did, then at best she understood it incorrectly. Reports that were intended for specialists, which only a human geneticist would understand, in the hands of a nurse. That had to go wrong, of course. No, she was probably simply furious with me and then she tore some misunderstood lines out of context. You can feel free to read my technical articles yourself. Then you'll see that there is nothing to it. In the end, she was sorry about all that again. She didn't even present me with the letter, but hid it because she knew that it was exaggerated. And with that we should put a period at the end of this unpleasant matter. My son, get yourself straightened out again, for the sake of your mother's memory. Don't risk your future with such embarrassing scenes!"

For a moment Rafael would have liked to have believed his father. His soothing voice trickled like balsam on Rafael's wounded longing for a strong arm that could lead him through the chaos of a violent world. The way his father had protected him from the furious doctors was the way he had wanted his father to be as a little

146

boy: One who radiated safety and security, a man of integrity, one who was trustworthy. Immediately afterward, however, Rafael tasted the poison in the calming balsam, and the trust that had flickered briefly disappeared at once. He was like a child who has been burned, who has let himself be fooled briefly by the beauty of a glowing flame, only to remember immediately the experienced danger of the fire.

His father had made his mother look bad once again. He had imputed stupidity, hysteria, and disobedience to her. If only she had swallowed the anti-depressants that her husband had prescribed for her. Damn it, you did not solve marriage conflicts with pills. If only she had let her husband explain the research reports. Damn it, Mother was not his pupil. She possessed a clear understanding and was very well capable of judging her husband's deeds. And she became depressed for the very reason that she could no longer bear her husband's deeds. No, he could not let the old hypocrite get away with his clouding of the issue.

"Don't think that you can talk your way out of this situation again with nice words," Rafael snarled. "That's all lies again, like your whole career. Why should your own wife accuse you of horrible crimes, if she had no evidence for it? Fine, she didn't haul you before a judge, which I actually think is too bad, for then we would already be somewhat further along with finding out the truth, and you wouldn't have been able to hide from your responsibility all the way into your hale and hearty retirement years.

"Your entire world view is totally schizophrenic. You very seriously believe in that nonsense of genetic destiny. Whoever has good genes is a good person; whoever has bad genes deserves to be eliminated. You Nazis believed that nonsense, and for that reason you sent the 'bad' people to the gas chambers. And you still believe today that through the elimination of bad genes you could create the good human being. You reduce man to biology and dismiss his soul. And then you are amazed when the darkest mysticism forges ahead in your inner life."

"Inner life, mysticism," the old man grumbled. "Such things can only occur to a psychologist. If you want to have a serious discussion with me, then stay on scientific ground."

"Yes, yes, you old Nazi. Anything that has something to do with your personality – you don't want to hear about it. But just imagine, psychology has contributed a lot to the explanation of fascism and didn't stop for Hitler in the process. – *If Providence has led me here, then it must have given me an assignment: to lead my homeland home into the German Reich* – I'm sure you were there in 1938 on the Heldenplatz. So then you know that Hitler believed in the power of Providence. And what is Providence? A strange fate entity, a divine force, where there is supposedly no God? Providence is linked to the old doctrines of predestination, to the karma of the Indians, the kismet of the Mohammedans, and the Original Sin of St. Augustine. Hitler believed in a pseudo-divine assignment to create the Third Reich. He acted on the basis of a religious delusion. That is the so-called rationality that you're always talking about."

"I didn't know that you also studied theology," Albert Makord said bitingly while tapping his forehead with his finger. "But perhaps I should have put you in the seminary. Then you could cry your eyes out with the Pope in Rome today about the injustice of the world."

"Yes, yes, go ahead and mock the Christian inclination toward social justice. You had nothing in common with that. You fell back into the atavistic belief that humanity produced: the belief in power that is increased through human sacrifice. Like the Babylonians and the Phoenicians, you sacrificed to the god Moloch and sent human beings into the fire. The more that were sacrificed, the greater your power would be. To a certain extent you Nazis are the resurrection of an old Babylonian sect that believed in the power of burnt human flesh. And you projected that fanatical false belief into genetics. Through bad genes, the god Moloch branded those people whom he selected for the sacrifice. Social Darwinism, which suggests that evolution brings to pass the annihilation of the weak, served as a small intellectual bridge."

"My son, now I'm really worried about you. Just what are you fantasizing together there? The National Socialist world conspiracy as a spiritual sectarianism – that never existed. Not even the ultra-left critics claim that. Perhaps I should call my colleague at the Wagner-Jauregg Hospital. A little narcotic drug couldn't hurt, in order to bring your visions under control."

Rafael was determined not to get sidetracked by his father's diversionary tactics. For once the truth had to be told. No matter how often his father would yet deny it, once the words were spoken, he could no longer erase them, and they would slowly make their way into his consciousness:

"Yes, go ahead, make fun of me. You've always done that. For far too long I fell for it and doubted my own mind because your system of denial sounds so logical, so perfect. Mother shattered against it. She was taken in by you for far too long, until it was too late and she no longer had any strength. But she finally caught on to your tricks. She discovered the facts that expose your entire system of lies, and then she no longer wanted to have anything to do with you. After she was unable to curb you in your superiority, she preferred to withdraw from your world once and for all. Doesn't the fact that she simply didn't want to live anymore give you something to think about?"

Now the old man became furious: "Damn it all, what can I do about the fact that she suffered from endogenous depression? Don't you think that I would have preferred to have a cheerful, loving wife? That wasn't granted to me. That's fate, which one must endure with dignity."

Rafael was jubilant: "There it is again, fate, Providence, inherency. Fate is responsible for everything that you don't want to see. You blame Providence for your suppressed mistakes. You can coolly torment women. If they fall to pieces because of it and become depressed, what can you do about it? It's all endogenous, caused by a strange fate of the mind. You can persecute, torture, and oust people – if they take it badly, my God, there's the proof that they had bad genes, and that almost justifies exterminating them.

"It wouldn't hurt you to look up a little psychology. Then you would know that through brainwashing you can make a 'genetically' inferior one out of any living entity in a very short time. Professor Seligman put dogs in a cage where they were subjected to continual electrical shocks. In a very short time they had all the symptoms of an endogenous depression. In the Milgram experiment, through authoritarian commands normal people were brought to the point of tormenting and torturing innocent test subjects. Rene Spitz demonstrated that children without support and care become demented, quit developing, and finally die. And that, completely independent of their genetic predisposition. The inferior children that your colleagues killed at the Spiegelgrund in Vi-

149

enna were such deprived, neglected children. Their deaths, even from a genetic point of view, were totally unnecessary. They only needed to been given the right family care, and they would have recovered. But after they had been violently separated from their families, they became weaker and weaker, sicker and sicker, more and more demented, and then they simply had to be euthanized. Through improper medical treatment diseases were first created, which were then eugenically 'cured.' What an epitome of stupidity. Just why didn't you euthanize yourselves? Because I have never come across anything more demented in my life than National Socialist medicine."

"Son, son, you're really in a bad way. Where did you get all that? None of that happened." Albert Makord shook his head in fatherly concern. "A person who has visions needs a doctor. Even our federal chancellor recently stated that. If this discussion between father and son has had any result at all, it is this: You urgently need medical help."

"So that you can silence me, too, like the euthanasia victims? No thanks."

"There are also wonderful medicines against paranoia..."

150

24

Moscow, October 1991

Told from the point of view of Valeri Suchov

Valeri Suchov set out to pick up his orders of the day. He got on the subway and rode from the student dormitory toward the city center. His destination was the headquarters of the KGB.

However, he did not head for his destination by a direct route, for he had to be careful that his disguise as a student was not penetrated. So he changed trains twice, during which he only got onto the departing train at the last moment, so that it would be hard for anyone to follow him. He entered the large Gum Department Store, as if he intended to buy something there, but then left it quickly through a backdoor. Only after an additional ride on the streetcar did he approach his destination, while ascertaining several times that nobody was following him.

All of that was routine, tested often, and precisely planned. It would also work today. Nobody would discover his true identity as an agent. For his fellow students he remained Valeri, a student of biochemistry, a perfect cover for a twenty-one-year-old young man.

However, if Valeri really thought about it, his cover was not simply a disguise. Biochemistry actually did interest him, and he was an enthusiastic student. He was very thankful to the KGB that they were financing his education. During the last semester he had also signed up for genetics. He wanted to understand and study all of the biological foundations of the human body. That was his great passion, and he felt instinctively that biochemical research would lead to fantastic results in the coming years.

Strictly speaking, his education was his only passion. Otherwise any emotion was foreign to him. Strictly speaking, Valeri had no feelings at all. His acquaintances sometimes called him Iceberg. Valeri approached life coldly and objectively. He did not fall in love; he knew no anger, no fear, and no pain. And this lack of emotion felt very pleasant to him; after all, it led to the greatest possible efficiency. Valeri was not held back by any scruples or any thoughtfulness.

151

Perhaps it was this straight-line, get-it-done mentality that had fostered Valeri's rapid rise in the KGB. He was sometimes amazed that as a youth fresh out of school he had already been accepted into the elite training program of the secret service. He probably had to have a secret patron, but he did not have the slightest idea who it could be, because he did not even know his own family.

Valeri had grown up in institutions. If he had parents, he had been separated from them so early that he could not remember them anymore. He grew up with the military drill of the communist Comsomol movement, which wanted to form the Party cadre from simple workers' children. That constant training from childhood on had probably formed his character. In any case it had hardened his body. He was familiar with every hand-to-hand combat technique and knew what to do in the most dangerous situations. He was extremely hardened. And it was perhaps for that reason that he knew no fear.

Valeri was an elite soldier, and that made him extremely self-confident. He was certain that he had a great career ahead of him, if only because in the Soviet Union careers were controlled by the KGB anyway. His firm had its fingers in everything and gave him a worldwide network of connections. No matter in which position he was placed in the future, there would be a party of mountain climbers ready and waiting to pull him to the top. So he could be satisfied with his life.

Nevertheless he was amazed that he was now already being entrusted with very tricky operations. Whenever anything went wrong in the country of Russia and had to be cleaned up, then Valeri was sent to the front. In his clean-up assignments he could not make the slightest mistake, for everything had to remain secret, of course. Yes, the public could not even become aware that an operation had taken place, much less that the KGB had its fingers in the pie.

Valeri was a sweeper. His specialty was liquidations.

Valeri was quickly outside the KGB building again. In his vest pocket he had a list of ten names and some addresses. He looked briefly at the paper: It was only psychiatric facilities that he was supposed to visit. His superior had only babbled something about a failed experiment whose consequences now had to be eliminated, before the new fanatics around Boris Yeltsin got wind of them. In times like these you never knew, of course, what the counterrevolu-

152

tionaries would yet reproach the communists with, once they had all the secret documents in their hands. Initial voices were already demanding that the secret archives of the national government be opened to clear up the crimes of the past – so this was now the result of that accursed glasnost, with which the impractical dreamer Gorbachev had ruined everything. Just what did he know about politics and about the efforts of the various levels that were needed in order to hold the world empire of the USSR together?

How was that idiot able to become General Secretary of the Communist Party of the Soviet Union anyway? A regrettable industrial accident. He had wormed his way into the good graces of KGB Director Andropov and fooled him into believing that as his successor and protégé he would continue the time-tested policies, only to break his promise immediately when he was in power. Oh, well, the just punishment of fate had now caught up with him, and Yeltsin was exposing him to ridicule before the eyes of the world. Gorbachev's days were numbered, but with him unfortunately also the days of the Soviet Union. So there were some things to be cleaned up, before unauthorized eyes obtained too much insight; that was clear to Valeri. And cleaning up was Valeri's job. For that reason he did not ask many questions, when his superior put the list of people to be liquidated in his hand.

The rest was routine. In the first clinic his KGB identification opened all doors for him. Thank God, or, better said, Stalin, the supervising ward attendants were all faithful members of the Communist Party who gave Valeri entry to all the rooms and quietly disappeared when Valeri got to work. In the medicine cabinets he found everything he needed. Haldol, morphine, rohypnol – Valeri mixed a lethal overdose that would even have stopped the hearts of elephants. The pleasant thing about it was that the medications were not at all obvious in the blood of the patients, because they had to swallow them every day anyway. If one of them then somehow got hold of a bit too much of his medication, well then he had probably perfidiously saved up a few days' rations in order to irritate his attendant and send himself into the next world with suicidal intent. You never knew, of course, what these paranoid schizophrenics were up to; they were simply not responsible for their actions and that was all there was to it.

153

Valeri put on a white attendant's jacket, put the syringe with the poison cocktail in readiness on the examining table, and went in search of his first victim. In the waiting room he soon found him. He examined the face and the name on the basis of his list and had no doubts. Antonin Hrdlicka, 50 years old, apparently an exiled Czech, he had to be the one. "Come along, you have to go for an examination." With those words he grabbed his victim by the hand and dragged him into the examining room. The screams of protest did Antonin no good. The insane people who were standing around were used to the screams. They only felt confirmed in their view of a dangerous world, where you were always threatened and could be picked up at any time. Now it had simply caught up with Antonin, as it had caught up with Igor yesterday and would perhaps catch up with Syatoslav tomorrow. What were they supposed to do about it?

In the examining room, Valeri, who was as strong as an ox, clamped the patient's upper body and arms tightly with his left arm, so that he could look into his eyes while he plunged the needle into his shoulder with his right hand. This was a moment of special intimacy that Valeri was addicted to, like a junkie to a drug. He wanted to see the looks on the dying people's faces, when the light went out of their eyes; he wanted them to take the face of their angel of death with them into the next world as a final memory, when their strength left them. That was why he held his victims in his arms the way a mother holds her baby. Wasn't he the midwife of a new life on another level of existence? Didn't he deserve to look into the deepest depths of their souls like a mother, before they started their journey? At that moment Valeri loved his job.

Antonin's eyes, which had opened wide with fear, became even larger as the medications streamed hotly through his veins and he looked into Valeri's faultless face. "Those eyes, I know those eyes," he stammered. "They look like..." Before Antonin could say the name that was on the tip of his tongue, his voice broke and his head sank back. *So, he's at rest*, Valeri thought to himself, and he attached no further meaning to the insane man's words, for just what would a schizophrenic recognize? It had probably been only a hallucination anyway.

The other two patients of Clinic A were sent to their new existence in similarly rapid fashion, and the patients from Clinic B and

Clinic C caused no difficulties for Valeri's experienced arm. They didn't even find time to confuse Valeri with crazy last words, as Antonin Hrdlicka had done, because Valeri worked at such an efficient pace. There remained only the large eyes that were petrified with horror, and they were like jewels in Valeri's collection, which he enjoyed raking in.

At about five o'clock Valeri had completed almost his entire day's work, and he was extremely satisfied with himself. Nine angels on one day, let somebody try to match that. In a few hours he had created work for the undertakers and coroners for many days. Yes, speed was simply his trademark. And there had not been the slightest complications that his superiors could have complained about. They would probably soon have to recommend him for a medal or a promotion; the Lenin Medal was Valeri's favorite, if he were given the opportunity to choose.

There was only the last woman on the list, and then he could go home and consume a festive supper with Crimean champagne. After all, every year he received a special allocation of twenty bottles of champagne, and he saved them for successful days like today.

Nina Antonova from Novosibirsk, she won't cause me any special problems either. He proceeded exactly as he had done in all the other cases – showed his KGB identification, mixed the poison cocktail, put on the attendant's coat, identified the patient and dragged her into the examining room, and gazed deeply into the eyes of the patient whom he had embraced for the death kiss. Just as he was about to push the needle into the patient's arm, her gaze struck him like a bolt of lightning – those eyes, what was it about those eyes? Valeri clenched his eyelids together as if someone had sprayed onion juice on his corneas. Then he looked at her a second time, and it was the same thing again. It was as if he were looking into a mirror: Her eyes had the same blue color as his own, the same long lashes, and the same curving of the brows. It was as if he were looking into his own soul, as if he were sending himself on the journey, and that paralyzed him for a few moments so severely that he could not inject the needle.

The patient used the opportunity of that brief moment, slammed her knees between the legs of her tormentor, tore herself away, and ran out of the room shrieking.

Valeri was dumbfounded, as he followed his escaped victim with his eyes. He shook his head, as if he wanted to shake off the daze of ten vodkas.

Such a thing has never happened to me before, he thought to himself. *But it doesn't matter, postponed is not cancelled. I've accomplished enough today anyway, so I'll just do this job tomorrow. My boss will overlook it.*

He did not notice that he was already breaking his routine for the second time, which consisted of the fact that first he never let his victims get away, and second, he never postponed an assignment until tomorrow. Even with a lot of reflection – and reflection was not his way anyway – he could not have explained to himself why this victim in particular had rattled him so badly. Nor did he know the reason for the similarity in their facial features.

25

Linz, November 16, 1991

Inspector Wimmer was fed up. Another lousy day in his office, which had not gotten him any further. How he hated studying reports. He would much rather have been outside on patrol, where the ice-cold wind of crime blew around his nose, or at least the dank Danube fog of the November days in Linz. Reports, nothing but reports, all kinds of printed paper – he had not imagined that his profession would be that way. But it did not help at all. Meanwhile police work was ninety percent bureaucracy and nine percent the collecting of apparently senseless minute details. That left one percent detective work, where you were permitted to use your gray matter to put the details together to form a theory. It could even be endured, if the detail work led to a clear picture with which you could conclusively solve and close a case. Then you would endure the ninety-nine percent dirty work and in the end stand there as a glowing hero.

But that was not how it was. In almost all cases, the parts could naturally be put together to form different pictures, as with a Chinese tangram puzzle. And it did require Buddhist equanimity to accept the fact that in the end all of the pictures were of equal value, that is to say, were equally probable, when compared with each other.

Since Wimmer had already drunk his ten cups of coffee today, his stomach had rebelled once and for all, and there was also no longer time for a circuit of jogging or the police fitness room. All of his possibilities for diversion were exhausted. Therefore he had two possibilities:

He could give in to his ill humor and curse God and the world, which, however, would intensify the problem with his stomach lining. Or he could actually practice Buddhist equanimity. He remembered that the judo master at the police academy had once added a few lessons on meditation and liberation of the spirit to the hand-to-hand combat training, and now he would try out that Asiatic nonsense. He could use some equanimity now, whether it had anything to do with Buddha or not, because his theoretical puzzle was simply falling apart in his hands.

So he sat down on a cushion on the floor and tried to sit with crossed legs. The threatening creaking of his joints announced to him that he had not done any stretching exercises for years and apparently considered gymnastics to be an extinct custom of an Australian tribe. He placed his hands on his knees, formed small circles with his thumbs and index fingers, closed his eyes, and tried to empty his mind by concentrating on his breathing. After five minutes, all he felt any longer was the pain in his thighs, which abruptly led him back to the pain in the pit of his stomach.

I could have also had that cheaper, thought Wimmer's mind, which was not empty at all. *Those slit-eye contortions are simply not for me. It's better for me to be vexed with my ruined hypotheses.*

What made Wimmer so furious was the fact that he still had neither proof that the snotty young Makord was a murderer nor any evidence at all that the big unknown man actually existed. No matter how he turned and twisted the facts, his two hypotheses remained equally probable. And he didn't even have the famous gut feeling that would have pointed in the right direction.

He had to get rid of his anger somehow, before the hydrochloric acid caused the ulcer in his stomach to rupture. To throw his anger in somebody's face, perhaps to harass the suspect a bit, yes, that would be quite nice, but he really did not have any new questions, and he did not want to make a fool of himself either.

Then it came to him like a bolt out of the blue. Of course – Puchner! Puchner was the right victim for today. That bastard had been sitting around on the medical documents for a week without making a sound. That was outrageous! He should have found the solution to the puzzle long ago, and he didn't even call. It was his fault that Wimmer was still brooding around without a clue, like an egg-laying kangaroo. That rotten situation had to change immediately.

"Do you know how late it is?" moaned Puchner, whom Wimmer had apparently dragged out of bed with his telephone call. "Yes, my little darling, I'll be with you again immediately. It's only the inspector. I'll take care of it quickly."

"You can forget your little darling right now and get your ass over here. Otherwise you'll find out just who I am. I've been waiting for your report for a week, and today I want to finally know what's going on. My strong arm is screaming for an arrest, and if you don't give me a suspect, then I'll just take you. Ha, ha."

"Can't it wait until tomorrow? Yes, Dear, I'll be right there." Puchner's voice was soft and sugary.

"Apropos little darling, didn't you tell me that your wife is away for advanced training for a week?"

"I'll be at the police station in five minutes."

Wimmer's stomach nerves relaxed immediately when he gathered from the mixture of contrition and fury in Puchner's voice that he had hit him in the right place. *Such a policeman's life does offer its little pleasures,* he thought cheerfully as he rubbed his hands.

When Puchner arrived a little later and gave Wimmer a poisonous look, the latter almost had a guilty conscience. "Nobody will learn anything from me, and I don't even know who it was," he said reassuringly. "Although, just out of curiosity, it's your young assistant from the coroner's office, isn't it?"

When Wimmer noticed that Puchner's face had taken on the color of a green mamba, he quickly changed the subject to relevant topics: "So, as I said, I'm very sorry that I disturbed you so late, but I really need your expertise concerning the medical documents from the suitcase. You know what I'm talking about."

Puchner's chameleon face changed slowly back to expert gray as he began to regain his composure and pulled the documents from his briefcase: "It really wasn't easy to make head or tail of this chaos of notes, but at last I got on the right track." Puchner gave a long, thoughtful sigh, as if he wanted to use it to emphasize the pains he had taken.

"Well, tell me what you found out."

"Now take it easy. It can't be explained that easily. In any case, they deal with purposeful breeding of human beings."

Wimmer was tense with curiosity: "You mean what the geneticists are writing about these days in the newspapers, that it will be possible to create perfect human beings through gene therapy? Those are dreams of the future that haven't been worked out legally by the judges yet. Genetically engineered corn is even prohibited in Austria. Why should it be any different with the genetically engineered human being? Ha, ha, ha."

Puchner acted mysterious: "When you understand what this Dr. Frankenstein describes in his documents, then you won't feel like laughing anymore."

"Now spit it out. Did he perhaps snip around on corpses? But you do that all the time, of course. In that light you should actually have liked the material."

"Worse, much, much worse. He experimented with living human beings."

"What did he do? Did he operate without anesthetic, like Dr. Mengele?"

Puchner paused meaningfully before he answered. "He subjected women to torture and violence in order to find out who could best survive such extreme stress. He let the hardiest ones live; the fearful were killed. From the surviving women he formed his test group and had them raped in order to arrive at a second generation of test subjects. Meanwhile the third generation of rape victims is already growing up in Russia."

"But that's sick! Who would do such a thing?"

"In dictatorships anything is possible, because there's no democratic control and the secret services have a free hand. Our report, to be precise, is divided into two parts. Part one takes place in fascist Germany in the concentration camp. We know that medical experiments were conducted on living people there. Part two takes place in communist Russia in a specialized clinic or in a gulag camp. There, too, medicine lent itself to military experiments on human beings. There, too, there was no control of any kind."

"You spoke of three generations of human test animals." Wimmer was incredulous. "That had to have lasted for fifty to sixty years. How can that have been possible?"

"Well, both parts were apparently written by the same person. In Germany he calls himself Markosky. In Russia his name is Mayinski, a not particularly imaginative deceptive maneuver. He must have been caught and carried off to Russia by the Red Army at the end of the war. There somebody recognized the significance of his research and gave him the means to continue it."

"But what is the significance of an experiment that's based on the raping of dozens of women?" Wimmer was slowly getting dizzy. "I don't understand that. I don't even want to understand it.

160

I'm used to a lot of things, murder, mayhem – but planned rape, that's too much, even for me."

"Think of the ethnic cleansings in Yugoslavia. There they also talk about purposeful rape as a political device. May God grant that the Serbs won't really do that! In any case, our Mr. Mayinski had the idea of being able to breed an especially brutal, insensitive race through rape. Do you understand the military significance of such an attempt, assuming that it were successful?"

Wimmer understood: Without feeling and brutal, the ideal soldier. Every army in the world would vie eagerly for such hard specimens. The action films of Hollywood were full of ice-cold executioners, let them be called Terminator or Rambo. A soldier without feeling could not be stopped by anything. And no secret service in the world, neither the CIA nor the KGB, would be able to resist the temptation to try breeding such soldiers in a secret project.

"Now do you understand the explosive nature of these documents?"

Everything was clear to Wimmer now. Every secret service, every mafia would stop at nothing to get those documents. Nor would they hesitate to commit murder to get the documents back, if somebody were insanely reckless enough to steal them.

Wimmer had his motive for murder. The unknown dead woman had stolen the documents. She perhaps wanted to make them public or sell them for money, who knew which it was? And the big unknown man had had no scruples of any kind in cutting her throat to prevent that very thing.

Well, wonderful. Things would soon get interesting in Linz. KGB, Russian and Italian mafia, CIA. They would all be fighting for Wimmer's ominous material.

Perhaps he should quickly apply for early retirement. Or better, give the documents to the CIA immediately, with the request for acceptance into the Witness Protection Program.

26

Nina was in a panic, and anyone else would have been the same if they had been in her situation. The ice-cold stranger had tried to kill her, and he would try again, she was certain of that. Nina did not know whether or not he was already lying in wait for her in another room or in the corridor. She looked around herself fearfully. He did not seem to be pursuing her. But what good was that? He wanted to kill her, and he would do it.

The panic had an astounding effect. While most people become mindless and thoughtless with fear, Nina was suddenly able to think clearly again. It was like liberation from the chemical bonds that held her mind in their clutches. It was as if the adrenalin really cleaned out her nerve cells and cleansed them of all the pharmacological rubble that had been making her life difficult for years. Nina's mind functioned logically and soberly once more, as it had probably once done previously, before she had fallen into the hands of these criminal psychiatrists. She quickly analyzed the facts:

Her life was threatened, and here in the psychiatric ward she would not survive another day. There was no point in asking the doctors for help, for they were probably in cahoots with the murderer. Or, what was even worse, they would not believe a word she said and pass off her talk of a murderer as a new attack of paranoid schizophrenia. She had to flee as quickly as possible and no longer had time to think up a well-considered plan for it.

She had to get the ward keys in order to escape undiscovered. Those could be obtained most easily in the offices of the doctors and the attendants. So off again into a clothes closet; she already knew the routine. She had no luck this time in the offices of the assistant doctors, because the doctor on duty had just lain down for a nap. His loud snoring conveniently kept her from opening the door. Nor did things go any better for her in the office of the attendants, because two of them had just sat down to play cards. That left only the chief physician's room, but that was the one that was most difficult to get into, because he usually locked it when he was not working there. As Nina eyed its entry door from a safe distance, both longingly and fearfully, suddenly a female attendant came running, screamed at the top of her lungs "Professor! Professor!" and stormed in through the door. Immediately after that, both of them stormed out again, with the curious secretaries following them. All of them ran in the direction of the patients' waiting room.

That was her opportunity. Nina slipped through the open door and searched the room. She hoped to find perhaps a spare key or even the entire key ring. If she were lucky, the professor was an absent-minded professor, and in the excitement that prevailed in the ward right now, something could remain lying around. But that would have been too beautiful, and miracles occur in a psychiatric ward extremely infrequently. All of the cupboards and drawers were locked or filled with useless patient indexes. Just as Nina was about to look for her own index card, she heard the hasty steps of the chief physician, who was apparently storming back into his room. Nina had to hide quickly. The closets were out of the question, so all that remained to her was a door that she glimpsed behind the chief physician's desk.

She quickly slipped through it and found herself in a small bathroom, apparently the chief physician's private bathroom, with a shower, washbasin, and toilet. *Yes, yes, communism does have its privileges ready for those who are somewhat more equal than the others. Everybody is equal, but the members of the establishment are a bit more equal than the others.* Everything was there: shaving brush, perfume, facial cream, eye shadow, makeup. Wait a minute. The professor did not need all of that himself. There was a woman involved. One woman? The chief physician probably went through the nurses one after another. That was nothing new. Perhaps even pretty patients could buy themselves a few things to make the march easier on their way to insanity, who knows?

While Nina began to rave at the sight of this accumulation of cosmetics, which were rare in Russia because they were hard to obtain, she was brought back to the dangerous reality by the chief physician's voice in the next room: "Comrade General, I really must protest," bellowed the chief physician indignantly into the telephone. "Now your lackeys are coming to my ward in broad daylight and killing my patients. No, I'm not crazy and I'm not imagining anything. In section B there's a male corpse, and it exhibits the handwriting of the KGB as clearly as if they had left me their visiting card in order to exclude any doubt. No, I'm very much acquainted with those things. As you know, I left my service in the KGB with the rank of colonel. So don't try to tell me anything. Normally I wouldn't even be complaining, but is it clear to you whom you liquidated there? That was an absolutely intact member of test group C. He was still being used and hadn't been released for removal from the experiment. You yourself gave this experiment the highest military priority. How am I supposed to deliver useful results if you attack me from behind that way?"

"What, what's that supposed to mean?" The chief physician's voice suddenly seemed to tremble. "What do you mean, the experiment was broken off? Are you aware of what nonsense you're babbling? That's fifty years of research that you thoughtlessly want to throw in the garbage can. Not even a dimwit like you can come up with such an insane idea. Fifty years, I beg of you; that's my entire goddamned life that I've sacrificed for this project. That just can't suddenly be worthless. You yourself raved to me decades ago about what potential lies in this knowledge, how you want to base the military superiority of the Soviet Union on it. And haven't I already proved to you what all is possible with it? Think about your KGB special detail. That's my work alone. And now this. Comrade General, I beg you: be reasonable."

The chief physician had apparently become hot in his agitation. He hastily took off his physician's coat and threw it down on the couch next to his desk.

"What do you mean, the counterrevolutionary forces can't be permitted to discover that we've experimented with human beings? They won't discover that! It was all strictly secret. That can all continue to be covered up, even if the devil in person were to come to earth and make a democracy of Russia, which won't happen anyway, except as a pretense. Even if Yeltsin lets a parliament be elected, after two years at the most he'll be fed up with it and let everything be shot to pieces again. That's certainly no reason to simply erase the results of decades of scientific breeding. Nobody pays any attention to that. The test subjects look like normal people, and they are quite normal people. So who's going to prove anything against us in that regard? O.K., as far as I'm concerned, I can destroy my notes. I have everything in my head anyway. But please don't destroy the test subjects. We're not murderers, after all, at least we don't commit murder senselessly. General Grigorov, I'll

164

destroy the material right now. I'll get the case out of the safe. One moment. Stay on the line."

Nina peered through the crack in the door and watched the professor open his safe and take a black case out of it.

"So, Comrade General," the chief physician whispered conspiratorially as he opened the briefcase, "I now have all of the material here on my desk. Together we'll now go through the list of test subjects who will NOT be liquidated. Then, as far as I'm concerned, you can send your bloodhounds, and they can have my briefcase and throw it in the fire. Then all traces will be wiped out. But leave my little children alive. Here we have Antonin H. Unfortunately our conversation comes too late for him. And then Mirka Andrevskaya. What, she's also dead already? But Nina Antonova, she's in my ward. You will kindly leave her alone. As far as I'm concerned, we can change the names. They're all false anyway. In honor of KGB Chief Andropov, we simply used the beginning of his name to mark this test group, but now it doesn't matter. He's been dead for a long time, of course."

"Is that really your final word? I don't accept that. I don't accept that, and I'll know how to prevent your murderers from destroying my work, even if I have to throw myself in front of each of your victims to catch the bullets."

The chief physician hung up the phone noisily and ran snarling from the room. Apparently he wanted to ascertain for himself that Nina Antonova was still alive. In his rage he forgot to put on his coat again.

Nina acted. She searched the pockets of the coat, found the ring of keys, put on the white coat, and in a flash of inspiration reached for the black briefcase, closed it, and left the room with hasty but measured strides, in order not to draw attention. Behind her she heard the furious shouts of the professor. All of the personnel were hurrying around in confusion, and the place hummed like a beehive. In the hubbub she reached the entrance to the ward without being recognized, turned the key in the lock, and was free.

Nina inhaled the polluted air of Moscow's inner city as if it were saturated with precious flower pollen. What for the citizens of Moscow was at most an incitement to sullen carping about real socialism, seemed to her to be the wonderful fragrance of freedom that she had missed for so long. Even the odor of heavy metal in her nose was more natural than the mixture of barbiturates and tranquilizers that she had still been given that morning. She had, however, no time for introspective contemplation, for soon everyone whom the clinic could muster for the search would be after her. She ran to the nearest subway station, got on the subway, rode through a few stations, changed trains at a junction, and repeated that until her pursuers had to have lost her trail. Finally she locked herself inside a public toilet in order to be able to look at the contents of the briefcase without being disturbed. She did not understand the many medical terms in the papers, but discovered among the many medical histories her own. On it was again the telephone number that she had already called, along with an address in Prague in Czechoslovakia. From the medical report it became clear that this had to be her home address. So that was where she would go.

She took off the white coat in order not to draw attention to herself with it in public. In the process she discovered that the absent-minded professor had also left his pocketbook with checks and everything else in the coat. That would help during the acquisition of a train ticket. Nina grinned: "The professor as the one who helped me escape, who would have thought that?"

*

It was an accursedly bad day for the chief physician. First the dead man in the ward, then the impending liquidation of his life's work, and finally he was unable to find his surviving test subject anywhere in the ward. As if that were not enough, he discovered finally that his briefcase and his coat were missing, together with his money and keys. He could easily figure out that Nina Antonova had taken everything with her and fled. In addition, the search party of attendants came back without having accomplished their purpose.

Now the chief physician really had a problem. He could have reported the entire matter to the police or the KGB, of course. In a major roundup, the patient definitely would have been found. But he immediately rejected both possibilities. The police would arrest Nina Antonova, to be sure, but then they would sniff around in the briefcase and ask unpleasant questions. And if the secret project were uncovered, he would be as good as dead. Following today's

166

events, there was no doubt about the determination of the KGB to sacrifice all of the people who were involved, to cover up this scandal. On the other hand, working with the KGB would mean turning Nina over to her murderers, and he certainly did not want to do that. Strictly speaking, Nina's flight did suit his plans; that way at least one of his test subjects would remain alive.

No, he had to take care of the matter himself. Nina should remain alive, but he had to get back the briefcase with his research. And the whole thing was really not as difficult, of course, as it seemed at first glance. For after all, the chief physician knew where she wanted to go. In the briefcase, she would have to have noticed the address in Prague that was her home address. He would find her there.

This could not be the end. During his long life he had already survived very different crises.

27

November 20, 1991

"I know that what I'm requiring of you isn't easy for you."

Inspector Wimmer hated these moments. There would immediately be tears and lamentation. Emotional outbursts were the thing that Wimmer had the greatest difficulty in dealing with. That, of course, was why he had chosen this job for himself, a job in which a person very quickly left feelings behind. You trained yourself to see a corpse as a pile of meat that no longer had anything in common with a human being. Then you could even join the coroner in developing a dark sense of humor that had cleansed itself. For that reason, kidding with Puchner had a long tradition and they could no longer even talk with each other without being mean. From that point of view, the autopsy room was perhaps the place where Wimmer had the most to laugh about.

The relatives of the corpses saw things differently, of course. For them the morgue was the place where they realized once and for all that they had lost an important person forever. How they mastered the sudden outburst of grief, horror, or fear was different from person to person. Some broke into tears; others became hard as stone and silent. But each time the emotional tension could be felt when Wimmer led a witness to a bier on which, beneath a white cloth, the outlines of a human being could be detected.

Wimmer could have recorded a hundred different reactions and facial expressions, if he had been permitted to film the relatives during that moment of horrible recognition. In a sudden burst of gallows humor he began to grin broadly. It would be a nice sideline, to provide Hollywood with mimetic material for the many crime movies; the horror would then come across much more authentically, and Wimmer would finally have the time and the money to see those films in the movie theater. He would then change his occupation to film critic, morgue critic so to speak. Such a person was bitterly needed. Wimmer's experience, of course, came only from the television set that he sometimes turned on after midnight, but the dissection room scenes on Austrian television were simply pitiful. He and Puchner could easily have improved them.

Puchner's sober face brought Wimmer from his dreams back into the morgue. Hollywood was far away and now it was important to do his job. Wimmer had asked the snot's young girlfriend to come here. Of course the snot had come with her, and even his lawyer had not let the opportunity pass to get on Wimmer's nerves once again. It was only an attempt, of course, but since Vera looked like the corpse, maybe she did have something to do with the woman and could perhaps identify her.

The attorney was already firing away: "Inspector Wimmer, I want to point out to you that you're subjecting my client to an impermissible mental strain. Miss Kurkova doesn't have the slightest idea at all concerning who this corpse might be, and there isn't the slightest clue that she ever met her while she was alive. For that reason we must assume that this official act will accomplish nothing toward the identification of the corpse. But we can certainly assume that after the excitement of recent days – for which you, by the way, Inspector Wimmer, are responsible because of your unjustified accusations – Mr. Makord and Miss Kurkova will experience an extreme degree of stress that could lead to a nervous breakdown. For nothing and for no reason. Do you really want to accept responsibility for that?"

Wimmer's belly cramped momentarily, as if it had transformed itself into the fang-lined jaws of a tiger. He would only too gladly have torn the attorney apart, he was so angry about his officiousness.

"Would you please let me do my work? I don't prescribe to you how you should compose those court petitions of yours, which could legitimately be used as toilet paper and whose only purpose is to hamper the work of the police. So, at least now get out of my way. And you, Miss Kurkova, are perhaps more important for solving this case than you think. So, don't let this little exchange of words spoil your concentration. Everything that occurs to you now can be important for us. Puchner, please!"

The coroner pulled back the sheet that covered the corpse.

When Vera caught sight of the waxy, pale face of the dead woman, she was peculiarly touched and simultaneously impassive. She did not know this woman, she was sure of that. Nevertheless,

169

she felt a deep sadness, which seemed, however, to be kilometers away, as if it did not belong to Vera, but to some other person. Then Vera was that other person, and she herself was a hundred kilometers away, and the autopsy room was a small point in the universe that had nothing to do with Vera. Then Vera metamorphosed into the dead woman, with a young woman bending over her, who looked just like her. Finally she felt as if she had entered a dream in which that face had appeared to her for years, only to immediately distance itself from her further and further, until it disappeared as a point on the horizon. Vera burst out weeping each time that she awoke from that dream, and she did not know why. Abruptly Vera was shaken by such a fit of weeping even now.

"Now see what you've done," Wegener scolded in the policeman's direction. He placed his arm protectively around Vera and tried to lead her away from the corpse.

"Leave me alone!" Vera tore herself loose and ran out into the corridor, with Rafael behind her. Wegener and Wimmer looked into each other's eyes with grim perplexity. Puchner spread the sheet neatly over the dead woman again, as if he wanted to quickly do away with the cause of this embarrassment. Which in reality was not necessary, since the woman had already left the world.

Rafael caught up with Vera in a corner of the corridor, where she slipped to the floor and stared straight ahead with lifeless eyes.

"What's the matter, Vera? What's the matter? Did you recognize the woman?"

Vera's gaze froze even more, and now she seemed light years away, and it was a vain undertaking for Rafael to try to reach her. He tried to talk to her and shook her by the shoulders. As a psychologist he was worried that Vera had had a derealization or depersonalization experience, in which the patient no longer knows who, what, and where he or she is. The depersonalization could end in a schizophrenic push, if the patient could not be brought back to reality quickly enough.

"Vera, Vera, look at me! Look into my eyes. It's me, Rafael. I'm with you. I'm with you. Come back to me, come back!"

Finally Rafael got through to Vera, by staring firmly and penetratingly into her eyes, and when vision returned to Vera's pupils, she was again seized by a crying fit. Rafael sat down next to her and took her gently in his arms. He held her carefully, as if by so doing

170

he intended to catch the force of her outburst of feeling. "Go ahead and cry, my darling. Let the tears come, and then you'll soon feel better."

Finally Vera had gotten hold of herself to the point that she wanted to talk. "You know, I can't explain what's wrong. It's so strange to see somebody who's your spitting image for the first time. And then she's already dead, before you can ask the first question. It's an absurd feeling, when something is totally foreign to you, but nevertheless quite familiar. I've never seen that dead woman before, and yet I know her somehow. For years I've dreamt of that dead woman, as if I knew that I would meet her today. On the other hand it's the sort of image that suddenly overcomes a person, one that seems to come from another reality. That seems quite real, although it can't be real. As it was in the moment when you wanted to sleep with me and I was certain that you were a rapist. Rafael, I'm going insane. Tell me that I'm not going insane!"

"No, you're certainly not insane, Vera," said Rafael soothingly, but in reality he was not at all that certain. Depersonalization phenomena, emotional instability, and psychiatric reference delusion — everything was there that causes the heart of a psychiatrist to beat faster. Rafael had to prevent Vera from falling into the hands of the people at the Wagner-Jauregg Hospital.

"That dead woman awakened something in me that had been buried, a very old feeling that I buried a long, long time ago. It awakened a longing to have somebody be there for me, somebody who would give me security. And then the pain was immediately there at having lost her for all time."

"Could it be the longing for a mother that you never had?"

Vera began crying again, as if she wanted to confirm that Rafael's interpretation was correct. "You know, I lost my mother so soon. I was still so little. I still needed her so much. It hurts so much, when you lose your mama. It hurts so infinitely much. I learned to live with it. I forgot it. But now, where somebody lost this dead woman, whom I don't know, now I feel it again. It hurts so much to grow up so utterly alone. It hurts so much."

Rafael rocked Vera gently back and forth, as if he wanted to rock her to sleep. During many therapy sessions he had learned to symbolically take the place of the lost parents of his patients, and

171

that knowledge now came to his aid. Vera's weeping slowly became more peaceful, and finally she became quiet and relaxed.

"Excuse me for disturbing this intimate shared moment." Inspector Wimmer, who had observed the two of them from an appropriate distance, now ventured closer to them. "If you're ready, then in spite of everything we should now take the young woman's statement." As he spoke, he looked at the floor like a boy who had just smashed the soup bowl at supper and was hoping to receive his dessert anyway by behaving as if he recognized his guilt.

"Vera doesn't know the dead woman. She's never seen her before," responded Rafael, as if he wanted to place himself protectively in front of his girlfriend, who now urgently needed peace and quiet in order to process her experience.

"I object to this interrogation with all necessary clarity and will...," Dr. Wegener interjected, but a bitterly angry glance from Rafael quickly silenced him again.

Now peace and quiet actually did prevail. Vera's relaxed sadness spread through the room and enshrouded Wegener's bustling activity, Puchner's pretended objectivity, and even Wimmer's rough armor. The inspector was changed by it for a moment, as if he were reminded of a soft side of himself that he had ignored for so long. He crouched down in front of the cowering Vera and began to speak in a gentle voice that surprised him about himself.

"I'm sorry that you had to experience all of this. Believe me, if I had been able to do so, I would have spared you that sight. And I'm grateful to you that you acceded to our request. I'm certain that your memories, whether they occur to you now or at some later point in time, will bring us further along." Wimmer was amazed at the paternal, concerned tone in his voice, where he had never had a daughter who would have enabled him to discover that side of himself.

"Are you sure that you don't know the dead woman?"

"I don't know exactly." Vera became approachable for Wimmer's questions. His voice calmed her and mediated to her a security that she urgently needed in this state of dissolution. "I don't remember ever having met that woman. Although, on the other hand, she also seems familiar to me because she looks like me. Quite honestly, I simply don't know."

172

"Let's assume for the moment that the similarity can be traced back to your being related. Who could then know something about this woman?"

"My grandma in Prague. She's my only living relative."

"Can you bring your grandma here to Linz for me, so that I can question her?"

"Yes, I can do that. But it will take some time to convince her. Grandma doesn't like to travel. She has never left Czechoslovakia."

"I'm certain that you can do it. And your grandmother will perhaps bring light into this darkness. Perhaps we'll then learn who the dead woman is."

*

Now Wegener was in the bad mood that was normally characteristic of Wimmer. When the attorney left the autopsy room, he could not get rid of the impression that he was leaving the place as a loser. His clients did not seem to need him. Wimmer had seized the position of trust that actually belonged to the attorney. Since he now urgently needed some attention, Wegener now sought out the man who had already trusted him for decades – the old Makord.

"That's what happens when you let a psychologist get to work," grumbled the old chief physician, when Wegener had told him about Vera's scene in the autopsy room. "Whatever my son touches, it ends in maudlin sentimentality. God, how I hate that talk of grief and tears."

"They're now going to bring Vera's grandmother from Prague," the attorney informed his client. "If she reveals the true identity of the dead woman, then your son will probably be out of the mess."

"So, so, the grandmother," growled Makord ambiguously. "The grandmother will clear up the case. What a Punch and Judy show." Then he noticed that his fingers were nervously fiddling around with this suit buttons, and he quickly clasped his hands behind his back.

28

Terezin, May 1, 1945

Told from the point of view of Adolf Markosky

The end was near. Hitler was dead. All of Germany was over-run by the Allies, and Berlin was in the hands of the Red Army. It was time to leave.

As a last island of Nazi rule, the Protectorate of Bohemia and Moravia protruded from the flood of hostile armies. *What an irony of fate*, thought Markosky, *that we Nazis have to give up our first plunder only as the very last thing.* But none of that mattered now. In a few days the Americans and the Russians would be arguing about who was permitted to occupy which part of Czechoslovakia. They were already making bets about which of the two would liberate Terezin.

The SS comrades were visibly nervous. They were still able to calm down with shootings, smoking out vermin, and liquidating deserters, but they themselves knew that all of that no longer made any sense. Secretly they discussed whether the Americans would seriously carry out their Morgentau Plan: All of Germany would become a potato field; all men would be sterilized, SS men first, of course. That would then be the inglorious end of the glorious Aryan race.

While some took heart in the morbid image of heroic death, others began to plan their withdrawal. Still others hoped that the Americans would still accept Goebbels's offer to push back the Red Army with the remains of the German Army after all. Good soldiers were needed everywhere, and the next world war was already preprogrammed.

Markosky was not concerned about any of that. He exhibited an almost stoic calmness, free of any fear, as if his grand experiment of freedom from pain had finally taken possession of himself.

His field was plowed. The potato field could go ahead and come. Markosky had achieved everything that he had undertaken. His research had progressed to the point than no army in the world would be able to destroy it. And above all, he was certain that no army in the world would want to destroy it. Quite the contrary, they would fight over it.

Let the Allies castrate the German nation, let them de-industrialize the German economy – they would let the German scientists live. The competition for Germany was not a run toward Berlin, but rather a competition to see who would get more German scientists in their clutches. They would use the German miracle weapons to bring down the Japanese Empire or to attack each other, depending on how they felt. And Markosky was sitting on a miracle weapon. So he could quietly wait to see who offered him a higher price for it.

He calmly went through his documents to determine whether or not everything was correct, in conformity with the grand plan that he had conceived. On his desk lay neatly ordered stacks of paper. Each one consisted of individual medical histories, which in turn characterized the unwilling participants of certain test groups. There were those who had been raped by SS men, those who had been raped by subhuman Slavs, rape victims of the first, second, or third generation, and rape accumulations over several generations. Even more important than those initial stacks, however, were two that he had cleverly written on blue and pink paper. It was not without paternal pride that he went through the records of the babies of his women. Blue for boys, pink for girls.

He had initially considered having the boys liquidated, since they could hardly be taken into consideration as future rape victims. Then, however, the fortunate idea came to him that they, of course – assuming a bit of brutal training – would yield the perfect rapists and were therefore needed to cross the offspring produced by the rapes with each other. Now he needed only another twenty years to breed and sort out the next hybrid generation.

Then he would have his perfect pain-free generation; he was certain of that. And with a bit of luck genetics would then have developed to the point that genes could be transferred to other people. He would then go down in history as the savior of mankind, as the man who had freed the human race from fear and mental illnesses once and for all. He was sure to receive the Nobel Prize.

But he still needed some time. "Give me four years," Hitler had begged his people and had nevertheless miscalculated somewhat in the process. It was actually too bad that the Third Reich was now coming to an end. Markosky was not sorry that Germany was losing the war; he was completely indifferent about that. But he would never again be able to carry out research as undisturbed and unrestricted as he had been under the protective umbrella of the SS, and he was sorry about that. In the democracies the maintaining of secrecy was much more difficult, and as soon as the matter was uncovered, the experiment would perhaps be broken off in a decisive stage, because of legal restrictions. Just think about that. He breeds the ideal gene man, and then some parliamentarians come, people who do not have the foggiest notion about things, and they prevent him from being bred. For moral reasons, they would then say, because fiddling around with the human genotype is not permitted.

He already saw them before him – those narrow-minded people, incapable of thinking beyond the edge of their plates, possibly even infected by this Jewish psychology that always wanted to have the effect on the subconscious considered first, and which always knew how to prevent any medical progress by expressing forebodings about its negative mental consequences. Those Freudians had taken over the position of the priests who constantly held the people's spiritual abysses up in front of them and in so doing robbed them of all vigor. No, his material would not be in good hands in a Western democracy. Although the American secret intelligence agency would indeed keep something secret that could be used for military purposes. Then he would simply have to spend his life in some secret bunker in Nevada. In an emergency that would be alright, but on the whole it was not very attractive.

But there was still the glorious Soviet Union, of course, as a dictatorship just as perfect as the Third Reich, also full of camps in which camp doctors were needed, with the same idea of the superman, the socialist superman, to be sure. Aryan or socialist superman – that actually did not matter. The deciding factor was that they wanted to have supermen, and for that they would need Markosky. And the Red Army would certainly not be disinclined to free up some money for the breeding of fearless elite soldiers.

Whether in Nevada or Siberia, whether it was the KGB or the CIA, somebody would build Markosky a new research facility, he was sure of that. First, however, he had to ensure that his material safely survived the next few days. He reached for the telephone receiver and dialed the number of the Lebensborn Institute in Prague.

"*Heil Hitler*, Banner Leader, I simply wanted to find out if you have already started the ball rolling for transporting the thirty-five infants, as I requested."

The Lebensborn Institute director's answer did not satisfy him. Markosky's voice became angry: "Damn it, Banner Leader, there's no thinking for you to do. The deportation of the infants to Terezin is a decided matter, and the order has come from the highest level. Now don't play the children's rescuer. Of course those subhuman babies will be liquidated. No, it's not immaterial that in a few days everything will be over anyway, nor is that any reason for us to let this brood live now. Do you know where those infants come from? They're the children of Jews and subhuman Slavs that we would only have left alive for research purposes until they reached sexual maturity. After the experiments were conducted they would have been destroyed anyway. Do you want these vermin to fall into the hands of the enemy and for the enemy to possibly present them as evidence for what has happened in our camps? Do you really want to accept the responsibility for that? Do you finally understand?"

Since the correct answers apparently came from the receiver now, Markosky's voice became calmer once more. "No, you don't need to carry out the liquidation there. What kind of light would that cast on the Lebensborn Project? Bloody corpses in the children's home – ugh! No, we can do that much less conspicuously in the concentration camp. Do we understand each other now? Good. So send off the children's convoy now. Then it will arrive here before the Red Army."

Markosky took a deep breath. It had cost him some effort to maneuver the Lebensborn director, who was incompetent with fear, in the desired direction. Then a smile emerged on his face. *I did get him to do it*, thought Markosky. In these last days it was simply only possible to use destruction and shootings as arguments. The truth that he actually did intend to save the children, before somebody else got any stupid ideas, was something that nobody would have believed coming from him anyway.

177

But that was not right. There was a group of people that had to believe in this miraculous rescue and probably also would believe it. And if he succeeded in that, he could suddenly change his butcher image for the better and in the end stand there as a rescuer and benefactor. And the best thing was that nobody would guess his real motives. He smiled again. Markosky as a rescuer of the mothers; he liked the image. It could be developed.

He had all of the women in the camp line up on the parade ground. He adopted a pose in front of them, put on a sympathetic, almost sad facial expression, and began to speak with an unusually warm-hearted voice: "Women and mothers of the Terezin camp, I...know your sorrow. I know that in recent years you have gone through horrible things. But in a few days those horrors will be over, when the armies of the Allies liberate the camp. Then we, the men of the SS, will be made accountable. And most of you are looking forward to that day of reckoning. That's certainly understandable.

"But before you pass judgment on us, you should know the whole truth. During all those years I always acted and felt like a physician. In an inhuman dictatorship we were forced to carry out orders and had to take harsh measures to preserve appearances. If we had released you, then we would have been locked up and liquidated just like the inmates of this camp. We could therefore not prevent the brutal action of the Hitler dictatorship, but we were able to tone it down to the extent that it was possible.

"Think about it briefly. Didn't you receive the best medical treatment from me, the right medicines? Didn't I always cure you? Many of you became pregnant in the camp. Well, you can't prevent soldiers from claiming their natural rights, as sorry as I am about that. Perhaps one or the other of you also fell in love with an SS man. After all, they don't look that bad. But as a physician I didn't ask about the reasons for the pregnancy, but ensured that your children came into the world healthy. Certainly, after they were born, your children were taken away from you and you never saw them again. I'm so sorry that you had to believe that your children were dead, but there was no other way. How would I have faced the SS leaders, if you had all learned the truth? My beneficial activity in this camp would have immediately ended."

178

In the rows of women there was restlessness. Olana sensed the skeptical amazement that came over some of the mothers next to, in front of, and behind her, while others remained apathetic, because they did not believe a word that the Nazi pig said anyway. But the hope that the children were still alive spread like a glowing fire.

"But if I took the children away from you, then it was only because they would not have survived for a week in this camp. Infants in a labor camp – that would never have turned out well. I knew that, and you knew it, too. I took the children from you to take them to a safe place where they could survive, and only that was important to me. And I swear by everything that is sacred to me that each of your children is well. They were all cared for and raised by nurses, in a nearby children's home. None of them died. Nothing happened to any of them. They are all healthy and well!"

Tears flowed down Olana's cheeks. She thought of the little Mara whom she had rocked in her arms after her birth. She had been so pretty, an angel's face; the little mouth had soon twisted into the suggestion of a smile. Olana had even sung her a lullaby, and then came the horrible pain, when the child was torn out of her arms. Since that day she had racked her brain with the uncertainty of what had happened to Mara. It would be so beautiful to be able to hold her in her arms again.

"Women and mothers of Terezin, your suffering is coming to an end. And as proof that you can trust me, in a few hours a convoy of trucks will arrive here, which will have your children on board. May this be the beginning of a happier time for you and your children. And may God forgive us that this happiness could not begin until today."

Olana could not do anything else. She fell to her knees and clasped her hands to her face. She did not notice at all that her face and neck became wet. She felt only her wildly pounding heart, as if it had just begun to beat again – to beat for her child.

When the convoy drove onto the parade ground, it was surrounded by clusters of screaming women who stretched their hands desperately toward the children who were gradually handed down to them by the nurses. *A touching picture*, thought Markosky, who was looking down at the scene from the window of his office. *Let somebody try to top that.* He was satisfied with his chess move. His

179

test subjects were saved, for nobody would take care of them as well as their own mothers would. And he had gathered enough data to find the children's whereabouts again, when it was time for the next breeding phase. In a communist dictatorship, the necessary measures could be just as easily arranged as they could in a fascist dictatorship. And in case it did not work out with the KGB as he anticipated, then he had just won himself enough advocates who would testify in court that he had become the "savior of Terezin."

It was now time to prepare for departure. Maier was supposed to burn all the documents that could not be transported or that had become superfluous. But just where was Maier? Not a trace of him in the entire camp. He had probably already left, like many of the others had also done. He could not be blamed for that.

Markosky went to his desk to pack his documents. But they were no longer lying there. Had he put them back into a drawer? Markosky tore apart his whole desk, but the papers remained missing. Somebody had probably caused them to disappear. Did somebody want to avenge himself on him? Were there already informants going around collecting evidence?

It did not matter. There was no more time to wonder about it. Then he would simply have to rely on the notes in his head. It was high time to disappear.

29

Wimmer eyed the old woman who had sat down in front of his desk. He hoped with all of his policeman's heart that she would bring him the solution to the puzzle. This murder case had already been glowing for too long in the pit of his stomach, and it slowly but surely endangered the continuation of Wimmer's caffeine abuse.

"So you can confirm the identity of the dead woman? I'm sorry that I must ask you to repeat again what you already said at the morgue, but I must now put all of that in my report."

"Yes, the dead woman is my daughter Mara. She was born in the year 1944 and grew up in my home in Prague. Is that sufficient for you?" Olga's gaze was strangely empty, as though her last tears had already died decades ago, and as if she had not just learned that her only daughter was dead. Perhaps the certainty of that death was a feeling that she had already known for so long that Olga now did not want to present the officer with the spectacle of a grieving mother. With her sullen voice she tried to keep the stranger away from the final thing that had remained to her: away from the intimacy that arose from the fact that only the mother and the daughter knew what had really happened.

But it was that specific intimate knowledge that the officer was panting for like a dog for a bone. And although he sensed the invisible wall that the old woman had erected around herself, he was not willing to respect her soundless grief.

"I'm sorry, but you do have to tell me a little bit more. Above all, I would need to know how your daughter came to Linz, what she intended to do here, and who was interested in killing her."

"What she wanted here? She wanted to visit her only daughter. Is that so hard to understand?"

"No, no, every mother likes to visit her daughter, that's clear. But why didn't the daughter know anything about this visit? And why was she lying as a dead woman in the bed of her — how should I put it — her son-in-law? And what is most remarkable, why didn't the daughter recognize her mother, or why did she refuse to identify her? You know, in recent days we've turned over the most abstruse theories in our minds here, about cloned people and people who have been aged, and about insane scientists who conduct genetic experiments. And all of that only because it simply seemed impossible that the dead woman and Vera Kurkova could be mother and daughter. A clear statement would thus have saved us from pursuing many false avenues in our detective work. That's why I would now really like to learn more about the background."

Olga gave a deep sigh. There was no way out. This blowfly of a policeman would not leave her in peace. He would not stop digging around in the entrails of her soul, probing and stirring them, until the pain erupted from her that she had kept in check for so long. She had changed her name to wipe out all traces of that wound. She had learned for an entire lifetime to maintain her dignity by denying her enemies the satisfaction of feasting on her collapse. There had been many such enemies, and now the inspector stood for the enemy who was not worthy to be permitted to recognize Olga's pain. She probably had to surrender some things; that could not be avoided. But she would defend the land of her soul centimeter by centimeter and only let the enemy enter it as far as was absolutely necessary.

"That's too many questions all at once, don't you think? Regarding question one: How should I know who killed Mara? I wasn't there. Don't you think that I'd like to know that myself? Otherwise I wouldn't be here. After all, that's your job, and I can't do anything about it, if you don't put things together.

"Regarding question two: She probably went to the apartment of Mr. Rafael Makord because she obtained the address from me. Vera wrote to me so enthusiastically about him and told me on the telephone that I absolutely had to become acquainted with him and come to Linz. She gave me both her own and Rafael's addresses, so that there would be no way for me to miss them, no matter when I came to Linz. I passed both addresses on to Mara.

"To question three: Vera couldn't identify her mother because she didn't know what her mother looked like. She didn't grow up with her."

Now it was getting exciting. Wimmer was wide awake: "What's that supposed to mean? Was Vera an orphanage child or something? Didn't Mara want to raise her child herself? Was she a bad mother who left her child in the lurch?"

182

Olga sighed deeply again. She had expected it. The enemy had just lengthened his drill bit in order to be able to penetrate deeper into her soul. But now she could not remain silent, for that would have meant letting the memory of her daughter be dragged through the mud: "Yes, you patriarchs would like to see it that way. Your first thought is always that the mother is to blame, if a child lacks something. But usually the opposite is true. The bad mothers are the victims of the men's violence. That's the way it was with Mara. She was abducted."

"Abducted by whom and when?"

Olga did not like to remember what she now had to talk about: "During the suppression of the Prague Spring in 1968 she was arrested by the Russians. She disappeared without a trace, and I heard nothing from her for twenty years. Then just two weeks ago she stood at my door, exhausted, older, and half sick. I almost wouldn't have recognized her. Thank God, I was still living in the same two-room apartment as in '68. Otherwise she would probably not have found her way home. Viewed from that perspective it was a late blessing that in real socialism we did have the right to a place to live, but had no chance for a better apartment."

"Where was she in the meantime?"

"Mara's statements were hard to understand. She was confused and under the influence of long-term psychopharmacologic drugs. They had apparently taken her to Russia and put her first into a camp for political prisoners and later into a psychiatric hospital. There they shot medicines into her until she reached the point that she no longer knew who she was."

"How did she finally succeed in fleeing?" Wimmer shot off his questions like arrows in order not to give Olga time to think.

"Somebody tried to kill her. In panic she stole her chief physician's ward keys and some documents. Among the latter she also found my address and some money. She reached Prague by train. At the borders she hid in the lavatory. She was discovered in spite of that, but a Polish border policeman felt sorry for her, and he let her go, when he heard what the Russians had done to her."

"What did they do to her?"

"Well, twenty-three years of imprisonment without reason and without a trial is probably enough, isn't it? She went half crazy at the thought of her little daughter, whom she had to leave behind with me in Prague. She didn't even know what had happened to Vera, whether or not she, too, had perhaps been abducted. I was able to prevent that, thank God."

"Vera grew up with you?"

"Yes, Vera did well with me, although, how would you do, if you had to grow up without your mother and father? I was so proud of the fact that Vera developed normally and knew nothing about the entire evil past. And now everything has caught up with her. Now she is experiencing all of the grief of the Kurkova women."

"What do you mean by that?" The police officer had smelled a rat and suspected that there was more to it.

But Olga quickly corrected herself. She at least did not want to provide any insight into her own story: "Well, from the documents that Mara had taken with her, she concluded that the chief physician of the psychiatric ward where she was confined was misusing her and many fellow patients for human experiments. It was a question of genetic experiments, in which the perfect human being was supposed to be bred."

"The genetically perfect human being, yes, that's the big fad right now. Those documents are thus probably worth money. But that probably means that the chief physician will miss those documents enormously." Wimmer grinned.

"Yes, and with that you also have your answer to the question of who could be interested in Mara's death. Mara was still in a complete panic. She didn't want to stay in Czechoslovakia. She was certain that the chief physician would send somebody after her, with the assignment to kill her and bring back the documents. Once on the train she thought that the chief physician himself was after her. She wanted to return to the West as quickly as possible to turn that black briefcase over to the authorities here. That's why she traveled on to Linz the very next day."

"Tell me, did Mara give you a description of what this chief physician looks like?" Wimmer asked the question as hungrily as a leopard that had crept up to within striking distance of its prey.

"Naturally! She was obsessed with the man who had tortured and tormented her for decades. She spoke of almost nothing else."

"Could you describe the man?"

"According to Mara, he was approximately six feet three inches tall, seventy years old, partially bald, lanky build, and in good physical condition. She even drew his face for me, so that I was warned if he should show up."

Wimmer knew enough. It was the burglar who had escaped from him in the police station. He had to be Mara's murderer. He had a motive; he was in Linz at the time of the crime, and he very certainly had no alibi.

"Dear lady, could we perhaps make an artist's sketch of this man? You only have to remember Mara's drawing. Our police artist will do the rest. With that we would have a chance to catch your daughter's murderer."

*

Olga did a complete job. The face of the phantom was so characteristic that Wimmer believed that he recognized the face of the man who had knocked him down in the darkness. The rest was police routine. The artist's sketch was faxed to all the substations, and the search was on. Wimmer only had to wait now until the bird came into his net.

During the next two days Wimmer did not leave his office. He even slept there out of concern that he could miss something. On the third day the telephone rang, and his colleague Peilsteiner from the Donaulände substation was on the line. "We found your suspect. He's living in the Tourotel, tenth floor, room 1011."

"O.K., stay there. I'll be there immediately."

When Wimmer had reached the tenth floor of the Tourotel, the rest came off like in a police textbook.

Wimmer placed himself to the right of the door to the room, before Peilsteiner knocked and loudly called, "Room service! We're bringing your order." When the door cautiously opened, Wimmer saw first the arm with the loaded pistol that slowly moved outward from the doorframe and pointed at Peilsteiner. It was an easy thing for him to knock the pistol out of the enemy's hand with a forceful judo chop. And in memory of the beating that he had taken in the police station, it was like a public celebration for him to punch his fist into his opponent's side and, when the latter curled up in pain, to end the whole thing with a blow to the neck. "This time you

185

won't get away from me, you dog," he grunted with satisfaction, as he looked down at the opponent who lay on the floor. In the process he certainly noticed the somewhat horrified look of his colleague, who was amazed at Wimmer's unusually violent aggressiveness and also showed little understanding for it. But what did he know about the troubles of the higher-ups in a long, frustrated policeman's life? The little pleasures of the legally sanctioned brutality still had to be permitted to him, especially when they were also necessary and justifiable in preventing an attempt to escape by the kind of man who lay in front of him.

30

When Rafael woke up that morning, he again felt as confused and grumpy as he had felt during his early professional years in the hospital, where, as a young psychologist, he had daily figured on being slapped down by his boss. The old gentleman was in the habit of demonstrating his mental superiority to his young assistants through questions to which actually only he himself could know the answer. This customary humiliation routine was doubly funny with regard to the ward psychologist, because in addition to the dominance of the older man over the younger one, the supremacy of medicine over the auxiliary science of psychology could be proven anew every day. Rafael had hated his boss for those humiliations, almost as fervently as he had despised his father for his visibly displayed arrogance. Nobody was surprised that the shy psychologist soon resigned from service in the hospital and went into private practice "in order to realize his potential," as the ward gossip secretly said in mocking him.

With some aloofness, after he had cursed all the anger from his soul in the freedom of no longer being subject to instructions, he viewed his old boss more forgivingly and could even admit that with respect to medicine he really had learned a great deal from him. That had the consequence that what had previously been such a clear delineation of the front between evil physical medicine and good psychology softened somewhat, and Rafael was no longer so certain that the arguments of the medical men did not have just as much in their favor in some things as the theses of the psychologists. Who could know what was true or false? He ended this discussion in his mind with the wise conclusion that there were simply different theory structures, each with its own advantages and disadvantages, and that no individual, so not even he himself, had a private monopoly on the only eternally valid wisdom.

In recent days his relationship with his father had developed like the previous one with his boss. Rafael became more forgiving and even caught himself reproaching himself for having taken his father to task too severely and for having unjustifiably suspected his father of fascist crimes. At the price of the renewed confusion over what was good and evil, what was right and wrong, he began to concede to his father that he perhaps actually was an honorable medical man who was inspired by the wish to heal and to help. He occupied himself seriously with the hypothesis that his many aggressive accusations were perhaps only the expression of an adolescent father-son conflict that was caused by the premature death of his mother. He had often experienced that in his practice, of course: when a mother and wife dies prematurely, then the bereaved develop a pathological grief reaction in which the father and the children secretly blame each other for the mother's death, because the fury directed at the other, the defined culprit, is easier to bear than the pain caused by the irreplaceable loss.

While he brushed his teeth, Rafael recapitulated once more what had caused this change of mind in favor of peace with his father. It had probably been the conversations with Vera's grandmother, who had come to Linz and contributed so much to Rafael's exculpation and to solving the murder case. Now it was clear that Vera had lost her mother; that the dead woman really was her mother; and that Rafael himself could not be her murderer, since the police had caught the real murderer on the basis of Olga's description. For Rafael everything had ended well; for Vera, on the other hand, it had ended badly. Vera now had to live with the fact that her mother had been held prisoner by the Soviets for twenty years and had finally been murdered. Compared to that, what were Rafael's ridiculous conflicts with his father, who really had always taken care of him and had offered him a normal home with father, mother, and child? What was a normal generation conflict in comparison to this horrible story of internment, separation, and death, which Vera had to grow up with? And what good was Rafael's distrustful digging into the fascist past of the citizens of Linz, which was based purely on suppositions, where the real and obvious criminals came from an entirely different direction?

No, perhaps he should seek reconciliation with his father, drink a glass of wine with him, and carry on a calm conversation with his only living relative. It would do the old man good, and probably Rafael himself as well.

While he combed his hair, Rafael firmly decided to do that. First, however, he had to take care of something else. He got on his bicycle and rode hastily to the police building, in order not to miss his eight-o'clock appointment with the police inspector.

When Rafael arrived there, Vera and her grandmother were already sitting with Inspector Wimmer in his office. The latter informed them all that the meeting was for the purpose of bringing the murder case of Mara Kurkova to a close, now that the identity of the corpse and the identity of the murderer had been cleared up. But some final questions and inconsistencies still remained open and had to be resolved in order to close the chain of evidence against chief physician Mayinski, since the latter was not prepared to make any confession.

There was first the mysterious briefcase that had been in the possession of the dead woman and had probably provided the murder motive for Mayinski. Wimmer handed the documents from the briefcase around and explained that in the opinion of the coroner they reported about genetic experiments on human beings in a concentration camp. The notes had wound up in the hands of the Soviets after the war, who had continued the experiments in Moscow. It was possible that the suspect Mayinski and the concentration camp physician Markoski were one and the same person. The covering up of those facts would be a clear motive for murder, which they now had to prove against Mayinski. The confrontation with the relatives of his murder victim would perhaps soften Mayinski up and move him to confess, and for that reason he was asking for the help of those who were present.

When the notes came into Olga's hands, she became silent and pale. She recognized the handwriting and leafed hastily forward until she came to the medical histories. Among the oldest ones she found the abbreviation O.K. and knew the facts. All of the rage, the humiliations, and the bitterness about what they had done to her erupted within her like a flood of memories that she had held back for a lifetime behind a dam of survival necessity. She turned more pages and discovered beneath the name of Nina Antonova the medical history of her daughter, and beneath her pale skin her veins swelled up out of boundless hatred toward the one man who had destroyed the lives of mother and daughter, and whom she would soon face. Yes, she would deliver to the officer the confrontation that he wanted, for she had waited for it all her life.

When Mayinski was led into the room, Olga's eyes constricted to narrow slits and her lips disappeared in her tightly closed mouth.

In response to Wimmer's question of whether she knew the man or could convey significant information about him, the words burst forth from Olga's mouth: "Yes, I know this man. He was a doctor in the Terezin concentration camp and was among my worst tormenters. In that camp I was raped again and again because this man and his colleague made the torturing of women their pseudoscientific pastime. You miserable pig! Wasn't what you did to me enough? Why did you also have to torment my innocent daughter? Back then in Prague I already knew that you abducted my daughter, and you wanted my granddaughter, too, because you couldn't get your mouth full in your sadistic craving. And why did you have to kill her, my little Mara, you pig? You killed her, you monster!"

Olga broke out in tears, and in the next moment she rushed at Mayinski to hit him. Wimmer and the guard who had brought the prisoner in were able to grab Olga's arms at the last moment and hold her back. They talked soothingly to the completely hysterical woman and tried to persuade her to get hold of herself again. Certainly this was all difficult for her, but now they had caught her tormenter, and he would not escape his just punishment. Olga sat there weeping and collapsed. Vera looked at her with perplexity, for she had only now begun to grasp what had happened to her grandmother, and what she had kept from her all her life, in order not to burden her with those horrible stories. In Rafael's head the images of the rapes in the concentration camp and of Vera's rape fantasies rattled along next to each other and formed an aha-experience of the kind that rarely occurs even in a psychologist's career. Wimmer was just turning toward Mayinski to confront him with the emotions of those who were present and thus put him under such pressure that he would not be able to maintain his denials. Then there was a knock at the door.

The door opened and Wegener's lively face looked in. "Apparently we've already missed something. Well, then it's time for my client and me to appear on the stage of events.

Wegener entered the conference room with Albert Makord following him. "Since Mr. Makord's son was accused for so long and apparently unjustly, and the good Makord name was dragged through the mud as a result, we probably have the right to find out what is behind all of that."

190

Wimmer, who felt massively disturbed at the high point of a successful production of police work, was on the point of declaring to the repulsive shyster with a growl that his client, for lack of party status and without an invitation, had absolutely no business being here. But he did not get to that point, because Olga's renewed and unexpected reaction now confused him.

Olga had gotten up from her chair. Her eyes were open wide, and her body seemed to have been transformed to a pillar of salt. As if in slow motion she raised her left arm and pointed like an avenging goddess at the retired chief physician of the Linz gynecology department: "It's you, you raped me again and again and could never get enough of your perverse sexual violence. Did you enjoy it? Ha! What did you actually enjoy about it, that you could have me, that you had power over me, that you could hurt me? I always asked myself that. I'd like to know that. Go ahead and say it before you disappear behind bars for all time."

Wimmer saw his plans failing, for if the old woman could not decide who was the culprit here, then her statement was not worth anything. "Just a minute, now who is actually who?"

"This pseudo-Russian Mayinski was Maier, the assistant. And the noble gentleman there was Adolf Markoski, the camp doctor, who thought up the whole insane project. Yes, you, look at me. Now you can no longer hide behind your power, you miserable wretch. You're Markosky." Her outstretched arm was still pointing like a fury at the Linz chief physician. "Do you know that your fine assistant killed my daughter, who was also your daughter?"

Rafael looked wistfully at his father. He would have made peace with his father, but it was all true; he had always sensed it.

Albert Markosky looked into the hate-filled eyes of his victim, into the sad eyes of his son, and saw in his mind the dead eyes of his murdered daughter...

And suddenly it was there again, the pain in his heart that he had deadened and suppressed for a lifetime, at the expense of all of the things that were coming to light on that day. His experiment had worked so well, and he had lived almost his entire life without pain.

But now the pain shot into his heart like a fiery ray and raged so wildly that it tore apart the fibers of that powerful muscle.

Heart attack – this time it really is a heart attack, Markosky diagnosed quickly before he sank to the floor and lost consciousness.

*

Markosky was not the only one who was carried away in an ambulance on that memorable day. Hours later, Wimmer, too, landed in the hospital, because his stomach finally went crazy. While with Markosky any help came too late and all attempts to revive him were fruitless, the art of the physicians would save Wimmer's life.

During the ride to the hospital, when he initially writhed in pain and then the anesthetic began to take effect, Wimmer recapitulated the last few hours, because he could not understand his stomach seismograph for the life of him. After all, things had gone extremely well. Why did his stomach lining go crazy on such a successful day? Where he had finally been victorious over the crime after all, shouldn't his hydrochloric acid have calmed down?

When the emergency doctor came to get the dying chief physician, Wimmer sent all of the relatives outside. He wanted to deal with Mayinsky at last in peace, before a new outbreak of feeling on the part of some participant or other prevented it again. But the old ass stuck obstinately and unemotionally to his claim that he had nothing to do with the murder and had only come to Linz because of the briefcase. He had not been able to get possession of it; otherwise he would have been long gone. Just why would he have killed his favorite test subject? After all, he had had twenty years to do that, if he had really wanted to do it.

Only when Wimmer threatened to call those nice Moscow telephone numbers that he had found in the briefcase, which presumably would lead to Mayinsky's superiors or to the KGB – yes, he would find that out and thus also have the murder motive handed to him on a plate – comically enough, Mayinsky only softened up because of those stupid numbers. It seemed as if the conversation with his superiors frightened him more than the prospect of a permanent cell in Suben Prison. Didn't he want them to know that he was in Austria? Well, it did not matter. In any case he was suddenly very willing to confess his guilt and gave a complete report about how he had pursued poor Mara to Linz, slaughtered her

192

with the knife, and put her in bed with the drunken Rafael in order to divert suspicion from himself. Signature on the report – and the case was closed.

Murder scene, corpse, murder weapon, written confession – everything was there. Wimmer had seldom celebrated a more beautiful victory over crime.

Why in the world did his stomach leave him in the lurch on this day of triumph, of all days? Wimmer did not understand it himself. Or could he no longer rely on his famous gut feeling?

The doctors diagnosed an acute stomach rupture and patched Wimmer back together again in an emergency operation.

31

December 6, 1991
The Day of Good and Evil

Rafael hated farewells. But fate was serving him that very thing abundantly.

It would have been enough, of course, to lose his mother prematurely. He had had that separation behind him for a long time. Soon he would bury his father, and with him all hopes of ever calling a normal, a good father his own. He had, of course, been ready to bid farewell to the image of the evil old man, but that was precisely what remained with him.

And now it was necessary for him to bid his lover farewell.

Rafael and Vera were sitting in the Linz railroad station restaurant, looking awkwardly back and forth between the marble floor and the classical plasterwork on the walls. In an hour Vera would get on the train for Prague. That much time still remained to them to clarify their relationship.

"The relationship between us wouldn't have worked out," said Rafael, finally breaking the silence.

"What do you mean by that? Did you expect me to get into bed with my uncle?" Vera had that crafty look on her face again, which Rafael loved so much about her.

"Half-uncle, I'm your half-uncle, to be precise. And after all, such a relationship sufficed for Hitler's parents, when they produced the little Adolf."

"Well, then look at how things turned out there. Those aren't particularly rosy prospects, Rafael."

"Vera, I know that you've gone through horrible things, and you have every reason to be sarcastic. But now think logically for once. If the two of us had children, they would bear a horrible legacy on their shoulders. Within them two terrible lineages would flow together, and that would lead to a constant conflict in their souls. My father was a rapist, your grandmother his victim. On the one side, our children would bear within them the guilt feelings and the guilt of the culprit, on the other side the rage, hate, and shame of the victim. Can you imagine what kind of psychological disorders are developed by such a divided individual?"

"Yes, but if we can't sleep together, we can't have any children either." Vera tried to turn the conversation away from the seriousness of the topic with gallows humor.

"It's not only because we're relatives that our love didn't have a chance. It also wouldn't have worked because of those terrible stories in the concentration camp."

"What do you mean?"

Rafael's voice became heavy. "Do you remember our failed evening, when you ran away headlong, because you saw a rapist in me? What you saw in me was what my father did to Olga. That is, you projected Olga's rapist onto me. You've carried the image of that violence within you since your childhood, because Olga and Mara subconsciously placed it in your cradle with you."

"But they never told me anything about it," Vera contradicted. "Just recently, during the police interrogation, I learned for the first time that my grandmother was in the concentration camp and was mistreated there. I was absolutely flabbergasted with shock, although after encountering my dead mother, hardly anything else could shock me. So why should I be afraid of something that I myself had never experienced? No, no, I think I felt that you were the same kind of bastard as your father. And now that I know all the crimes that he committed and how he destroyed the lives of innumerable women, I ask myself why I'm still sitting here at all and talking with a criminal bastard like you."

Rafael had to bring himself up short in the face of this aggressive attack, but the reproaches were familiar to him, of course, because he had tormented himself with them all his life. For that reason he escaped to the familiar bastion of psychological explanations:

"Vera, believe me, it's simply the case that the subconscious, suppressed family models are the very ones that are most easily passed on to the next generation. The very drama that could never be produced seeks out new actors who have to present it, until it becomes clear to the audience what it's about. But yes, of course I bear my father within me. Since childhood I've had to live with the guilt that Albert Markosky burdened us with, even if I, myself, could and can't do a thing about it. That's why I was always afraid of violence, afraid of women, afraid of treating women badly or injuring them. That's why you struck me to the core with your accusation. I always felt guilty, because I sensed what my father had done to the women. I was afraid to be a strong man, because in my mind strength equals brutality. That's why I failed at love. Thus my father destroyed not only the women, but also me."

"But Rafael, you're a loveable man. You're not brutal, and you'll find a wife who will love you the way that I would have liked to do." Vera took him by the hands and briefly thought about how she could end the conversation in a conciliatory way:

"When I was growing up with Olga as an only child, I always wished for a brother. You could be my older brother. Olga is old, and when she dies, you'll be the only one I have left. Let's be brother and sister. Aren't we like two lost children in a terrible world, like Hänsel and Gretl in the dark forest? We really could take each other by the hand and find our way out of the thicket together."

Brother and sister – with that Vera hit it right on the nose. Rafael, too, had wished for a sister, in order to endure the loneliness in the home of his parents more easily. Now he had found his sister. He remembered the book of one of his colleagues, in which the brother and sister, Orestes and Iphigenia had overcome the cruel world of their ancestors by helping and forgiving each other. Thus the two of them had been able to climb out of the cycle of murder and blood vengeance, and they both became happy. His colleague had called this shared accomplishment Origenia's solution, put together from the two names Or(estes, Iph)igenia. *Origen*, like the English word *origin*, the start and new beginning. Perhaps it was now time for that new beginning. Perhaps it was time to end the hatred between Sudeten Germans and Czechs. Perhaps all of the sorrow of this declining century was supposed to lead to the fact that his family now consisted of Sudeten Germans and Czechs. He would have children and Vera would have children. If they discussed the mistakes of the past openly with them, they would become friends, and the cousins would visit each other in Prague and Linz. After all, it was not far, just about two hours by train. Perhaps that unspeakable border would also disappear again, which had built up the hate between the two nations. And thus, just as Czechs and Austrians together had made the Danube Monarchy great, so

196

they would soon work together in building a Europe that was becoming united.

While they paid and walked to the railway platform, Rafael told
Vera about those thoughts. They decided to remain in contact, to
write letters to each other, and to support each other wherever they
could. And since Vera was following her mother's coffin to Prague,
in order to be on time for the funeral that Olga had organized, she
invited Rafael to visit the graves in Prague and Linz, where everything began and everything collapsed, on All Saints' Day, in order
that they might mourn together, digest everything that had happened, and later pass on all the knowledge of the horrible events to
the next generation.

All Saints' Day for a family reunion is original, thought Rafael to
himself and had to laugh. The new beginning was already stretching out its feelers.

As the train began to move, Vera waved from the window and
called to Rafael: "My brother Orestes, fight for your new era, in
which men and women meet each other free of violence. May love
be with you!"

And Rafael called back: "My sister Iphigenia, build the new
temple of womanhood, in which no woman can ever be injured
again."

Rafael waved to his Iphigenia for a long time, and he felt
lonely; and his heart hurt from all of the mourning for the woman
whom he had lost. In his aching heart, however, he felt that pain
paves the way for love. For only he who is ready to feel and who
opens himself to everything – only he can discover that love is in
his heart.

And as Vera's image disappeared in the fog, the face of another
woman was superimposed upon it, and Rafael felt that this woman
was waiting for him.

32.

Halloween
Linz, October 31, 1991

Told from the point of view of Valeri Suchov

It was time to strike. High time.

When Valeri thought about how far he had already pursued his victim across Europe, and how often the victim had slipped through his fingers, he became angry. And anger was an emotion that he seldom allowed himself. It was bad for business.

As if it were not enough that in the Moscow clinic he had let himself be confused by the strange look of that woman, the next day she had disappeared, and it had taken days before he had found her trail. His superior had found out that address in Prague, but Valeri had also arrived there too late. If he had not eavesdropped on the old woman who told her neighbor in the corridor that her daughter was on her way to Linz, he would really have had difficulties with the man who had given him the assignment. He was briefly amazed at the fact that he understood that conversation in Czech at all. But he was not a man of great ruminations, and so he raced after the train in a taxi and finally caught up with it in Kaplice. On the train he had soon found his target. Unfortunately, she sat in a full compartment, so that until their arrival in Linz Valeri had no opportunity to sneak up to his victim. After all, she would have recognized him again, and during the uproar that would then have ensued, the murder would have been possible, to be sure, but it would not have been technically very clean. And Valeri loathed sloppy work.

At the Linz railroad station the situation was similar. Masses of people on the platform, in the tunnel, and in the ticket hall, where the woman stored her case in a locker. Valeri wanted to be alone with his victim and without witnesses. So nothing remained but for him to carefully slip along after her. The victim walked in the direction of Blumauerkreuzung, turned right into Wienerstrasse, and walked through beneath the railroad viaduct. Near the large pillars beneath the railway Valeri was already about to draw his pistol, but then a screaming young woman came running toward him, who, in her hysterical panic, simply drew too much attention to herself. In the semi-darkness of the underpass he almost overlooked her; from then on it was better for him to leave his weapon in his pocket. The victim turned left into Anastasius-Grün-Strasse and entered a large apartment house. On the second floor, at the end of the corridor, she rang a doorbell several times, but nobody opened the door. Valeri peeked once more from the stairway around the corner. The woman was standing alone in the corridor. Valeri listened and it was deathly still. That was his chance. In this hand-to-hand combat situation he decided in favor of an ordinary knife, which was well suited to this domestic framework. He rushed toward his victim and stabbed from behind in the direction of her heart, since he knew that with a good hit, at most only a death rattle would cross her lips. But the woman turned around at the last moment, as if she had felt his presence; but instead of screaming she only put her hand to her mouth and sobbed violently, as if she knew that this last moment had to be swallowed like a bitter medicine. For a good reason Valeri avoided the look in her eyes and concentrated on his work. His next stab connected and the woman collapsed.

Valeri grunted with satisfaction. This woman had resisted him for a long time, but with a true master, in the final analysis any resistance is futile.

Only the disposal of the body remained. If necessary, that point could be left out, but an elegant solution would give his work the finishing touch.

Valeri reached for the door handle and noticed that the apartment was not locked. Such carelessness, when you never could know if thieves or murderers were terrorizing the area. Valeri carefully opened the door and listened to find out if anyone else was in the mausoleum that he had chosen, anybody whom he would then have to push over the Styx in a dignified double burial. The air seemed clear, so he dragged the corpse into the front room and closed the apartment door. Then he heard rattled breathing from the apartment and was strangely touched, for how was somebody supposed to die, without the master having laid hands on the person? That really would be too funny, if somebody had obediently hurried on ahead and executed himself, when he would have had the job done much more simply by Valeri. He peeked through the next doorway and grinned with amusement. A corpse was lying on the bed there, but it was more probably a drunken corpse. The man on the bed was still holding the bottle of *Eristov* in his hand, but was otherwise quite far gone. Half-empty wine bottles that were lying around bore witness that the man was probably more than far gone. Valeri suppressed the greedy desire in his throat and reminded himself of his principle of not drinking anything while working. He decided to wait a little longer, for this was the ideal opportunity for the final solution to his case.

When the drunk began to snore loudly, Valeri moved toward the completion of his deed. He dragged the dead woman into the large room and laid her carefully next to the intoxicated man. Then he stabbed hard a few more times so that blood sprayed over the sheet and over the unsuspecting drunk. Then he carefully took the poor man's hand and stirred it around in the blood of the murdered woman. After that he pressed the blood-covered knife between the alcohol-deadened fingers and pressed them firmly around the handle. At the end he took a new knife from the kitchen. *Borrowed is not given,* he thought to himself, *and I don't want to put the police inspector on the right track with an extra knife.*

Satisfied, he looked at his work. Let somebody try to imitate that. It gave him malicious enjoyment to think of how a Linz police inspector would tap around in the dark in the coming weeks. Looking forward to that fun, he did permit himself the last swallow from the vodka bottle.

When Valeri had left the building, he was finally able to take off his leather gloves. He blissfully breathed in Linz's metallic night air. It was a good day. He could finally head for home.

On the way back, when he met noisy children on the Blumau, who were storming out of a tramway, he remembered having read that in America, on this night of Halloween, the children played the trick-or-treat game. Disguised as ghosts, the children play bad tricks on stingy adults who do not give out any candy. Valeri smiled. The stingy man should have left him more of the *Eristov*. He had to be paid back for that according to the laws of Halloween.

When the drunk awoke from his intoxication the next morning, he would probably ask himself which evil spirit had played this dirty trick on him. Perhaps even the responsible police inspector would begin to believe in mysterious spirits when this case remained unsolvable for all time.

*

Valeri made one more side trip to Prague, for there, too, he had a clean-up job to take care of, in order to eliminate the last traces of that mysterious experiment, the meaning of which was not known to him nor did it concern him in any way. After completing his work, in a bar on the Moldau River he drank a double vodka in order to enjoy his accomplishment in peace, at least this time. He let his gaze sweep over the Karlsbrücke and the Hradčany Castle in what was for him an unusually thoughtful manner. And suddenly he had the indefinite feeling that this was a significant and strangely familiar place. The déjà vu of that moment caused him to think of the strange dead woman in Linz who had disconcerted him with her eyes in such an unusual way. Again it seemed to him as if he knew those eyes, just as he thought he knew this bar on the Moldau River, although he had certainly never been there before.

While Valeri tried to shake this psychiatrist's déjà vu shit from his mind, a stranger stepped up to his table.

"Permit me, Milton Johanson is my name. You don't know me, but I have an offer to make to you, one that you certainly can't turn down."

When the stranger sat down and began to talk, Valeri had the pleasant feeling that otherwise came over him only within the walls of the KGB headquarters. He needed this encompassing power of the large organization that knew everything and accompanied a person everywhere, in order to feel safe. And that very security was also conveyed by the stranger who acted as if his obtrusiveness were natural.

For that reason, Valeri was not surprised when Johanson identified himself as a CIA agent who was hunting for deserters from the KGB. CIA and KGB, the difference lay primarily in the exorbitant fees that were paid in the West. And once the USSR had collapsed, as everyone could figure out for himself, the career prospects in the East would be more than dismal. In the U.S.A., on the other hand, a CIA man could become president, as glowing examples proved.

201

Valeri nodded dreamily and ordered himself the next double. When Johanson talked about the mysterious black case full of scientific documents that the CIA absolutely had to have, an incredulous light went on behind Valeri's curtain of alcohol. Naturally, that case – his next to last corpse had locked it in the locker at the Linz railway station. The chief psychiatrist from Moscow had been so eager to get it that he had a falling out with his KGB superior, out of pure panic at the thought that this case would be confiscated by the KGB without being given back to him. Valeri had learned that only yesterday during his telephone conversation with the Lubyanka. For that reason alone the chief psychiatrist was on the termination list and was Valeri's next job as soon as he was back in Moscow. The case must really contain material that was worth a lot of money.

While he was drinking his third double, the situation became quite simple. It actually did not matter for whom he would obtain the black case. Both his KGB boss and the CIA agent were very eager to get it. But the American offered more for the same work. U.S citizenship, a princely salary, a house on the Potomac River, Halloween pumpkins for Valeri's future children. It was not difficult to make the right decision. A short time later Valeri was on the train to Linz.

*

The rest was routine. Valeri concluded astutely that the final hand movement of his corpse had served the purpose of enabling her to swallow the locker key, in order to keep it away from Valeri. The poor woman had probably thought that Valeri had only pursued her because of the case. Since the corpse was in the custody of the police, they must have also found the case with the key.

For a professional like Valeri the break-in at the police station was a trivial matter. Although, as Valeri admitted to himself with relief, it certainly helped that Inspector Wimmer was not at the station that night and thus could not defend his booty.

So it turned out as it had to turn out. Valeri turned the case over to Johanson and accepted for it his new identity and the plane tickets to New York. *Val Kirk – what a dreadful name*, he thought to himself, *it almost sounds like Kurkova*.

Kurkova, he had noticed the name on the train to Prague, when he was studying the contents of the case without understanding very much. He grasped only that he himself was part of a big experiment that had produced elite soldiers. And he could be proud of that; after all, he had always felt that he was something unique. He also learned that Kurkova was the name of his next-to-last corpse, of the only victim who had ever flustered him.

*

A peculiar man, Milton Johanson thought to himself as he accompanied Valeri to the airport. *That glass-clear look in his eyes, the striking chin, the high forehead – fifty years ago he would have been readily accepted as an SS man. But how does an SS man get to the Soviet Union? Well, it doesn't matter. In the future we'll breed all that ourselves.*

*

Mara's death had not been in vain. Her grandchildren would grow up in the U.S.A. and make their careers there. They would belong to the elite and – completely free of fear and scruples – help in the process of demonstrating to the whole world the superiority of "God's own country."

For, the warriors go where wars are fought. And the superior warriors are employed where superiority is the means that is used to stomp the opponent into the ground.

And the next war will certainly come. And the miracle weapons will also be used. And no matter how many dictators get the surprise of their lives, the chimera of power will raise its head in a new place.

*

Markosky's corpse seemed to grin peculiarly as the lid of the coffin was closed. *I wonder if that's eternal peace,* thought Rafael, but he immediately rejected the idea.

203

Epilogue: The *Mu* Gene

Salzburger Nachrichten of July 21, 1999, Science Page

Sensing pain lies in a single gene
Mu produces receptors for natural opiates

Washington (SN, dpa) – Whether somebody feels pain or only a mosquito bite when receiving an injection does not depend on his toughness and self-discipline. The decisive thing is the influence of a single gene in the genotype. Neuroscientists working with George Uhl of Johns Hopkins University in Baltimore, Maryland encountered that in mice. They present the key gene *mu* in the Tuesday issue of the *Proceedings of the National Academy of Sciences*. *Mu* produces the receptors for the natural opiates in the body. The receptor molecule binds opiates such as morphine as well.

The more active the *mu* production, the more opiate receptors a person possesses, Uhl concludes. Accordingly, this individual reacts more weakly to a pain because the endogenous opiates have a greater effect on the majority of the receptors. Simultaneously, the number of receptors determines how a treatment with pain-relieving morphine drugs takes effect. Morphine drugs are absorbed by the same receivers on the cell surface, as opiates. This means that patients with an active *mu* gene and many opiate receptors receive help from morphine drugs more rapidly and more easily than others with the inactive gene and less receptors.

Deviations determine the number of receptors

According to what the researchers have learned, how many receptors a *mu* gene spits out depends on tiny deviations in one region of the gene, which they call the control center. According to Uhl, photographs of the human brain show that some people can have up to twice as many receptors in some regions of the brain as others.

Expression of Gratitude

Many people have contributed to the production of this book.

First I would like to thank my publishers, Benedikt Föger and Klaus Gadermaier, for accepting my project and getting it ready for publication. Their encouragement was of inestimable value. I also thank Ms. Kogler, the publisher's office manager, for her good organizational assistance.

My family accompanied me through all the ups and downs that were connected with the genesis of this book and brought me to the point of finishing it. My children helped me with their interest; my wife gave helpful suggestions. I express thanks for that as well.

I also thank the AP&P Company for the support contribution to the creation of this book, as well as Managing Director Albert Pleninger for the spiritual and moral support, and for his curiosity and openness with respect to new stories that are told by life. A firm that distributes its products throughout the world is probably also a good forum for bringing psychological ideas to the people.

Last but not least, I thank my many clients who told me their life stories and thereby contributed to the formation of the theories upon which this book is based. To be sure, it must be emphasized that any similarity of the protagonists of my book to living persons is unintentional and therefore purely coincidental. But since thousands of experiences of innumerable people have condensed to psychological models in my mind, that situation contributes to the fact that among other things *Without Pain* is a quick way to recognize and understand psychological entanglements. As such it is the practical continuation of my theoretical book *Die Kinder des Tantalus* [The Children of Tantalus]. Anyone who has read both of them holds in his hand the key to grasping every family drama.

In that sense, I wish the reader fun and excitement while reading this novel.

Rüdiger Opelt

In his preface to the first edition of *Die Räuber* (*The Robbers*), Friedrich Schiller wrote: "Whoever has made it his purpose to topple vice and to avenge religion, morality, and civil laws on their enemies – such a person must expose vice in its naked odiousness and place it before the eyes of humanity in its colossal enormity. He himself must wander momentarily through its nocturnal labyrinths; he must know how to force himself into feelings whose perversity causes his soul to bristle."[3] It might be argued convincingly that Rüdiger Opelt's attempt "to construct a psychological profile of some fictional perpetrators of the Second World War,"[4] and thereby "to show what violence causes within the soul,"[5] corresponds directly to Schiller's assessment of what is required to uncover the reality of the darkest abysses of human behavior.

Although the novel *Without Pain* unquestionably belongs to the genre of the murder mystery and has some of the characteristics of the contemporary international thriller, it is hardly typical of either type of novel, as they appear in the English-language book trade. The most significant difference lies in the visibly didactic intent of the author, who openly presents the narrative as a literary illustration of personal psychological theories that have been developed more theoretically in his nonfiction writings.

In that respect, it is important to note that what Opelt attempts to accomplish is not really something new. His approach, of course, employs typical twentieth-century literary devices such as stream of consciousness and personal internal perspective to magnify the reader's perception of what transpires within the respective characters, especially the villains. However, the resulting picture of the psychological factors that are pertinent to the development of the story is hardly more intimate than the one provided by the monologues of Schiller's villainous Franz Moor in *Die Räuber*. Indeed, a strong argument can be made that for both Schiller and

---

[3] Friedrich Schiller, *Sämtliche Werke* (Munich: Winkler Verlag, 1968), V, 733 (translation mine).

[4] P. 7 above.

[5] Ibid.

Opelt the central artistic problem is that of creating a convincing presentation of the psychology of evil.

Nor is the basic premise of *Without Pain*, the idea that the crimes of the present are a product of the sins of the fathers, particularly new or original. Not only is the same notion developed (in this case to a lesser extent) in Schiller's *Die Räuber*, but it is presented in many other works of literature, ranging from the dramas of Greek antiquity to mainstream literature of the twentieth century. It is especially interesting, however, that Opelt's treatment of the timeless problem of the conflict between good and evil has obvious and direct ties to important works of eighteenth-century German literature.

If the only real link between Opelt's novel and earlier works by German authors lay in similarities inherent in the respective psychological treatments of amoral villains – Adolf Markosky and Franz Moor – whose motivations for ruthless, unfeeling, and vicious actions are focused in extreme self-interest, it would be difficult to argue that the relationship of this narrative to the German literary heritage is more than coincidental or trivial. There are, however, other indicators that tie the narrative specifically to ideas that were developed very intensely by Johann Wolfgang von Goethe. Such relationships suggest that *Without Pain* is actually further removed from the literary pattern suggested by the label "murder mystery" than a superficial reading might indicate.

One of the most visible connections to ideas developed in Goethe's works lies in Opelt's very calculated depiction of the Nazi villain Adolf Markosky as a Faustian figure. Endless pages of literary analysis have been devoted to Goethe's presentation of an inherent duality in man that is capsulized in Faust's declaration that two conflicting souls dwell within him. It is clearly no accident that the man with two identities in *Without Pain* – the vicious, unfeeling Nazi doctor and rapist, Adolf Markosky, in his earlier life, and the respected, apparently benevolent chief physician, Albert Makord, in his later life – concretely reflects Goethe's polarity. Opelt hammers that fact home in the later pages of the novel, when he identifies Rafael Makord's father with an appellation that combines the two names by which the man had been known during his life: Albert Markosky.

An additional link to Goethe's thought is apparent in the words spoken by the two innocent young people, Vera and Rafael, as they part near the end of the novel. It is particularly significant that in defining their new relationship as that of brother and sister, they identify with the classical Greek siblings Orestes and Iphigenia. In her final words to Rafael/Orestes, Vera/Iphigenia admonishes him to fight for a new era of nonviolent humaneness. The parallel to the title figure from Goethe's play about Iphigenia is pointed and clear. If nothing else, Goethe's Iphigenia is one of the dramatist's strongest advocates of humanism. Viewed from that perspective, Rüdiger Opelt's novel is, despite its modern setting, not simply a period piece, but also a work that deals in an interesting way with timeless and complex problems of the human condition.

When Schiller defined his artistic purpose in the preface to *Die Räuber*, he suggested that one responsibility of dramatic art was to function as a force for the promotion of virtue and moral behavior. In so doing, he made an initial presentation of ideas that he later refined and stated more directly in his essay "*Die Schaubühne als eine moralische Anstalt betrachtet* (The Stage Viewed as a Moral Institution)." If we accept the idea that Opelt's novel *Without Pain* was conceived with a similar purpose in mind, are we not ultimately brought to the point where we must ask the question: Is the crime novel, or more specifically the murder mystery, to be viewed as a moral institution?

Well, maybe...

Lowell A. Bangerter